D1262044

1968

By Richard Stern

Fiction

Golk [1960]
Europe, or Up and Down with Baggish
and Schreiber [1961]
In Any Case [1962]
Teeth, Dying and Other Matters [1964]
Stitch [1965]
1968 [1970]

Plays

The Gamesman's Island [1957]
Dossier: Earth; Twenty-Four Blackouts from
the Middle Electric Age [1966]

Edited

Honey and Wax; The Powers and Pleasures
of Narrative [1966]
American Poetry of the Fifties [1957]

1968

A Short Novel,
An Urban Idyll,
Five Stories, and
Two Trade Notes
by
Richard
Stern

**Holt, Rinehart
and Winston
New York
Chicago
San Francisco**

"Milius and Melanie" was
previously published in
Hudson Review, Autumn 1968.
"Veni, Vidi . . . Wendt" was
published in *Paris Review*,
Spring 1970.

Designer: Ernst Reichl

SBN: 03–084529–7

Printed in the United States
of America

CONTENTS

A Short Novel
   Veni, Vidi . . . Wendt, 3

Three Stories
   Ins and Outs, 79
   Milius and Melanie, 92
   East, West . . . Midwest, 113

An Urban Idyll
   Idylls of Dugan and Strunk, 131

Two Slight Stories of Abuse
   Gaps, 175
   Gifts, 188

Trade Notes
   Story-making, 199
   introductory, 207

for Nicholas, with love

A
SHORT
NOVEL

The author is grateful to
Easley Blackwood for composing
the two measures on page 53
and for the row on page 54.
He is also grateful for the
conversation of other composer
friends, Robert Lombardo and Ralph
Shapey. They are not responsible
for the opinions of the fictional
composer, Wendt.

VENI, VIDI ... WENDT

From Los Angeles to Santa Barbara, a paradisal coast bears the permanent exhaust of the automobile: shack towns, oil pumps, drive-ins, Tastee-Freeze bars, motels, service stations. At Ventura, the coast turns a corner which sends the Santa Ynez mountains east-west and lets the sun hang full on the beaches for its long day. A hundred yards or so off the highway there are a few sandy coves almost free of coastal acne. One of them, a mile north of a red boil of tourism called Santa Claus, is Serena Cove. A wooden plaque over the single-gauge railroad track gives the name. Cross the track to a cyclone fence. Behind that, in a lemon grove, is an amber villa shaped like a square head with glass shoulders. This is the Villa Leone, for which our place was the Changing House. (The villa has been turned into apartments.) Our house was—is—low, white and gabled. It has one grand room windowed on three sides, three bedrooms, a kitchen, and three bathrooms, two of which function. It is hidden by odorous bushes, palms, live oaks and great, skin-colored eucalypti, some of whose sides have been gashed by lightning. A wall of honeysuckle ends the driveway; behind it, the south lawn leads thirty feet to a red-dirt bluff covered with vines threaded with tiny blue flowers. They hang to the beach, a half-mile scimitar of ivory sand. Three other houses, hidden from ours by palms and trellises, share beach rights. You see them from the water, glassy monocles snooting it over a subdued sea.

Actually not the sea, but the Santa Barbara Channel

which is formed by the great private islands you see only
on very clear summer days. The islands are far enough away
to preserve a sense of the sea, but, like a lido, they break
waves down to sizes which keep you from worrying about
small children.

We were there ten summer weeks, in the last five of
which I wrote the first version of an opera. I've never had
an easier, less-forced time, and although, now, back in Chicago, I see that what I did there on the coast was not much
more than take out the ore, and that I now have to build
the factory and make the opera, at the time I didn't know
it. During these weeks I never turned back to see what I'd
done. Day after day I coasted (yes), writing away, feeling
the music and story come with an ease which, till then, I'd
never known.

Everyone seems to know that opera is on its last legs. In
fact, music itself isn't doing too well. A fine song writer,
Ned Rorem, says that the Beatles are the great music of
our time; I suppose they are more inventive than most.
Our best composers spend a lot of time stewing about
audience-teasing and other art-world claptrap. Only Stravinsky seems like a wise inventor who happens to use music
instead of words or mathematics. And he is enjoyed more
as a Dr. Johnson than as an enchanting musician. A man
like me who's spent himself writing a musical drama is led
to feel his work has no public significance, that, at best, it
will be endured by a few friends and an occasional audience
bribed by free tickets and a party in honor of the composer.
("Honor" because he endured the long boredom of working out what bores them only an hour or two.) An "enforced loss of human energy," wrote Mr. Khrushchev about
armaments. Of course, writing music is not enforced
(though one must pass time doing something), and music
is a few wrongs up from armaments.

Though down from political action, as the hierarchy of
1968 had it; and I was influenced by such mis-estimates as
well as by my inner tides. I lent a very small public name
and an equivalent public gift to the better-known victims of

institutional brutality. Last spring I marched in the Loop,
collected fourteen draft cards, made a speech in the rain by
a Meštrović Indian, was photographed, televised, went
home to look at myself on the local news, and had bad
hours waiting for the FBI to turn me into the local Dr.
Spock. In short, paid the debt to my consciousness of
being in so frivolous a trade.

On the one hand, I dream of my own Bayreuth, the
Wendt Festival, with, not mesmerism and fruited myth,
but classical wisdom and common sense made engaging
and novel by the least duplicitous of contemporary musical
lines. On the other hand, I feel the shame of luxury, of a
large—rotting—house, of privacy and silence, of a livable
salary and easy schedule, of an entrée into the little circles
in which I whirl—college music departments, two-day festi-
vals in Mexico City and The Hague, occasional mention
in a news magazine's music section.

For this opera, which, with luck, will be given a trun-
cated radio performance in Stockholm and a workshop run-
through in Bloomington, Indiana, I'm trying to do, I suppose, what writers do in prefaces (or what my Uncle
Herman did fifty years ago as advance agent for Barnum).
I'm writing an account of its genesis or composition to serve
as a kind of a trailer (which, as usual, precedes what it
"trails").

Any thoughtful man who types the solitary "I" on the
page as much as I have these past weeks must consider its
perils. This is a great time for "I." Half the works billed as
fiction are just spayed (or Styrofoamed) memoirs. This
week's literary sections are on Malraux's *Anti-Memoirs*, apparently an unravelable mixture of real and fictive "I"s,
pseudonyms, *noms de plume* and *noms de guerre*, mixed in
with fictional guises and life roles (in which "the man" tells
Nehru that he is a "Minister of State" the way that Mallarmé's *cat* becomes *Mallarmé's* cat). I suppose this need to
multiply oneself is one of the billion guises of libido. (Professor Lederberg found gender in bacteria; perhaps gravity
itself will turn out to be the lust of particles for each other.)

That genius Nietzsche, whom I still read in a Modern Library Giant bought at fifteen after reading Will Durant's *Story of Philosophy* . . . No, I'll begin again; I'm not writing autobiography. Nietzsche asks, "Aren't books written precisely to hide what is in us?" Granting the exceptional concealments of his time, isn't this still the case? I know the authors of some of the frankest books ever written. The books are mostly trailers or self-advertisements, letters to women saying, "Here I am, come get me," or to parents saying, "This is the reason for my condition." Or sometimes, they're just brilliant drugs of self-assurance.

Every book conceals a book. But as the great old fellow (F.N.) says, every thinker is more afraid of being understood than misunderstood. Wants uniqueness more than love and gratitude.

In Nietzsche's day, the pose was to be *simply* grand, in our time, to be *complexly* grand. The good artists I know are more credulous than *smarter* people. (So you hear stories of their naïveté or—its other face—mean shrewdness.)

Writing your own story, you can report, pose, and judge all at once. Not as blissful a cave as music, but not bad at all.

So here's my little *Enstehung des Walpole's Love* (*Opus 43*), my yet-to-be-finished opera. I pray it's not a substitute for it. (In fact, I'm willing to send a Xerox of fifty pages of score to anyone who sends ten dollars and a self-addressed, stamped return envelope to Holt, Rinehart and Winston, Inc., 383 Madison Avenue, New York, N.Y. 10017.)

> [*Owing to personnel changes in our office, Mr. Wendt's invitation must be considered null and void. H., R. and W.*]

2

I don't begin at the beginning, but with my then seventeen-year-old son, Jeff-U. (For Ulrich; I'm Jeff-C, for Charles. Ulrich is the great-uncle from whom I inherited not the

two hundred thousand I expected, but fifty.) Oedipal
miseries were, I thought, ruining my summer. They were
at their worst when Jeff-U invited his friend Ollendorf to
stay with us.

I was not anxious to have Ollendorf around. The presence
of an outsider inhibits me, if only for a time and from
walking around in my skin. Though notches up from the
loudmouthed adolescent ignoranti who fill up our Chicago
house, he would be extra presence, an absence of dear absence; he'd be swinging baseball bats against the vases,
tackling Jeff-U into Sackerville's stereo; I'd be forking over
six hundred for that in addition to the hundred and eighty-
five it cost me every week just to hook our trunks up in
Sackerville's place. (Which turned out to be Donloubie's
place.)

I did not want him.

But there was small recourse: Gina, my almost sixteen-
year-old, had had her amical quota with Loretta Cropsey.

I laid it on the hard line. "He can come if you, One,
specify dates: ten days and not an hour more; and Two, he's
got to fly into Santa Barbara, which means the three-thirty
out of San Francisco. And Arrival Day counts as Day Number One."

Since Jeff-U daily stretched his six and a sixth feet of unemployed body upon a bed from one A.M. to one P.M., it
didn't strike me that Ollendorf's afternoon arrival constituted an important loss of a vertical day. "Besides which,
it takes half an hour to get to the airport. And before that
you'll have to work your way into a T-shirt. Even shoes.
Maybe even a pair of socks. Not matched or clean, of
course, but you can see, there's more Ollendorf to the day
than his arrival at the house." (Not that Jeff-U wore the
same piece of clothing three consecutive hours. Except for
dress shirts, which I told him to pay for himself. Since
which the San Ysidro Laundry had been deprived of his
custom.)

It turned out I won't let him pick up Ollendorf anyway
because (1) he could drive only our New Yorker, Sacker-

ville limiting the Volkswagen to "licensed adults," and
(2) "I'm not going to burn a quart of fuel to fetch your
effing pal when I'm up at Goleta anyway." (I rehearse the
chamber group Mondays.)

He wished to telephone Ollendorf. "Sixty-five cents won't
kill you."

"*Kill* me?"

"I paid for most of the calls."

"Not the tax."

"Here's a buck," fingering the besanded back pocket of
the early-afternoon pants for one of the crushed bills which
remain from spring poker triumphs and his grandmother's
indolent generosity—substitute for the physical birthday
presents which would force her into the dangerous byways
of Fifth Avenue.

I take the buck. "This covers about ten percent of them."
If it's but a week of weeding nasturtiums or washing windows, I am bent on seeing his hairless arse erect before
one P.M. Without myself having to chain and toss it into
the local office of the California State Employment Service.

Of course, he knows what I'm about, knows I bait him,
but though down to fourteen bucks (if I haven't overlooked
some of the pockets or the change which overflows to every
couch and bed in the house), he throws me another bill.
Which I don't make him pick up or unroll; because if his
theatrical arrogance caused him to toss a five instead of a
one, he will be down to nine bucks. (I didn't unroll it until
I was in the john: I have theatrical bouts as well. It was,
unfortunately, a single.)

3

Every other weekend, the cove fills with the landbound
children of my Los Angeles relatives and summer colleagues.
(Especially those unable to keep progenitive tools from
progenitive work: George Mullidyne has six, the odious
Davidov has pumped five into the beauteous Patricia, and

even the emeritous Krappell manages to churn junior Krappells out of his third wife.) They turn our half-mile of beach into an anvil.

I buy twenty-four cans of pop at a crack; they don't last an afternoon. The be-Pepsied urine threatens the brim of the channel and, for all I know, brings on the underground coronaries which the *News-Press* attributes to "settling of the channel fault." The last of these, 4.5 on the Richter scale, had our chairs leaping around for half a minute, and, up the coast, severed an oil pipe which poured a hundred thousand lethal gallons over the lobster beds of Gaviota. (Note: Winter '69, after the rig across the way leaked millions: I hadn't seen anything.) But I found a local grease called Gorner's which looked but didn't taste like pop. Two giant bottles last a week. (The better mousetrap.)

Three days after I made the first sketches for *Walpole's Love*, my Aunt Jo, her son, Sammy, and his three children, Little Lance, Indian-colored Sabrina, and my favorite, the Golden Triangle, Mina, drove up from L.A.

Sammy's a cetologist at La Jolla. He spends his life in a bathing suit taping the conversation of whales in the green-and-silver tanks of the Marine Biology Laboratory. Whales, it seems, are the wisest of creatures, fearless, sensitive, co-operative. They tend their distressed kind, nudge them to the surface, and skim their pallid flanks for circulation. (Such stuff goes well in Santa Barbara, where the daughter of Thomas Mann used to escort a dog she taught to type to parties where parakeets supposedly chirp *Traviata*.) In such pursuits, Sammy has grown whalish himself. A pink cigar of a man, he rolls out of his Squire Wagon with children, mother, and fly rods. (At the service of the deep during the week, on weekends he murders there.)

Mina is Jeff-U's age. Two strips of psychedelic cloth hang on five and a half feet of intoxicating flesh. Her vitaminized breasts are those of Hungarian spies; her golden triangle—how I imagine its secretive fur—her pure, thick lips, her winking invitations to the ball I think are meant for me. I have seen her beauty spill over since sixty-four. Even then,

she was ready, lolitable. (We watched that film together
on the late show. How she understood.) But then there was
Wilma Kitty (wife and children waited economically in
Chicago), I had less reason to act out Nabokov's dreamlife.
But while the earth gnashed hot jaws under channel waters
and the Impulse to Lobsterhood searched new stuff, I
dreamed madly of opening Mina's Northwest Passage. (One
day, driving her east, to Grinnell or to Penn State; at dusk,
by Winnemucca, Nev., or Provo, U., we pull in to a desert
motel, we swim, Mina, you and I, in a silver pool and come
back dripping to our cabin, brassy droplets on our golden
flesh. Silent, regarding, we strip wet suits—I have lost ten
or fifteen more pounds, my pectorals are weight-lifted into
buttresses of depilated chest—you walk to me—no, turn
from me—flipping suit from ankle, I pull your back to
my front, Hungarian breasts within my palms, and you,
struggling for me, go belly-down upon the double bed,
glorious snow-white rearward twins aquiver for the loco-
motive rod.)

Aunt Jo is gray, gap-toothed, powdery, hard of hearing,
repetitive, with our family appetite for the fortissimo mon-
ologue. When she, her sisters, and her surviving brother, my
father, the Optimist, assemble, it looks as if an Eastern
rice village on stilts has been given life. (All are on canes.)
They enter, four octogenarians with octogenarian spouses.
(The spouses, except my father's, are all second mates: this
family survives. Survives and kills.) They surround the
children with their gifts, old arms, and puckering lips.
"Open, darling, open and see what Aunt Jo [Belle, May]
has brought her precious." They vomit triumph, praise,
self-adoration. All is right with the world. (Why not? It
has endured them.) The cities they inhabit are crimeless,
the water pure, the streets immaculate, their children
extraordinary, known over New York, Scarsdale, the world,
on the verge or aftermath of incredible deals—mentioned
in *Textile Week*—their grandchildren are peerless beauties
of rare and promising shrewdness. The gashes of their lives
(children dead in auto accidents, bankrupt sons, psychotic

grandchildren, doomed conditions, stymied lives) are scarred
over with such noise. They stagger into the living room,
drop into sofas, and, huge voices aimed at the room's
imagined center, begin their simultaneous, uninterruptible
spiels. Canes gaveling carpets for emphasis and control,
voices crashing against each other, they solicit, they demand
recognition of their life performances.

Only one mortal thing can suspend their arias: Food.
Velia's thin, West Hartford voice inserts, "Would you like
a bite?" Convulsion of struggle, sofa arms crushed, canes
gripped to bone, the gravity of sagged flesh reversed by
visions of repast. And commences the Long March to the
table. There, stunned moment of formality, who will sit
where? Velia leaves them struggling—monarchical whales—
but appetite dissolves precedence, they fall to, moaning
about the splendor of the vittles; though their old hearts are
sunk at the thin New England provision, the cellophaned
corned beef, the thin, pre-sliced rye bread staled in the
Protestant markets which magnetize Velia, and, for sweets,
dry wafers in lieu of the thick snail curls of raisins, nuts,
and caramelized dough, or the scarlet tarts, the berries
swillingly augmented by terrific syrups. No, nothing is right,
but then how should a thin-nosed aristocrat know what
keeps old Jews alive? Mouths liquid, they compliment—
and so enrich—the sober fare. They live, they eat; the juices
flood. This is what ancestral migrations have aimed at.
(Children of the Book? Yes, quick. Sons and Daughters of
the Schnecken, the Custard Tart.)

Aunt Jo and I sit in Sackerville's beautiful living room,
Japanese-free of furniture, windows on three sides, in front,
the flowered lawn, empalmed, honeysuckled, grassed to the
great bluff over the ocean. The noise is of bird and wave,
the Pacific is blue, snowy. Aunt Jo takes my arm, pulls herself up by it so that her lips are at my ear. In a voice that
is part puzzlement, part revelation, she says, "The Lord has
been good to you, Jeffrey."

The gap-toothed, powdery, great-nosed face tosses back
toward the drained cans of pop, the scarlet paradise flowers,

the spread and noise of children, and what?—the pretty, apparently undemanding, apparently giving wife. She remembers the commissions from Tanglewood and Fromm, the write-ups in *Time* (three harsh slaps), the full-fledged attack by Winthrop Sargeant ("The complex aridity of Wendt's music, commissioned, composed, performed and —hopefully—buried in the academy") which she has read as professional compliment. And this is all set in the ocean-cooled, semi-tropic poster-dream of paradise.

"Things *look* good out here, Aunt Jo."

We both know that childhood friends are dead in the wars, drunk, bankrupt, or, at best, anonymous. She knows the deceptions of the present, this powdery old aunt whose first husband died returning a crosscourt volley from her sexagenarian racket and whose second was struck by a Yellow Cab as he hurried to her summons at Madison and Seventy-Second Street.

I press the skin bag under her elbow and lead her where lawn and bluff meet in the line of insane-looking palms (spiky umbrellas, vegetable porcupines). On the beach below, dowitchers snap beaks for red beach ants, waves flush iron gleams. (Their metric genius is something I try and try to figure and employ.)

I hand Aunt Jo into a rattan chair, squat beside her ropy legs, and keep my ear alive. I am figuring a sequence.

Yes, for the other night, after a dismal sixteen months in which my only opus was a setting of Definitions from Hoare's *Shorter Italian-English Dictionary For Wind Instruments, Radio Static and Audience Coughs*—I tried to be of the brave new laboratory-world, and it crippled me— mooning on the beach, watching the murderous oil rigs lit like rubies in the channel, I hit upon Something Grand. Out of the Blue. And, while Velia snored in the double bed, I sat at Sackerville's cypress work table and sketched the plan, laid down the lines, established a tone row, and worked it all up around a story.

Yes, the opera. In this day and age, surrounded by aleatory gamesmen, vatic pasticheurs of Mozart, phony

pholkistes, electronic adolescents, employers of blow-torch-
ers, Caged mice, and concrete crapistes, I fell into this
antique pit.

And it's no surrealist cop-out, no twigged-out Clarsic
(*Carmini Catulli* or miserable Yeats play with less action
than a cigarette ad), no neo-Wagnerian *Geschwätz* but
something new, fresh, off the morning paper. Urban dew.
In brief, the story's about a police sergeant and a black
hooker he woos with precinct and other stories. In particular with the old eighteenth-century story—he's a night-
school reader—of the icy bachelor Horace Walpole, blind
old Mme. Du Deffand who loved him hopelessly, and then,
decades later, young Mary Berry, whom the old Walpole
loved and who milked him of his wit and knowledge as he
had milked the old Deffand. Girl and cop conjure between
them the characters, who show up on scrims, on a screen,
and on the stage (like the Czechs). The musical lines drift
with the actors, or, like motifs, fade into other time schemes.
No dominant style (the sign of this century), no batting
the company into shape. Deffand sounds like Scarlatti and
J. C. F. Bach, Walpole like Haydn and early Beethoven,
Berry like Beethoven and early Wagner, the sergeant like
Arnold Pretty-mount, Igor the Penman, my dear Webern
(the musical laser) plus a bit of Elliot C. and Pierre B.;
the hooker will swim in every love song, east and west,
that can squeeze into the tone row. Yet the lines are never
to blur, there are but chordal shadows round the sparse,
informative line.

"Sam found marijuana in her drawer last week."

"What?"

Aunt Jo waved at a gold twig in the blue water. Mina on
a mattress. "She said everyone takes it."

"Foolish, foolish. Hardly started, they want life to have
italics."

"Maybe if you speak to her, Jeffrey. She respects you,
you're the artist in the family, she thinks it's wonderful to
have a famous cousin." (Aunt Jo received one of the ten
Who's Who in Americas my mother bought the year I

joined the Kansas morticians and General Electric VPs.)

Gravel scutters—my sequence has dissolved—a car pulls in the driveway. A gray Bentley. Must be a mistake. No. Donloubie.

Donloubie is the owner of Sackerville's place. He has come on a mission, foolish and remote as himself.

"Murder."

Two days before, this golden corner had suffered its first Caucasian murder in ten years. Donloubie's neighbor, Mrs. Joel, the candy-maker's wife, was found under the closed lid of a heated swimming pool (ten yards back from the Pacific).

Donloubie is hunched, muscular, immensely rich, is said to own much of Columbus, Georgia, his wife a goodly portion of Jacksonville, Florida. The Santa Barbara story is they met and married to stretch their desmesnes until they touched. Mrs. Donloubie has contrived the Theory of Three. The week before, Slochum, a broker, was found at the foot of stone stairs in a pool of his blood. Now Lydia Joel. "Who'll be the third?" ask the Donloubies. (Slochum was drunk, fell and broke his own neck.) The Donloubies tremble. They alert housemaids and chauffeurs to departure. But can they depart? Their neighbor has been found floating in eighty-five-degree water, gray head bashed with unknown instrument. They cannot flee the coop, despite the fabulous tracts of Florida and Georgia which underwrite their Bentleys and their orchid garden.

Donloubie comes to his tenant's tenant. I am a University Professor, the only one he has ever known. The University conjures up for him the investigation of exotic fauna. Can I suggest a way of getting sophisticated sleuths into the case past the befogged and bungling local officers? "Perhaps your criminologists up there." He means the University of California at Santa Barbara. Doesn't he know I am as remote as can be from university life, that I am a summer-quarter visitor, that I know no one but two colleagues in the music department and a few student instrumentalists

and composers-in-the-egg? The Donloubies have lawyers,
brilliant manipulators of their tax returns and real-estate
transactions. Is he afraid to let them know his home touches
a house of violence, that he himself has been questioned by
police? God knows.

Donloubie appears on our—his, Sackerville's—lawn with
his Japanese chauffeur who carries a tremendous basket of
fruit. Nectarines, peaches, plums, Kadota figs, Persian mel-
ons, a pair of golden scissors agleam within leathery grapple
of dates. Aunt Jo rises in tribute to this gorgeous heap. Donloubie, unknown to her a minute earlier, has *sur le champ*
become a Personage of Note, a future embellishment of
her litany of triumph. She receives him, I am sent for a
chair and shout Jeff-U off the Angel Baseball Game to fetch
it. (Argument coagulates in his long face. He is invited to
stay, his social charm contrives important business with
the National Broadcasting Company.)

Donloubie gives a nervous appraisal of this half-forgotten
sliver of his holdings, frowns at an active sprinkler on the
south lawn, an unshaven quality in the wall of honeysuckle
—I see anew with his landowner's severe eye—but he is on
deeper business, he hardly knows what. His gray-blond
haycock, his reddish eyes, his sixty years of salted tan, his
beauteous chestnut sport coat and fifty-dollar Charvet shirt
command the lawn.

Did I know, he begins, that Mrs. Joel had had eight
housekeepers since the first of January, that she was a
vicious, half-mad woman, that Mr. Joel, slavish in devotion
though he was, was on the verge of having her committed,
that he had begged him, Donloubie, to keep an eye out
on her while he, Joel, gallivanted? Yes, indeed, and the
blond cock tossed but did not—a wig?—waver in the air,
old Joel had greater interest than in, ha-ha, Tootsie Rolls;
for a man of seventy-six, Joel was in—if the Missus will
excuse the phrase—terrific sexual form, that if he, Donloubie, were not an old acquaintance—not friend, mind you
—and had he not received a call from the man at the very
time the miserable woman was having her head beaten in,

he, Donloubie, would look very closely at Mr. Joel's where-abouts.

Fascinating, but where do I fit in?

—Well, I thought you ought to know, for one thing. I feel responsible as your [pause] host.

Very nice, but isn't—

Yes, perhaps, but I was from a city where they—as it were—specialized in murder, and therefore, surely, in its investigation. Then, too, I was in contact at the University with all sorts of knowledgeable types. He was not entirely persuaded about local competence in these matters, and since he and Mrs. D. were friends of the deceased, if one could be a friend of a totally disagreeable woman who so antagonized her servants that they dropped off like leaves—though, oddly, the present housekeeper, a rather genteel woman, by the by, had stayed more than three months—at any rate, as neighbors, friends, and, too, as people who both were obligated elsewhere yet felt they could not leave until at least the preliminary matters were cleared up, they wanted to bring in proper investigators. I, surely, or, at least, *perhaps*, could help them find someone, either in Chicago or at the University.

Strange, but it was a glorious basket of fruit, the man did not summon me to write a dirge for the dead woman—I was once offered such a commission, as if my lyric mathematics could serve an antique ritual—the man was clearly anxious to talk, yet nervous about talking to Mrs. Erwin or any of the very few locals he deigned to talk to, or who deigned to talk with him. It wasn't clear how Donloubie—strange name—perhaps a Creole—came to own Columbus, Georgia (if he did). In fact, it occurred to me then and there that his wealth was squeezed out of young girls' thighs and bloody needles in the port streets of Marseilles and Genoa, and that he was damn scared the dumb locals might dig up this history, that even the local rag would publish it, and that, who knows, he would have to give up the Pacific villa he'd chosen to live and die in. I had better try out those dates on the neighbors' cat.

"The Missus and I would like you and yours to come for a drink this evening."

Sorry, pressure of society—we are invited to a party—ditto tomorrow—no party—but he is unstoppable. "Monday, then."

"Splendid."

Aunt Jo shines with solution. "Jeffrey, call the FBI."

Donloubie's tan fingers sink to the basket of fruit, grip a melon, raise and jam it against the dates. "Missus. Donloubie learned to dial a phone some years ago."

The cock of hair waves, the red-pit eyes shiver, the mustard sport coat and hundred-dollar beige slacks rise from the rattan. "See you Monday, Professor. A strategy session."

"I'll be there, Mr. D., don't worry."

"Donloubie don't worry, Professor."

"And thanks for the fruit."

"Enjoy it in health. Good day, Missus."

The chauffeur is spun from the house, where he and Jeff-U have divided the misery of the California Angels.

I too have had it, the breathy clucks of the old aunt, the local bloodshed, the noise rising up the bluff. "Aunt Jo, will you excuse me a bit? I've got to," and left hand is up to tap the hair above the ear. The Composer's Aunt understands.

Past Jeff-U and Cleaning Velia into the bedroom, where the Muse has stripped her toga, and where, conjuring up the golden body of the impossible cousin, the composer pours generative sap across Sackerville's rough sheets.

The Party

That is, a select company invited to participate in some form of amusement.

Tonight's amusement: musical assassination.

The company: Davidov and Mullidyne, the University

musicologists and their wives; Donald Taylor, my old side-kick from Hindemith's Harmony Class at New Haven. Invited, but not attending; a Montenegrin serialist employed by the Disney Studios; Mme. Hortense Reilly, local alto and graduate of Mme. Lotte Lehmann's Santa Barbara master classes; and Benedict Krappell, sociologist, emeritus, whose musical credentials were playing double bass for Damrosch in the twenties to support—his words—his academic habit.

The inviter/selector: Franklin B. Ritt, an ex-Morgan, Stanley broker and active Patron of the Arts whom I'd met in a Spanish museum five years ago and with whom I have been semi-annually afflicted ever since. (Ritt takes no planes, and stops off in Chicago changing trains.)

The ostensible purpose of the gathering was to introduce me to the musical high life of the area. As I already knew Mullidyne, Davidov, Krappell, and Donald Taylor, that left the Montenegrin, Miss Reilly, and Mrs. Ritt. Or, as it worked out, Mrs. Ritt, a woman of either great discretion or puissant ignorance. Between "I'm so glad at last" and "So sorry your wife," she said not a word.

Of course, in such company, it didn't show.

"They all know your work," said Ritt in telephonic invitation. Stunned by this rare celebrity, I did not sufficiently examine the reticence of the verb.

Velia does not take much stock in human variety and seldom goes to parties. Besides, her small capacity was exhausted by the Angeleno Wendts. "I'm not going. It'll be one more hellish evening cutting down every absent musician in the world."

This is not my line. An exception to the celebrated viciousness of my fellow craftsmen, a good piece from them gets a loud cheer from me. "Perhaps La Mullidyne will have some tidings about psychotic blackies, and you can feel at home."

"That's sweet talk in front of Gus." (Gus is fathoms deep in a game of solitaire.)

"I said we'd be there at nine. The party's in our honor."

"Your honor."

"I regret the dependent state of the second sex, Velia, but you'll have to play along with it till the kindergartners have had their day. You can star tonight: you're two thousand miles closer to hot gossip than they."

"I don't feel like starring. I don't feel like going."

I fear—to the point of idolatry—the unreason of women.

"Come on, Vee, it'll put color in your cheeks."

"If I'm so pale, I'd better not show myself. I don't want to humiliate you."

The bee's suicidal aggression is one of the pathetic drives of nature. And poor Vee's.

> La pauvre femme n'est pas méchante
> Elle souffre, tu sais, d'une détente.

This in the bathroom getting on a maroon turtleneck (cotton, to spare myself in heat and pocket) and California sport coat, a rose-and-magenta plaid. Large teeth white in the sunlit skin, blue-black eyes, remnants of black hair, I conjure irresistibility out of the mirror. Though who'll be there to resist? Draggy crones, perhaps one with splendid legs and chest, a wrinkled Frau Musicologue who'll drop her lip my way and, *piano piano*, "Call, I'm in the book."

To Jeff-U, in his sixth straight hour before the enchanted glass: "Get your arse erect and go play Casino with Mom." Rage and disdain darken his long face. "I thought you were going to read *The Possessed*. A whole month, and you're still in Part One. Gina read *Martin Chuzzlewit* in two days, she's halfway through *Children of Sánchez*, and you can't fight your way off Page Sixty-Five."

"I don't feel like reading."

"Then write. I bought you that notebook for graduation."

"Why'n't you get off my back?"

"Oh, that's lovely filial talk. Once more, and I'll whack the indolence off your bony hide."

Jeff-U is mortified by skinniness. Strong and good-looking,

he feels he has to knock everybody dead with perfection.
Horrific vanity of adolescence. Now and then I look at
Erikson or some other Guide to Life's Hard Stages, and
muzzle my particular fury in generic analysis. Not tonight.
"You get no backtalk from NBC. No criticism, no testing.
That's the source of your infatuation with that machine,"
and I slap the button which blanks the screen. Jeff-U
continues staring at it. "*Amour-impropre.* Your mind'll
sink so snake-low it'll be unable to rise. You'll perish an
idiot. A McLuhanite bum. And looka the mess here."
Moated by a carton of orange sherbet, the butts of four
frankfurters, a quarter-filled bowl of tuna fish (he never
finishes anything), pear cores, two cans of Pepsi (he must
have bought them himself). "What a spectacular bloom
of human culture."

"Good ni-ight, Dad," D gliding to B flat. Softening my
heart, transposing the exchange. A dear boy, wiser than his
savage pa, and no power-mad know-it-all, no instant-revolu-
tionary, pimpled Robespierre shrieker, no louse-ridden
Speed-lapper, hardly a drinker (innocent fifth of vermouth
in his closet, beer to fatten up), not even a bad driver.
Only vanity, sloth, and narcissism blot him. "All right.
Take it easy," and I pull out the button of the magic
casement.

Why does the party count? I suppose for the musical
jaws within which lay Patricia Davidov.

Another tale of Middle-Class Adultery (Genus: The
Academy; Species: Music). Human beings have comparatively few ways to express themselves. We swim in a sexual
sea, we measure our affective lives by sexuality. Patricia
Davidov was the yeast of *Walpole's Love*. Or, at least, what
happened with her was partial expression of what it also
partially expressed.

She was there, a long, golden, big-boned woman, and
across from her, the dark-faced, sandal-wearing, tieless,
white-toothed megaphone and music-hater, Davidov, author of *The Blindness of Donald Tovey*, *The Deafness of
Ludwig Beethoven*. (Democratic hater of titles, Davidov

removed Sir Donald's "Sir" and, ignorant lout, Beethoven's
plebeian—Dutch—"van.") This dissertation, bound in the
black spring binder which constituted its only public
presence (i.e., it was never, could never be published, except
by a vanity press, which Davidov's vanity would prevent
his using), this dissertation graced my desk the entire
summer and was returned in a manila envelope, unread, to
Davidov's box. Unread, except for certain comic dip-ins,
here and there, when this musical wild man lashed the
finest noncomposer analyst in English or, yes, emptied the
cerebral intestine which substituted for his neural matter
upon the sublimities of Opera 109, 111, and 131. Davidov's
egoism permitted him to struggle against only the greatest.
(The drunkest punk takes on the greatest gun of the west.
Except that Davidov had not been shot down, could not
be, for he was down to begin with, could hardly have
reached lower depths.)

    We sat amidst Ritt's Collection. This fantastic assem-
blage of the abortions, blotches, and illegitimacies of gran-
deur needs a word. In Ritt's hillside house, an immense
stucco-garage affair, this insanely penny-pinching prodigal
had collected or piled every cut-rate piece of artistic junk
his wide travels had brought him near. There were litho-
graphs by the nephews of Matisse's nurse, oils not of Carraci
but of Garraci, dreamscapes not by Redon but Virdon,
abstractions done by imprisoned mensheviks, graffiti from
Bombay streets, earrings fashioned from the teeth of
Goering's schnauzer. The statistical improbability of so
flawless a pile of criminal merde bespoke the kind of genius
which marks California. With San Simeon, the Franklin
Ritt Collection is the prize of California Schweinerei.

    In this setting, pictures smeared on walls, clumps of
sculpture squatting by perhaps-ashtrays, within this prison
of creative shit, there were its living voices, Davidov and his
junior partner in crime, Francis Mullidyne, and their beautiful wives, one on each side of dear old Donald Taylor (tiny,
bespectacled, timid celibate who had deserted the musical
zoo for his antique shop in the Paseo and satisfied a scholarly

itch by writing articles on eighteenth-century France). (It
was his article on Madame Du Deffand which launched my
libretto).

The musicological jaws were biting the throats, ripping
the flesh, and drinking the blood of every composer living
and dead (with the conspicuously humiliating omission of
J. R. C. Wendt). Within the hirsute, vibrant nostrils of
Davidov, I read a terrible question: What somatic deficit
kept Bach from the proper mode of human expression, murder? What sickness glued Einstein to his numbers, de-
frauded Shakespeare of dirk and pistol? Where had I gone
wrong, squirting out musical sperm instead of poison?

Even Donald Taylor, minute, and cyclops-eyed behind
fishbowl lenses, was forced from timidity to question the
Davidovian Scheme of Musical *Schrecklichkeit*. "I don't
follow that bit about Schubert, Bert."

Charmer Davidov responded that if it were a pair of
tight trousers, Donald would follow it close enough.

A company gasp, except for the impassive Venus whose
Davidov-inoculation was renewed each night.

Into the gasp plunged the fury of Wendt. "You're a
creep, Davidov. Why Ritt here trots you out as social
decoration, I don't know, unless to let his guests enjoy a
sight of the sewer. As for me, I've had it," and having
calculated that a man with a mouth like Davidov's is probably at least the coward I am and that my extra fifty pounds
and six inches will pacify if not tranquilize him, I get up,
snarling.

Ritt mentions something about seeing his "latest buy,"
Donald Taylor says he guesses he'll come with me, Davidov
manages, "Wait a mo'. Wait a mo' there, buddy. We gotta
talk this thing out," two of the ladies are shivering too
much to respond to my farewell nods, the other, the long
golden obbligato to the malodorous Davidov, puckers and
opens her lips in recognition of the farewell blast, perhaps
divining that it was she as much as her husband who excited
it.

The Bleeding Jellyfish,
or Masters and Servants

with—for bows to antiquity and other concessionary spice
—one epigraph from the saint of English humanism, Dr.
S. Johnson: *"There is nothing, Sir, too little for so little a
creature as man."* (which has, with its hidden injunction to
the objects of Gallupian inquisition to regard the recalci-
trance of small things before blowing stacks of utopian fury,
more force in the Age of Gallup than in Dr. J.'s hierarchical
time) and, for musicians, another from A. Von Webern:
"Life, that is to say, the defense of a form."

or The Persistence of Uoiichh

1

Eight A.M., slow getting started, not from Ritt's select
company and bargain booze, but from sheer sludge of time,
skeins of fat in blood, layers of surrender stacked in the
passage from sleep to waking.

Up, on with shorts scissored from denims shrunk in the
Carpinteria Laundro-Mat, haul Gus off the morning cartoons and descend the three tiers of sixty-nine pine steps
(only this morning do I notice the pretty mathematics)
to the empty beach.

Gus: "You better not run onem pockmark things."

—Em pockmarks is bloodworms.

I avoid them, raise heavy, archless feet and clump up the
beach trailed by Gus. When he senses a race and goes into

high, my overreacher's need levers my gross pins, and I
beat him by a mile. With frequent stops to assure him that
I'm watching his progress, really to mute the hard pumping
in my not—quite—unflabbed chest, the diaphragmatic
tremor after deep breaths. This morning, I look round
from one of my markers, a nude, fallen eucalyptus, and Gus
is furiously waving me back, his stickpins flailing the terrific
morning air. I lope back, Air-Rider Wendt. Gus, gorgeous,
blue-eyed, big-mouthed head split between hysteria and
joy, points me to his feet, where lies, sits, squats, a frightful
purplish glob of what I would elsewhere take for the fecal
deposit of a hippopotamus; or perhaps the aborted hippette
itself (gluey within the placenta). Vomitous, wrinkled glob.
Uoiichh.

—Look, Daddy, a jellyfish.

Shall such things live?

Closer, one sees incipient differentiae, rubbery pincers, a
kind of mouth. Gus nudges it with a eucalyptus prong. The
thing gathers itself, wrinkles up for a kind of progress. (Is
this what our wrinkles spell?) The pincer shifts, the ocean
rolls closer, a bubbled fringe breaks round the glob. "It
lives," I said. "It's alive."

—I'm going to bring it up to Mom.

—She'll collapse.

—You carry it.

—You're out of your little mind, lovey.

—I'll get me the bucket.

—Leave it alone. Let it go back to the ocean.

Which almost happens as the next wave, lapped by its
twin, floods the creature and brings it homeward a foot or
two.

"I'm gonna get the bucket." Since I have a sweet sight
in mind, the presentation of this uoiichh to the sleeping
Jeff-U, I say nothing. The little pins mill up the first tier of
steps.

I regard this miserable presentation of the sea. Wordsworth had not wasted a cubit of his verse on such as this.

Yet it by no means deserved the terrible fate Fellini gave its giant, plastic cousin at the end of that rebuke to (and wallow in) grotesquerie, *La Dolce Vita*. Among jellyfish, it holds its glob high.

The water embraces it. I pick up Gus's prong and urge it seaward. At which, there issues a squirt of thin, pathetic ink. Gus is back, fist round the loop of a metal bucket. "What happened?" A wave comes up, flushes feet and fish. "Help me, Daddy."

Gus puts the bucket edge on the jellyfish's. An inch of glob is on the metal. And then again, squirt, tiny hemorrhage from hidden wrinkles. "Gus, this jellyfish is bleeding. He's in pain."

Gus laughs at this splendid joke, takes eucalyptus prong in right, bucket in left hand, and tries to fork up glob. Another discharge barely misses his foot.

I take the branch, throw it into the water, and detach his fingers from the bucket. "Leave it be."

Oddly enough, no tantrum. But we run no more, ascend with the story of our discovery to awakened Davy, who doffs pajamas for shorts, runs to the beach, and ascends to tell us he can't find it. What relief. The Wounded Vet has made his way home. (*Histoire d'un Uoiichh.*)

2

On the wall of the Davy/Jeff-U bathroom (unusable toilet) there's a painting, "one of a series by Emil G. Bethke interpreting the world of ophthalmology." This Kandinsky cluster of globes—eye, earth, lens, sun—"illustrates the persistence of roundness, a simple derivative of the roundness of the eye, the solar bodies and the very instruments with which we examine them." I discharge medusa-shaped phlegm into the sink and meet Herr Bethke's globes. ("Medusa," for I have looked up "jellyfish" in Sackerville's big *Webster* and seen the picture of the rag-of-bone-hank-of-hair creature named by some witty naturalist.) My yellow-brown glob trailing its thin throat reins supports the thesis of Emil Bethke's art.

Roundness. Persistence. Tonal row. Row nothing. It is roundness, circular. A trap.

In Chicago, the Department's musical electrode, Derek Slueter, corners me weekly with the latest advance in musical slavery, "Dumbandeafer's Solipsism for Electro-Encephalograph" (a pianist playing while hooked to the apparatus whose record of his reactions to being hooked dictates what he plays).

To Slueter, Wendt: "I compose for liberation, not tyranny."

Secretive, snaggle-toothed, Jesus-bearded boy, he smears Game Theory, movies, computers, and synthesizers on our departmental head (and budget). The peace of Santa Barbara is, in no small measure, a Slueter-less peace.

Yet today, at the cypress work table, I sink not into the delicate shoals of my dear Deffand's exchanges with the icy bachelor, but into the calluses, cancerous boles, and labia-shaped knots. One week ago, they drove my fantasies, then me to the Ali Baba Café on Salsepuedes Street, where I slipped in behind the blue-lit teamsters, soldiers, adolescents, iron-eyed, gray-headed ex-sailors and watched the bumps and jangles of Miranda, the Gaza Stripper, almost stiffened enough to ask the mini-skirted dank blond waitress what time she finished. In the living room here there is a table made of a stump of eucalyptus. Its almost flesh-colored (Caucasian) gap faces the couch. I have not been able to joke about it. The persistence of need, a prison.

This morning, everything underlines enclosure: the staves I rule on the white paper, the sharps turning keys which fail to open doors, the annual striations of the cypress, the marine wrinkles raised to purplish bars of cloud. The persistence of uoiichh.

3

We sit, the four of us, Donloubie and his Missus, Velia
and I, in a stupendous room before fifty feet of treated glass
within which preen five miles of crescent beach and untold
acres of moon-and-oil-rig-lit ocean.

The room is modeled after the Double Cube at Wilton,
but "fifty percent larger," says Donloubie, stranding my
small mathematics. A crystal mass, twenty feet above us,
draws mild glitter from a hundred gold and silver objects—
trays, decanters, dishes, whatnots. Soft light seeps from
ivory walls indented with bas-reliefs of mermaids, plastery
mock-ups of stonework in the Church of the Miracoli.

We're couched on fifteen curved feet of gold and rose
drinking some vodka concoction reddened by a raspberry-
like offspring from Donloubie's hothouse. A black-tied,
hunched-up butler (not the chauffeur) approaches with
heaped tray.

"Ooh," says Missus D., "China Chicks." Butler leans
with his great offering, I study the crusted containers of
herb and dribblings, reach for a couple, and then—they
are so small—as the servant withdraws, reach again, causing
him to miscalculate, so that the tray tips and one of the
tiny globs falls over the edge to the golden tundra of carpet.

—Swine.

Donloubie, eyes like red ice.

I, momentarily taking this qualifier to myself (who
better?), flush, swallow, cough. Butler, hide leathered by
frequent whips, mutters apology (to me, Donloubie, or
perhaps the injured Chick), scoops, large tray perfectly
suspended in one hand—had they recruited him from the
defunct Twentieth Century Limited?—and begins a second
passage of the Chicks. Persistence of roundness. Velia
utters profound Thank Yous against Butler's perhaps-
humiliation. His back, in retreat, humps an extra centimeter,
hours nearer its grave.

Masters and servants were having and giving bad times in Santa Barbara. The police had arrested Mrs. Joel's housekeeper, Mrs. Wrightsman. Donloubie: "Not that I blame the woman. Joel said his missus threw her dinners on the floor."

Is the floor Santa Barbara's sacred space?

Perhaps to Mona Wrightsman, who, bent there to retrieve her spurned veal chop, there gathered the final fury of a hundred such rejections, from there rose to the vicious spurner, and, there standing, rage and pan still hot, beat and beat again the thin, hated skull.

Home, I read in Roger Caillois's *Man, Play and Games* of the romantic toys of boys, the practical toys of girls. Had the child Mona been given miniature skillets? And Butler, had he been given by mistake a broom instead of a three-master? (So China Chicks instead of China Clippers.) And Mrs. Joel, who refused meal after meal, not to find what slaked her appetite, but—Donloubie's version—to fill the day's tyrannic quota—what were her Christmas gifts? Dolls? Which cried when squeezed? Ninety-five-pound Caesar in rose bathrobe and puffy slippers (Mrs. Wrightsman's doll) to be swatted, sponged, stripped, lifted by those muscular arms, carried to lidded pool, dumped, and lidded up again.

Velia, in rebellious connubial servitude, once again determines nevermore to take master-talk from Julius Charlemagne Robespierre Wendt, turns her back to him and reaches bed-edge. Wendt, Servant, if not Sum, of Appetite and Ambition, conjures up from opposite edge the golden spread of the Musical Anti-Christ Davidov's wife, and breathing, grunting, manacled, and sinking, covets, covets.

Names and Games, Tales and Flails

1

News drifts in muted to our still cove. Plains, mountains, and deserts do something to televised accounts of Cleveland riots, political treks, the Politburo in Prague, or even, just north of us, the trial of Newton, the Black Panther. The palms, the waves, the dowitcher trills, E flat, G, make it all remote.

Chicago devotee of The New York *Times*, here Velia skims the eight-page *News-Press* and reads California history. She likes to snow me with unexpected expertise, and hides her sources under pillows, behind Sackerville's pathetic library, or her boxes of Modess. A literary Geiger counter, I find them all. I leave no print unread, cookbooks, cereal boxes, Jeff-U's *Pigskin Prevue*, Davy's *Mad*. From the toilet seat I spot behind the blue Economy-Size box, Professor Bean's *California, An Interpretation*, and read how this hundred million acres of mountain, desert, parboiled valley, and paradisal cove received its name from Calafia, Queen of California (an "island between India and paradise"), a black beauty who trained griffins to feed on men. Recruited to fight Amadis of Gaul and his son Esplandian at Constantinople, her winged assistants chewed up both sides. Broken, she turned Christian, married Esplandian's son, and took him back to California. All splendiferously rendered by García Ordóñez de Montalva, and read by the deputies of Cortez who sailed up the difficult coast the year after downing Montezuma.

Friday afternoon, for the first time in my daily racket encounters with Jeff-U, my arm could not deliver the cannonballs which plunge him into errors, despair, and double faults. My smart drop shots, volleys, slices, cuts,

and crosscourt lobs were countered by confident drives.
Jeff-U bounced up and down in wait for my patsy service
and swung like his dream of Pancho Gonzales. Six-two,
six-one. I walked off with a dry-mouth whistle, asweat from
black eyes to limp crotch, drove wildly home on the freeway,
neck too sore to check the approaches, honked at by swerv-
ing Jaguars, missing the Serena turnoff and forced to double
back from Summerland along the railroad track.

Saturday, after three hours of fluffing Walpole's aria at
Mme. Du Deffand's death, music which I must repeat when
Mary Berry hears of Walpole's death, I was ready for revenge. I hung around Jeff-U's prostrate form, his immense,
bony, but well-made back (ah, I thought, I have given him
something, Velia's back being a less-distinguished feature of
her body, curved by some displacement of vertebrae into
a flattened S). The back was being tickled for a penny a
minute by Gus and Davy, alternately.

"Wanna play?" asked Jeff-U. Cut-rate Medici of Titilla-
tion.

The boys said, "Yes."

I said, "Why not?" and we were off in Sackerville's VW
to the beautiful court set in the California oak grove of the
Montecito park. There in Act II of the agon, I lost the
first set 6–1, went silently into the second, won the first two
games, lost the third out of sheer weakness, not having the
strength to serve consistently hard, arm aching with pre-
visioned defeat, lost the next four, and then, going to
position on the base line, heard Jeff-U say his finger was
blistering, and "Let's quit," meaning, "We've made the
point, why continue?" I left the court silent, trailed by the
three boys—the little ones having played during warm-up
time—and went in silence home. There, before my shower,
I sat down at the little upright I'd rented for our room, and
worked out with terrific speed a perfect aria. I haven't played
it over, haven't dared, but I feel its rightness, its place in the
score, its power, felt its words (a line of French, then one of
English) as the sybaritic bachelor imagines writing a letter
to the dead woman who, from the screen, interprets his

words in such a way that they drive small, elegant stakes into her heart.

The explosion—to use the word which in the 1960s stands for every exacerbated encounter, chemical or human, mental or physical—the explosion at Jeff-U came out of the void the next day, an hour before he is to call for Ollendorf (who changed flights at the last minute and arrived a day early). "Better put clean sheets on your bed for him," said I.

"O.K." He gets up, surprising me a bit by the speed of his accession. "I'll put one sheet on."

—Better put two.

—He's my friend. I know what he wants.

I get up and follow him to the linen closet. "Take two, please. Your mother and I are his hosts, it's up to us to see things are done right."

—Bullshit.

I take this in stance for a bit. He has gone inside with the two sheets. I follow, notice his bathtub is filled with sand. "I've asked you to keep the sand out of that bathtub."

—That's Davy. He comes in the back way, washes his feet in there every day, five times a day, and the sand just stays there.

"Will you clean it out please, before you go?" My words are polite, but, Walpole-like, there is the undercurrent of menace in them.

—Let Davy do it.

"I realize you've had a tough day, a tough six weeks," I say. "I know you're exhausted from having your back tickled, but I want you to clean it, so your mother doesn't have to further twist her back doing it herself."

"Eff-u," says Jeff-U. (Despite almost universal literary freedom, I am a child of repression in print and usually refrain from writing out what is a not infrequent presence in my speech. ((Let the Edwardian guff of this sentence express my feeling.)))

I approach him, eyes aglitter with rage. "You say that to me once more, and I'll knock the living crap out of you."

His eyes show scare, but he forces his voice through it. "You better not hit me. Ever again."

At which, the rage of days touched off, I shove him across the room onto the bed. He yells, his legs, very long legs, sneakered, start kicking wildly, pumping him up. I crowd him, daring more violent response. "You effing bastard," is the response.

I punch his arm hard.

He leaps up, I punch and miss, he gets out the door, and now amazed (for I've never hit him like this), as well as fearful and furious, he calls to the closed door of our room, "Cmere, Mom, cmere, Dad's trying to *hurt* me."

And I, hearing the wonder in this, O brave new world that has this in it, feel my fire flooded, doused, and think, My god, this is Jeff-U, little beauty-boy whom I showed off to Mlle. Boulanger in Paris (a picture keeps this memory refreshed), to whom I gave milk bottles in Cologne reciting the *Inferno*, singing the *Well-Tempered Clavichord*, dear companion and confidant, and he is just learning that I am —*was!*—trying to hurt him.

I stride out, whisper in the muted menace-voice of Jimmy Cagney (fellow alumnus of Stuyvesant High School, along with Lewis Mumford and Daniel Bell), "Don't upset me like that again, Jeffrey. Never again."

"I'm not upset," he says.

My rage starts up, my tone rests monotonous. "You haven't the emotional richness of a pebble," and go into the bathroom, heart throbbing terribly, mind so swept with self-disgust, disgust at Jeff-U, disgust at my violent failure as a father, I'm unable to speak to him with any ease at all for four or five days, even with Ollendorf there. (Ollendorf turns out to be a jolly, decent boy, who comes in on a happy roar and jokes the entire two weeks he remains.)

2

Velia has accepted an invitation to a "peace-making" dinner
at the Mullidynes.

"Why did you accept?" I yell. "You know I can't see
people when I'm working."

Not quite true, sometimes I have to see them. "Is that
effer, Davidov, coming?"

"I assume that's what the peace-making is about," said
Velia, who has had a triumphant version of my squelch,
without, of course, its sexual basso rilievo.

The Mullidynes live in the hills on the lip of the desert.
Donald Taylor drives us up in Ryan, his convertible
(brought from a man named Ryan who never put the top
down but liked the style of convertibles). The drive is
up the Riviera, Santa Barbara spread out like a cupful of
Genoa, then into the strange broken, mocha-colored hills
nudging and nuzzling each other, the most artful, Cézanne-
looking hills I've ever seen (and I was once in Aix-en-
Provence for the playing of the *Drang Nach Bach* songs, my
opus 9).

All the way, the body of Patricia Davidov rises from
those hills to calm the agitation raised by the menacing ap-
parition of her husband.

But when we arrive at Mullidynes' house—a fine eyebrow
on a noble hill—the Davidovs are not there. Nor do they
come. Had he refused? Or had Mullidyne managed to un-
hinge his lower jaw? (The evening supplied the answer.)

Mullidyne is quite decent out of Davidov's presence.
And his wife turns out to be quite remarkable, very long
and soft and smart, a cabinetmaker, fisherman, linguist,
mother of an immense, well-mannered and—tonight—in-
conspicuous brood, an honest person who does not press
for intimacy yet is quickly your intimate. (Life—she seems
to say—is too short for anything else.) Finally, a marvelous
cook. We have a terrific kidney dish, I see the Escoffier

open in the kitchen, it must be Number 1339, *Turban de Rognons à la Piemontaise,* "Fill a ring with *rizotto à la Piemontaise* (2258), press into the mold and keep hot." And, after, marvelous melon balls and strawberries from the valley. Says Sandra, in a voice you would expect a rose to have, "I wanted to have valley grapes in hard sauce, but Chavez has called for a boycott of table grapes. I don't dare buy them." Velia, who has just lugged home a mountain of green grapes, receives a punishing stare from me, and says "I'm not a Californian."

"Don't buy them again," say I, though kindly. Velia has a new dress, a Finnish print (she has read the Finns have learned to stain materials a new way), full of blue and yellow balls and great stripes, a kind of sack but better formed, light, but you know (she says) you've got something on, a knockout, it almost restores her looks. (She had them, her legs are very fine, her body thin, but neat; but that's over.)

It is a night for stories. Of a pattern, as I see it four hours later, riding down the hill in the dark, each story so much more final in its way than a tennis match. (Though who knows. The people involved may have emerged from the fierce predicaments in which our memory abandoned them.)

The one that tells for me is about the Davidovs, but its trailer, another account of domestic fury also stays. It's Sandra's psychology professor at Duke, a man who, infected with J. B. Rhinitis, took to a Jungian strain of it, the so-called "substratum of certain memories which were 'not one's own,'" the apparent ability of some semi-mesmerized people to "recall" experiences of psychic ancestors, "Bridie Murphys," or "Viennese court ladies." His wife, a student of cell conductivity in frogs, expressed the contempt a lifetime's Scotch-Presbyterianism had schooled her never to express by telling him that she too had strange inklings of an antecedent life. "Oh yes?" he said, from his worldly, husband side. "Were you a cigar butt in Sir Walter Raleigh's mouth?" But weeks later, short of a willing subject, he decided he had perhaps overlooked a local treasure, and asked if she were still smoldering in Raleigh's jaws.

"No," she said, "but I was bending over the microscope last week when I had the strangest feeling that I was gathering fernshoots by a river with a name I knew deeply but which now sounds strange to even pronounce." She had never used, and he had never heard, the word "fernshoots" before.

He removed his Roi-tan from the ashtray, inhaled for steadiness, and asked what name that was. "Huai," she said.

"I'm curious, why do you think?"

"The River Huai," she said, "a broad river curling around a kind of cape of firlike trees."

"We can begin tonight," he said, and had her lie back on a couch, and switched on his tape recorder. There she registered her month's secretive research into fourth-century Chinese history. She was, she said, a Sinic farm girl living near river fortifications worried by Sienpi troops; her father Li Huang-ti, grumbled in Chinese—she'd spent twenty hours in the language lab, playing the records—about taking his turn as sentry on the wall. (Sandra's account was more detailed.)

The Jungian husband, blank, like most of us, to any Chinese history between Confucius and Sun Yat-sen, had the notes transcribed and taken to the American professor of "Chinese Civilization: A Survey," not at first revealing the extraordinary source, but when told that, yes, there was such a river, there was a repulsion of nomadic invasion attempts in the fourth century, said, "It's my wife," and asked if the strange sounds which issued from her were authentic Chinese. "I've never bothered speaking it," said the scholar. "Though I pick out what might be a few words. But here," and he smudged out a few characters, "see if she knows these characters. I'll transcribe the English sounds for you." That night, the Chinese peasant girl disclaimed ability to read, that was only for administrators of the rites.

So it went for weeks, until a book-length monograph was transcribed from the tapes, the West Virginia farm girl translating more of her feeling into fourth-century China than she had ever revealed on her own. Her husband was enchanted with this metamorphosis of dogged student of cell conductivity into naïvely sensuous Chinese village girl (raped by Uncle Su-i Chen, taken up as concubine by a weaver from Shang-Chi, dying of a sexually ignited pneumonia)—all mimicked on the stiff Grand Rapids sofa while he, the rapt psychologist, fell away from all his domineering cynicism and behavioral training. After he submitted the manuscript with full complement of annotation to, not the *Journal of Parapsychology*, but Basic Books, his wife told him over his four-minute eggs that she'd played this little joke on him, she thought it was the way to lead him back to proper experimental work, some of the books she'd used were in the upper shelf of the linen closet, would he perhaps return them to the library, they were overdue, and his first class was nearer to it than her lab, she would bring him home a nice sirloin for supper.

When she came home that night, he had not left the chair, she drove him to the hospital, and when, six weeks later, he came out, the term was over and she had gone.

Watching Sandra stroke her husband's browless little head (tactile conclusion to this gruesome tale), I thought, "Aha, this soft jewel of a woman, this fruit goddess with her great bowl of rose and golden balls, has suffered terrible blows somewhere, Mullidyne is her rock. He must have his facet of tenderness as she must have hers of toad. Soft jewel with toad in head. Such beauteous carats congeal only from secreted poison. Brutal father. Psychopathic mother."

"Tell about Davidov and Pat," she told Mullidyne in her lovely voice, and in white virgin's dress, passed the crystal bowl of strawberries and melon balls. Behind her, a great window showed night squeezing a line of sun-fire against the blunt point of the hill. "Davidov," said Mullidyne, and laughed. "Davidov." And with what one then could see was indeed a bit of forehead, contrived a wrinkle or two of frown.

Davidov, he said, sprang from the bowels of the Brooklyn ghetto. Ugly, squat, an atheist broken from an orthodox cigar-roller's home, "saved for scholarship" by the public library, where, each week, he read B. H. Haggin in The Nation and resolved to study music, not for love of music —"He's next to tone deaf"—but for love of the destruction he sensed—wrongly—in Haggin's devastating columns. Native shrewdness sent him to the top of Boys' High and into City College. In forty-two, despite feeble vision and flat feet, he was drafted, pulled like a rodent from New York, and sent, dazzled by fear, to a Kansas army camp, where he stayed, goldbricking and clerking. Knowing he'd need proficiency in an instrument to pursue musical studies, he got a local drummer to teach him the tympani. In forty-five, he was transferred to San Francisco, and aimed like a broken arrow for the Japanese invasion, but, with Hiroshima and the end of the war, was discharged in Oakland. He walked over to Berkeley, enrolled with his G.I. Bill, and became the first World War II veteran to get a doctorate in music, his dissertation, The Failure of Opus 111: An Analysis of Tovey's Critical Blindness and Beethoven's Musical Deafness. (The manuscript on my office desk had been revised for a publication which was never to be.)

In Berkeley, he taught two freshman Musical Appreciation classes. Enrolled in one, and soon auditing the other, was a beautiful co-ed from the Napa Valley named Patricia Mulholland, the poor, smart daughter of a workman in the Mondavi Bottling Plant at St. Helena, a cousin of the Los Angeles aqueduct-builder. That this long, great-titted, golden beauty with a famous California name should be hanging on every word dropped from his muzzle (my memory has altered Mullidyne's more straightforward vocabulary) so intoxicated Davidov that his lectures became wilder and wilder, more and more notorious. The destruction of every musical reputation past and present fused with the

discovery of sexual perversity or ineptitude in nine-tenths
of the great composers of musical history. He called the
fusion the Myth of the Castrated Orpheus. It had the postwar co-eds slavering at his very name. But Pat was there
first, and with the most, and, age seventeen, she let her
untouched cup run over the parched, violent instructor.
With the ferocity of a miser, he whisked her down to City
Hall, wrote Davidov after her name, and within a month
had impregnated her with the first of their five children,
two sons who but faintly darkened the generous gold of
Mulholland genes, three daughters who stooped under the
squat darkness of Davidov's. And down the coast they
moved to Santa Barbara's new campus, where he took over
as chairman—though then but assistant professor—of the
Music Department.

Here revolts began. First, his colleagues protested his
tyranny, obstinacy, and musical ignorance to the chancellor
of the University, who removed him from the chairman-
ship and threatened to withhold tenure unless he mended
his tattered ways, and then Patricia, who told him that she
loathed him more than any human being could be loathed,
felt she was married to the devil himself, and was now
ready to have affairs on any street corner with any man
who'd deign to look by her ever-swelling belly to the great
promise of her never-fulfilled-by-Davidov interior.

Under these twin assaults, Davidov, like rotten wood,
broke apart. While Pat picked up astonished flutists in his
own department, took them to motels, paid the bills, and
shed her extraordinary graces on their graceless heads (this
from the unbeautiful, browless Mullidyne), Davidov stayed
in the hot mesa apartment, warming the bottles, changing
the diapers, driving the kids to school, and hiring sitters
when he had to stagger to the University to give his but
slightly less fiery lectures on the febrile contortions of
Handel and Pergolesi. At night, he would call down the
list of graduate students, till he traced Pat's lover-of-the-
day, and beg him to release her for the night. Then, said
Mullidyne, he found me at Alabama, liked my little article

in *Musical Quarterly* on the "Harmonic Blunders in *Le Nozze de Figaro*," brought me here, and then, from the moment I arrived, poured into my ear his tribulations with Pat, with the Department, with the life he led, he, the great Davidov, who should be shaping the strong intellects of men who would rewrite musical history, transform the flaccidity of contemporary composers and performers, and water this Sahara of the Arts with the kind of criticism which had lifted literature from caveman grunts to the heights of Miller, Dahlberg, and Selby. "I," said Mullidyne, "who had my friend, Sandra, waiting here at the hearth for me, though we were on Anacapa Street then, couldn't tear myself away until Pat would grind up in their Pontiac— exhausted but triumphant—and brush past poor Davidov with, 'Did you remember to put the vitamins in Gloria's bottle?' "

What vengeance. Yet if she hated him, she hated herself worse. (This seemed reasonable to even Pat-lusting me.) "Sash here had to go to her sister's funeral and take care of her kids for two weeks; and Pat was on my doorstep every time I came back from class. 'I've told Bert I'm here, he's not to bother you,' and she'd lie on the couch, shoes off—she has beautiful feet, kind of thick ankles but terrific legs, I nearly went out of my frigging mind. She begged me to run away with her, I should leave Sash—Sash knows this—Sash, she said, was too soft for a man of my mettle, whereas she'd become hard on Davidov's brutality, she was basically soft as Sash but would stand up to me, improve me. And I'd just shake my head and say I wish she were happy but couldn't she make it for her children, if not for Bert. And she said, 'They have his heart. They can think of nothing but what's in front of them. Or worse, what's in front of each other. They live to eat, they lie around, they have no curiosity.' But I couldn't believe it, I thought the children amazingly good in view of what was happening in the home, helpful to their father, sympathizing with him, yet, as far as I could see, not harsh to their mother. And then she'd go, and half an hour later, Bert would call and ask what did she say, what did she do, and I would say, 'Please keep her away from me, she just complains of her unhappiness, she's such a child it's tragic." And he'd say, 'Just let her talk to you for a bit, it's better than her picking up these bastards in the street, maybe she'll talk herself out of it. At home, she never says anything, she never talked, ever, except dumb-ass women's questions, why this and why that, why's the ground down, why's the sky up, and I'd have to knock the shit out of her, here she'd been my own student, I'd given her a couple of A's, I still think she earned them, but she was probably just giving me back my own words and I was so blinded by my putz I didn't see what I was getting into, Jesus Christ, I wasn't made for this, Frankie,' and on and on, till I'd say, 'Bertie, I've got to go to sleep, Sash is calling me and forgive me.' He'd scream, 'You effing pig-sticker, you're nothing but a mouse-brain pig-sticker, I saved you from George Wallace and pellagra and you can't give me the time of day, you're an effing sonovabitch,' and so on, until the next day, or maybe two days later, he wouldn't call, but he'd know what time I went to pick up my mail, and he'd bump into me, and say, 'Francis, I was wrong, you and I are the same type, we're both married to dumb pigs, we both know music, we oughtn't to quarrel.' And it would start all over again."

Sandra, on the couch by her husband, smiled as if she'd not heard this story, as if her husband had repulsed the proffered detente with, "Don't say my wife's a pig. Or even yours."

"But she's still with him," said Velia. "I saw them holding hands downtown in the Paseo." (And my heart bumped in fury, at Velia, at Davidov, at Patricia.)

"What happened," said Mullidyne, "was some kind of contract he made with her. He let her have a round-the-world trip, and in the interval, he built her this house on the shore, it must have cost him sixty thousand even seven years ago, and he hardly had a nickel. He taught night classes, lectured all over, though nobody's ever heard of

him, he wrote book reviews at twenty dollars a shot, not
even taking time to open the books, just pouring them out,
on any subject, he did a stint on the roads in the summer—
he's still got muscles under that flab—everything, and she
came back after four months and she's stayed down there,
and I haven't been asked once, and though I see her at
parties, it's one nod and good-bye, and that's the way it's
been for seven years. Oddly enough, I still care for him.
And for her. He's a brute, yes, but he's got standards. He
cares deeply. He thinks, maybe wildly, but how many
think at all?"

Snaking down the Marcos Pass in Ryan, Donald Taylor,
as if reborn in the foam of these passionate stories, said,
"My God, how can Mullidyne take him? How can he go
on all these years with all that he knows about him?"

"He had to have his Misery Vitamins every day. Maybe
to have something to amuse that great wife of his," I said,
taking a look from mine.

My bed-reading in dear Deffand's letters offered a better
answer. Wrote the old poison pen about Buffon, the
naturalist, "*Il ne s'occupe que des bêtes; il faut l'être un
peu soi-même.*"

Gradations of Effing

1

That night, stimulated by this storied bowl of untasted
goodies, I slept with my dear wife for the first time in a
month. A certain, special pleasure, old acquaintance newly
met, though with P.D.'s imagined opulence fresh on my
mental bones, I was scarcely replete after the short-order
feast. (Of course the polar breeze of imagined betrayal gave
its own zing of sadness and soft revenge; what a rummage
sale sex is.)

In the Tacitean tradition, my Walpole was a great comparer; surefooted, though procrustean. This morning, while the lawn sprinkler makes instant rainbows in its whirl, and there is otherwise a stillness in pine, palm, and fir, it strikes me I want a musical comparison between such elegance of gradation and the rough-hewn, grandly uncertain gradation of my own mind. Music has splendid means of articulating such contrasts. I think my opera may be about the difference between oceanic passion and terrene order; policeman and prostitute, each a social control for other people's passion, summon up Walpole and Mme. Du Deffand to control their own. Something like that.

But it's not enough. Judgment and action live on fine-honed distinctions; verbal ones. ("Galba had the capacity to rule, if only he hadn't."—Tacitus; "Pitt liked the dignity of despotism, Mansfield, the reality."—Walpole.) Velia and the thought of Patricia offer different things. What to choose? (Maybe the policemen should fall in love with Madame Du Deffand. Like the detective in *Laura*.)

I'd waked up choked with such thought; or, not choked, soaked. In that estuary—inbetween—state, I heard a thickening of line, a gulf of bass, E C sharp D D flat. Pressure: and into mind Voltaire called out by Rohan's bullies, beaten in the street, Rohan, chaired, saying, "Spare the head. It can still amuse us," the crowd watching Voltaire, bleeding, mad with fury and astonishment, the crowd saying of Rohan. "Oh, that was decent. *Le bon seigneur.*" "Enough," says Rohan. Voltaire, up, bony, long, bemudded, back to the drawing room, where he had been the light of the company, answering their gaping faces with his story, seeing them freeze, sympathetic emotion not available for the likes of him; a solo bassoon, staggering in fifths, a clutch of cello, a slash of violin, and then, orchestral rumbling, a small structure building. From this day, Voltaire's dazzle will burn, the Revolution is ten years nearer.

Pressure. In the bed, a sense of leg, Velia's. I roll over, lift an interposed valley of blanket, the leg shifts away.

Cold, dangerous, selfish, womb-raddled, public-minded, hating.

Yesterday, in the San Ysidro Pharmacy, buying wine, I waited by the magazines till the afternoon *News-Press* arrived with the latest on the Joel case. By the fifteen-dollar cribbage boards and Japanese television sets for the beach, a barefoot girl, with fantastic legs and rear. Bare-armed, face pale, blond, a little blunted, but with that sense in the nostrils and mouth that she wanted someone. Her breasts. No great matter, but there, in an easy flowered blouse. White pants, a cozy for her beauteous rump. Wrenching legs. I looked up from *Scientific American* and caught her sense of being looked at. She came back, examined the paperbacks. Had she ever gone through a book? She came to the magazines. In a minute, I turned and brushed her arm. How old? Statutory-rape age. I couldn't tell. Hopefully eighteen, more hopefully twenty, but not unlikely, fifteen, sixteen. Too young, even in this new world where anything goes, where anything that can be called love is applauded—cows, leaves, watermelons, Krafft-Ebing sweetened for mass production—like "Château Laflute" made out of horse blood, cow urine, and the discarded skins of Marseilles grapes. The Revolution's won, we are all privileged, it is not kitsch, mass culture is for real, though it is plain style for all. I stoop for *Life*, my bare arm, tanned beneath short shirt, feathers the fantastic leg. All I need is "Can I give you a lift?" or "Shall we?" or "Let's go outside" or "I'll be in the VW." I have Sackerville's plates, I'll use a version of his name. There is a whole string of new motels, half-empty. Or, hell, in the fields, bugs crawling in us. *Life* has investigations of Masaryk's defenestration, and of thalidomide children learning to cope, a crack at American doctors who didn't know about the Heidelberg clinic where the child learns how to zip, walk, eat, and, as they put it, "toilet himself." Why doesn't every doctor call into the World Health O., which has all the stuff on a computer? Like that Hemingway story of the

doctor who carries the Guide to Medicine indexed for
symptoms and treatment. *Life* quotes one of the benevo-
lently lethal Rostow brothers, Never a time when so great
a percentage spent on armament, yet Donald Taylor told
me we're almost back at the Renaissance, when the Napiers
and Da Vincis refused to publish their lethal inventions.
Only vacant-minded puritans and bright tinkerers will work
on weapons. But there's the rub. I stoop again, the leg is
there. I take my seven-buck Château Lafitte and depart. I
will not be refused, I will not be arrested. (Though I know
the symptoms and the treatment, I will stick with my
disease.)

2

I look up Davidov in the Faculty List, dial, but hang up
before the tone, then sit by the phone and look at the
eucalyptus, a huge salmon, its terrible insides exposed by
the old fire bolt. I ring again.

A child's voice: "Davidov residence."

—May I please speak with Mrs. Davidov?

A flash of music, a terrific theme. I leap to score paper,
phone stretched in left hand, pencil notes, De, dom, dom,
dom, de, da-da, dada, da-da, dee de dom. Heavenly, and
then more, a flood, transpose, shift, work in the tonic, a
depth of bass, a figure.

—Yes? Yes? Who is it?

—Pat?

—Yes. Who's this?

Sigh: Defenestration of Inspiration. "It's Jeff Wendt."

"Oh. Didn't think I'd hear from you." Meaning?

—I want to talk to you. Not to Bert. Just you. Think
we can manage that?

Pause. "Mmm." I was in.

—Your body's on my mind. I want to see it. I want to
see you. I can hardly wait.

—Mmm.

—Can you meet me at the Safeway in fifteen minutes?

—Half an hour.

—I'll be there in fifteen minutes, in a yellow VW. I'll park as far from the store as I can, in the southeast part of the lot.

—I can't figure directions.

—I'll see you. What'll you be driving?

—A beat-up powder-blue Ford station wagon.

—I can't wait to see you. So long.

—Good-bye.

I haven't shaved. I haven't shat. Bowels crucial. At home, I shave, shit, and read at once. Velia has taken a picture of the three-ring activity. If I write a sequel to this memoir, in the new age of freedom, it will be the dust jacket. Here, the plug is too far from the toilet. I first squat. (The equalizer: Shelley, the Kennedys, Bonaparte, Walpole, Anaximander; Thales fell into a pile of it.) I am too nervous to let go. Then shave with my Philips, bought two years ago in Amsterdam after they played the *Quartet in No Movement* and after the only visit of my life to an official whore.

—You off?

—Yeah.

—I need to get a few things at the store.

Christ. The Safeway. "I'll pick 'em up. Give me a list." Grumble, but she writes one.

Jeff-U has my car keys, he has lost his ninth set. ("I suppose you never lose anything." "You jerk, I pay for what I lose and pay for the replacement. And still I haven't lost a key since nineteen-sixty-one." Arbitrary figure. "Or anything else. Not only is your mind a sieve, but your pockets are full of holes. And the main thing is, you just don't give a damn. Well, that is going to change, buster brown, you are going to be paying your own sweet freight very soon.") The keys are in his back pocket, along with a besanded dollar bill, gum wrappers, change, and, Lord love us, a hairpin with a blond hair therein. Nobody but Davy has blond hair in the Wendt family. My God. When has he had the time?

I have lost all feeling in my gavel. I may not be able to do my stuff. Fantastic.

But I'm there, baking on the asphalt lot, fifteen reflective minutes before the station wagon wheels up the ramp an indiscreet thirty miles an hour, whirls down the last row, then the middle, where I am, and finds a place two empty cars away. My God, she's a big woman.

—Hlo.

I lean in the half-open window. It is the east, and Patricia. The alba is the blast of a Jaguar. ("Ah," says Donald, driving into Montecito, "a Jaguar. I'm home." He saw a black Cadillac the other day. "What are things coming to?" There are more Rolls-Royces for these ninety-three hundred people than in any four blocks of Park or Fifth.) "Glad you came."

She has on one of these psychedelic prints which women with small figures can use as camouflage but which a great beauty like this doesn't need. All she needs is a strip of burlap, one single color with maybe one odd streak of another, the rest done by that great corpus delicti (though not, as yet, by me). "Where you wanna talk?"

—See that motel down the corner. That's where.

—Climb in.

I go around. The door is stuck. Davidov hasn't thrown a new car in with the house and round-the-world. She leans over, and it is then, lightly through the glass, that I catch the outline which cements the runny swamp of my belly, stiffens the gavel, the resolve, here in the noon parking lot of the neo-Aztec center (bougainvillea empurpling the latticework, a gnarled oak brought in from the hills to make a jungle nook).

The *patronne*, back from making beds and distributing packets of soap, comes in from her betwixt brunch-and-lunch coffee. "Wife and I have been driving since dawn. We need a quick snooze. Up from . . ."

—Fifteen dollars. You can have Number Three, not on the highway.

I sign in "Mr. and Mrs. J. Mullidyne."

We enter the blind-drawn, shadowy room with the double bed. Patricia kicks off her shoes, she is down to five-ten,
turns around, her face flushed, her pointed nose huffed with
breath, thin mouth open. She holds out her arms. I lean
toward the burst of orange and purple sun between her
breasts and kiss the rough material, wrap my arms around,
and drive her awkwardly backward to the bed. Our breath
would have terrified Mme. Du Deffand. (Did Walpole
ever breathe like this?)

A deep kiss, her mouth rich with Filter Blend. Is there
no Lavoris in the Davidov compound?

We rise. I take off my blue sport shirt, breathe hard,
flex muscles.

She rises, Venus, barefoot, bends for her hemline—she
has somewhere unzipped—removes the dress so that, like
a great banana unpeeled upside down, her immense,
beauteous legs show to the pants, then her waist, ribs, the
bra, marvelous, the neck. I manage out of my Bermudas
(despite new obstacle). I wear no underpants. She steps out
of pants, I kiss her copious rear, draw up my arms, hers are
unclasping her bra, I cup the haughty twins, flip off the
cloth, she is mine, I hers, *Himmelweiss*. We fall back,
we entangle, she mouths my home base, I hold back, agony,
she is no novice, fortunate Davidov, this Napa Valley bottling queen. I make my way out, down the valley, hands
on the hills, lower over the great hump, into the sweet
divide, oh my, why is this not my daily life? What have I
done not to deserve this?

What a sight from beneath, great palisades of peach, she
bounces, she jounces, I manage with beach-hardened legs
to upend her, I am on top, in the holy saddle. (Paul has
just issued the decree from Rome. God, I assume this
beauty is in touch with Dr. Rock's pill. Upon this rock.
Poor Paul, will you go to your last resting place innocent
of this huffing sweetness? In abundance, I think of the un-
derprivileged.) And then, as always, and not when called
for, the great maiden humming, noising, "Unck, oonck,
yeyeye," and there we are. "Og God, maw, maw, maw." I

try, I exert, I limp without fuel, she crushes me. Fiat. It is done.

I sink beneath, I work the tongue, oh crushing, those eucalyptic thighs. "Ahhhh," she says. My eardrums.

Done.

We lie. In a minute, I look over. The great body is working, it is gauzed with sweat. I feel a twinge of surge. It grows apace. I wait. It grows. I lean over, I mount. "Hello, Dolly," she says. We wrestle, we throw each other about. I enter, we somersault, we twist, we bite, we hug, we sniff, taste, we hurt, we work it up, we go, we keep going, we are there again.

Basta.

We hug each other. I sleep.

Awake. "We'll take a shower."

I can hardly walk. I am shamed to be seen, so limply small am I.

We're in the shower. We soap each other's hair, back, chests, the sun breaks on the line of sea, she touches my aching swell, it is tender, retreats, she is back at my rear, I lean into her, we are face to face, we kiss under the jerking spurts of water. Wet, we track our way over the polished wood onto the sheets, we work our way, I slowly, she but fed by what has wearied me, though inside, she squeaks, is tight. I come up to the mark, there is a muscular spasm, there is something else. "I love you," says foolish old undergraduate I.

"I love this."

We agree to meet tomorrow at the Safeway. Two o'clock. I will have a longer time to work.

3

It turns out (what I have but suspected and hardly cared about till now) that I am not the only one in the family making the record. Velia's notebooks, which I thought contained merely digests of her occasional course work at

the School of Social Service Administration (her pre-meno-
pausal contribution to urban wreckage) contain personal
observations as well. I should have married Roz, the con-
stricted Connecticuter, whose bowels would not move for
days (what a partner for Igor, the Hypochondrical Penman), or the culturally silenced Cholonese girl in the biology lab in Paris—was it Vo Ban?—who was so mad for
navel-licking and the presence of oranges in the love-bed.

This record-keeping, though it is much more than that,
is a late and perverse development. It must derive from our
reading, in succession (me, as always—almost always—
first), the novel of Tanizaki about the couple who leave
their diaries open to stimulate each other's jaded impulse.

But what purpose has Velia's epic catalog of my smells,
warts, and deformities (hairy toes, unbalanced ass, flabby
chest, hawkish nose—black hair rampant on snotty ver-
dure)? And is it intended for me? Or the children? (The
notebooks lie all over the house.)

And, astonishingly, there are analyses of the unhappier
traits of our (I assume) children: Gus's rages, Davy's stub-
bornness, Jeff-U's narcissism, Gina's sharp tongue. Are these
her notion of the proper Annals of the Gens Wendt?

She is moving the vacuum around, the striated hose
leashing the noise-box, which, she deeply knows, prevents
my work. Barefoot, I sneak behind her and stamp the green
circuit-breaker. She heaves, breathes fright, turns.

She has on yellow pants bought from Magnin's, a surge
of Californianization, but her legs and rear are so thin, she
cannot fill these glaring funnels. They droop pathetically
below her coccyx, jounce, unpressed by sufficiency. Her
face is red with repressed fury.

"I can't work with that." Courteously. "I'm sorry."

Her mouth sucks itself in, the cheeks dimple, not in
female courtship, but in advertisement of displeasure at
male peacockery.

"Translating your charming diary notes into music is a
job that needs concentration. I can't simply transcribe
them. I need a template. Music can't take such acids. Like

the body, it needs solid stuff, proteins." And I pat the limp
rear of the trousers. Her *beaux yeux,* a pure hazel, no one
has such single-colored eyes as Velia, how long is it since
they entranced me?

"You've been reading m-y private notebooks." That
ascension for Miss Berry, end on B flat.

—You left them on the right—the northwest—corner
of my very own work table. It was the clearest passage to
India ever not-supposed-to-be traversed.

—I can't follow that. I don't read your notebooks.

—I don't keep diaries. My notebooks are sketchbooks.
If you wash your hands, you can read them.

—I don't open your letters.

—I wouldn't say that.

—I haven't opened them in years unless I know they're
also meant for me.

When a marriage fails, the couple which has opened its
other's mail, ceases to do so. And vice versa.

She sits down on the golden couch and covers her small
face with her fine hands. Her grandmother's ring, weaving
bands of emeralds, diamonds, and sapphires, glitters from
the third finger, right hand. She hasn't worn her engagement ring for years. (Its diamond came from the navel of
the little gold lady on my Uncle Herman's favorite ring.
I won the ring in a Casino game when I was six. "That's
what you call Big Casino," said Uncle Herman, and could
not be made, even by Aunt Lillie, to take it back.) Velia
says, "What did you read?"

—About the hair in my rump, the cruelty in my voice,
the smell of my body.

—I was furious and controlled myself by writing everything down. Everything that annoyed me that day, I
mean.

—It was very well written.

—Thank you.

—I myself don't think it's advisable to do this. It's not
like taking a cold shower, or singing away your miseries.
It's more like gastrulation, or, let me put it this way. It

seems that internal organs are made from material on the egg surface. I mean, if you start showing, even superficially, your discontents and dislikes, like that face you made when I turned off the vacuum, or these little body Travel Notes of yours, the stuff won't go away. It'll seep and steep inside and become part of you. So a bit of care, or even living together as we are will become impossible. You know when we behave decently to each other, even on the manners level, we soon get to care more for each other.

Velia is crying. Noiselessly. Probably was during my physiological analogy. She asks whether it would be all right to go in the room. (The room where we sleep and I work.)

—Let me get my paper and pens out first.

She goes in, the yellow pants so pitifully ugly I can't watch them, they are now curled up, her face is in the pillow. I take up the sheet I'm working on, then put it back. "I can't work this way. I'm sorry I read your notebooks."

She is heaving and humping in the pillow. No response. The situation is transformed, the apparent meek—who were never meek, just quiet in persistence—inherit the earth.

I grab *World Scriptures* and *Ideas of Modern Biology* (source of my analogy), and, in the kitchen, open a plastic cup of boysenberry yoghurt, whip, whip the scarlet juice in the low-fat whiteness, and read about the fly-catching feedback of a praying mantis. And for minutes keep from myself Velia's state.

Hold off from that puritan, judaic, masochistic analysis which will show me as tyrant, betrayer and brute, and will see Velia as Ariel calibanized by me. Mencius's disciple asked why some are great and some little men, and Mencius said the great men follow that part in them which is great, the little men that which is little. Hypocrisy, arrogance, wrath, conceit, harshness, and *Dummheit* enslave; fearlessness, steady wisdom, alms-giving (I gave the Negro shoeshiner in the shopping center a buck while I waited for Pat), self-restraint (I've never hit Velia), austerity (I've lived for months like a monk), truth (*oui et non*), mildness (*non et oui*), vigor (I run on the beach), forgiveness (mostly), absence of envy and pride (not absence, but overcoming)—these are the divine properties which liberate.

"The success of a given population structure is the probability of survival and reproduction, the fittest genotype that which maximizes the probability." (So pills, abstinence, then sheer attrition of sentiment prevent more Wendts; more Wendts diminish the scope of existent Wendts; so lovelessness is the trait which maximizes the survival of the Wendt population.) Walpole, Mme. Du Deffand, and Miss Berry survive by not marrying. (The generic energy went into what makes them survive.)

Behold, thou art fair, my love; thou hast doves' eyes within thy locks, thy hair is like a flock of goats that appear from Mount Gilead, thy lips are like a thread of scarlet, and thy speech is comely, thy temples are like a piece of pomegranate within thy locks, thy two breasts are like two young roses that are twins, which feed among the lilies. Until the day break, and the shadows flee, I will get me to the hill of frankincense . . . camphire with spikenard, spikenard and saffron, calamus and cinnamon, myrrh and aloes, a fountain of gardens. Awake, O north wind; and come thou, south; blow upon my garden, that the spices thereof may flow out. Let my beloved come . . .

Yoghurt and boysenberry, magnolia, bird of paradise and plastic, honeysuckle and Velia, peaches, roses, VWs, New Yorkers, come my life, pasteurized homogenized DELICIOUS served just as it comes from the carton. Excellent with cheese. Net wt. 8 oz. Distr. by Safeway Stores, Inc., Head Office, Oakland, Cal. 94604.

History Is Made Morning, Noon, and Night
or
When Nixon Runs, the Grunion Don't

1

Ocean noises, a piper's flatted G. No one in the house, even Velia making safari to the sands. At the cypress table, my four pens, red pencil, point like a shrew's eye, cubes of india rubber, the stylus with which I draw my own staves, the Weyerhausered trees on which I commit whatever will be my residue (I am not what's swimming in the waves below). I usually don't compose at the piano. A defect? I simply hear the music, I trust what I hear, I have never felt discrepancy between the graphite smudges on the stave and the "sound" in my head. Orchestrating, or instrumenting, I am somehow up on almost every blown, bowed, plucked, or hammered sound. When I, rarely, "hear" something whose instrumental elements escape me, I just sit it out, going over sections and choirs like a schoolboy till it comes.

Honeysuckle hanging in the nasal follicles, doubling in the brain. Neural rust. Elicits a "shadow horn" (Ives's "shadow violin" in Decoration Day), and I have my orchestral narrative shadowing

Baritone sounds from horn, bassoon, cello, transforming, as if under water, a serial current born in the overture foam

and never absent, even in the silence which fills a gap in the row. Pacific. Continuity. Humanity. Genes.

Bonaparte's musing aria, "Robespierre, *fauve modeste*," as *secco* as a Mozart recitative, a carefully charged *Sprechstimme*, followed by a broken shadow of the row:

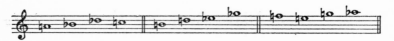

"Giii-nnah" (I can insert that call).

Three, *four* hours, I am still fresh.

Hand cramped. No erasures. Confident. I don't look back. This score will go.

2

I drive up 101 (El Camino Real) to get mail and library books at the University. A pretty, wise-faced Chinese librarian, barefoot and mini-dressed, tells me they've moved the Ms and shows me where. I take out Webern's Opus 5 (with the sonata movement in 55 bars), Eager S.'s String Concerto with its "motionless measures" (his term) and flutters of wind, some electronic gossip of Stockhausen (*Carée* with its pale glissandi at 67), and the latest *Die Reihe* (to up my adrenalin).

The mail is for Gina (envelopes bleeding impassioned afterthoughts: "Disregard stuff on TP—he just called from H's!!!"), Jeff-U (parietal instructions from Oberlin), an invitation to a McCarthy "Blow-Your-Mind" during the Convention (Chicago socialites in alert modulation; though not quite alert enough), a letter to my mother returned for misaddress (Santa Barbara instead of New York—no further comment today, gentlemen), and *The New York Review of* (Each Other's) *Books*, XI, 2, minus one of Eager's unearthly/worldly Swan Songs of an Octogenarian. (My—of course secret—competitor.)

I flip through the *Review*, whose effect is to make me wish

to top everything I read there except for the stravinskies,
which are sheer joy. I read H. Morgenthau's harsh entomb-
ment of Robert Kennedy (the marble thrown at the
corpse's head), admire its Tacitean errors (*capax imperii
nisi imperasset*), but, but, last Shakespeare's Birthday
(April 23) in Indiana, I went on the campaign plane and
made speeches (for what was not to be) to the Butler and
Bloomington Music departments. ("We tried to get Irving
Berlin," said Bobby.)

On the front cover, a Levine of Hubert Humph-er,
knitting with barbed wire, crocodile tear hanging off left eye,
fat face squinched half into John Garner, half into Mira-
beau.

I feel left out. The music world is fierce but not half so
fierce, not a tenth so populous with brains, pens, and venom
as the literary-political world, and of course, not within
light-years of influencing events or feelings. We have only
our subversive time-schemes to insert in half-deafened men
(fewer each year).

I don't know whether to leave the *Review* in the men's
room (where I've cleared my roughage—alerted by Morgenthau's citation of Cromwell's, "I beseech you, in the bowels
of Christ, to think it possible you may be mistaken") or
to take it home to raise Velia's conversation level and keep
her from her catalogs. Or—and this is what I do—take it
downstairs for the lovely Chinese girl. (That accursed Exclusion Act which kept this great race of brains and beauties
to so dangerous a minimum that the meeting of East and
West will, at best, take place above the Dewline.) As she
stamps the scores, I ask whether she'd like it.

Her face, scotched a bit at the cheeks (how smallpox must
have devastated her fruit-picking ancestors), is now alight
with sweetness; eyes, mouth, cheeks, even the ears tremble
with response. But no words. A shrug: I dunno.

—It's pretty good this week. Gass on Lawrence, Morgenthau on Kennedy.

—I'm an Ag. Sci. major.

"That's life," I say. "Thank you," taking up my books,

my *Review*, my marbles. I have an abnormally short torso
and long legs; the turnstile, which she releases for me,
strikes at the testicles, my torso hangs momently over.
Ag. Sigh.

3

12:30. An hour and a half before my engagement.

In the Volkswagen, zipping past Sandspit Point, ten
snooty palms surveying the bikinied beach, I suddenly want
to see some pictures. I haven't been to the museum since
'64, when Wilma Kitty and I surveyed it and each other in
confused simultaneity.

I turn off the Freeway onto State and park around the
corner from it. In the white courtyard, Greek vases, marble
torsos ("after Praxiteles," "after Phidias"), limestone bo-
dhisattvas, beaded, their small sweet breasts soliciting touch
(but there are French tourists looking on).

There is a wall of aluminum-and-black-enamel panels,
the trick being to arrange the aluminum squares so that the
thread differs from section to section, making in-and-out
peaks of reflected light, then diving in with a black-enamel
cavern; handsome enough, more work than arranging groceries and, happily, unaleatory ("Arrange the blocks as you
wish"). There's a splendid Zurbarán Franciscan (I remembered it), Tintoretto-lit, brooding, greenishly geometric. At
the desk I buy Macedonian gold-coin earrings for Gina's six-
teenth birthday next week.

The VW is being leaned on by a barefoot chicano who
smiles at me easily, without apology. "Never apologize, never
explain," the Balliol aristocrats were taught. Six hippies on
the grass are passing—is it called—a joint from pinched
fingers to pinched fingers. One is a beautiful girl with a
weeping willow head of hair who gives my long look a second look, pauses, looks too quickly away, but not before I
recognize her as a Mullidyne.

4

"How," asks Patricia Davidov, "can you tell that the house
has been burgled by a Pole?"

I am making a Greek cross for her verticality. We are between rounds on the second and, it turns out, penultimate
day of our affair. "Well?"

"The garbage can's empty and the dog is pregnant."
Her head rises from my stomach, and she gets a not-yet-,
not-ever-to-be-eliminated roll of my side flesh in her teeth,
then licks. "Salty."

"Who," I respond, "was Alexander Graham Pucinski?"

"Mmm," she says, arching a long neck northward, till
I lean southward far enough to place my tongue within her
mouth. Small revival. I slide around on the pivot of my
stomach. We are parallel, head to head. "Well?"

—Get in first.

—The first telephone pole.

"Mmm," says Patricia, great knees up, great feet on my
rear flanks. "What," she manages, "is a circle, huh, of, uh,
Polish intellectuals. Oh. Called?"

"Oh, Patricia."

Three-o'clock Augustan sun through blinds. On the wall,
sun-barred, a beautiful Japanese print of two ladies, hands
on their frisbie-shaped hats, skirts blown up to show sandals
like those by this bed, thongs between first and great toes.

—A dope ring. Now.

So be it.

But, oh, I am feeling it. Whosoever hath, to him shall
be given, and he shall have more abundance, but the
capillaries of my rear bulge sorely, my mouth is clogged
with canker sores, there is a drowsy numbness in my chest.
By mentality Cyrenaic, I am in body Stoic.

I flop. Patricia encircles me, front to my back, a divine
burden, but a burden, a weight. "Had it?"

—Had it.

She plants hands on the sheets and in push-up position attempts a sweet abrasion.

I turn slowly, struggling. Embrace and kiss, deeply sweet. But my legs are weary, my gavel without authority. If I could represent the future in the present, storing away for the hundreds of unsolaced hours the abundance of Patricia, I would even vote for Richard Millstone Nix-no. But nix, but no, Heinz has not yet canned her goods.

5

Full moon. The tide chart says high tide is 9:45. From Miami, Nixon has spooned up the worst of cornball syrups, his plugging history, and received the cheers of the hard-hearted and the surface-sentimentalists. The rich dropout, Scranton (of P-ay), leans to Mrs. P. Ryan Nixon and forms the words "terrific," for he can't match such poorboy sagas. Nixon huddles with the newsmen, faking an intimacy his face can't manage.

From down Padaro Lane, Davy's friend, Willy, walks to tell us that the grunion will come streaming in to lay their eggs at 9:54. We go down the steps to the beach. The moon is there, plowing the water silver, we kick off moccasins and wait, Davy, Jeff-U, Willy, Ollendorf, and I. The waves roll toward us, lap each other, come to pitches, crash, lap each other, fan toward the shore, our feet, the steps, leaving behind bubbles of fringe. But no grunion. No grunion eggs. Perhaps the rigs of some of the men gathered in South Miami have let lethal oils slip into the channel. Or perhaps, when Nixon runs, the grunion don't.

Exemplary Lives and Barbecues

1

Exemplary lives: Stripped of detail by model-seekers, the saints, heroes, and witnesses (Kierkegaard's men of significance) are reconstructed by the new democracy of neurosis: Everyone afflicted, the race is even. So new Bokes of Governors, Mirrors for Magistrates, Model Courtiers.

Webern. Banal except for his music and his death. The engineer-official father, the parochialism (though he conducted often in London), the poverty, the domination by and idolization of Schönberg, the friendship without (expressed) rivalry with Berg, the teaching and chorale-directing jobs (Jewish Blind, Workers' Chorus), the hated work in the operetta theater at Stettin, a couple of prizes from Vienna, the mountain-climbing, the uxoriousness, the absorption in children, then, broken by the Nazis (no funds for Jewish Blind, no Workers' Chorus), proofreader for his publisher, the war, air-raid warden, only son killed near Zagreb, he and wife pack rucksacks, age sixty, take to the roads to see their daughters, cooped up in house with son-in-law's parents, the sons-in-law return, Webern scarcely ever leaves house, timid, laconic, yet, September 15, son-in-law Mattl working the black market and currency exchange, has found him a cigar, he goes to have dinner, the Americans set a trap, Webern lights up first cigar in years, goes outside to keep smoke away from grandchildren and is shot by stumbling North Carolina army cook (drunk, trigger-nervous), twice in abdomen, once in lung, stumbles into house, "It's over. I'm lost." Webern's wife denied pension, soldier claims Webern attacked him with iron bar, he shot in self-defense.

Exemplary?

Schoenberg, dominating, fierce, teacher, writer (*Harmonielehre*, the *Letters*), painter, tennis player, world citizen, late father, excused by Austrians from military service (as was Lehar) after Loos, the architect, spurred by Webern and Berg, appealed, rejected, age seventy, by Guggenheim Foundation for grant to finish *Moses and Aaron* ("I have had some pupils of note . . . My compositions are . . ."), though pension from UCLA was seventy dollars a month, fading in L.A., which, said Mann, in the war was livelier than Paris had ever been (Vera Stravinsky concurring).

Stravinsky's life, looking in from outside, the finest, the intimacy with the best (known) of men, women, whiskeys, food, music, books, places (Vevey—Ravel down the street —Venice, Grasse, Hollywood), visiting the rest of the world, fine wives, children, but then, the mania for bowel talk, the materia medica, the morning headaches, the hypochondria (above the navel, the old seat of melancholy), the jousts with fakes, critics, imitators, thieves. The preference for thinking to understanding (the first continuity, the last conclusion), composing to composition (ditto). Yet in the Rio Zoo, before the anthropoids, he wonders "what it would be like to go about on all fours with one's behind in the air, and with a plaque on one's cage identifying one with a Latin binomial and a paragraph of false information." Is not the good fellow thus bravely exposed in those elegant books of R. Craft?

After my run on the beach in the dankest of all our Santa Barbara days, it strikes me I have been taken in by the charm, the silvery bustle, the off-the-cuff wit. (Glassy the currency of Bobsky and Eager?)

For us, heritors, auditors, watchers, better the laconic failure types (Giacometti, Webern), the mordant and silent (Schoenberg and Pound), the fabling, courteous, twisted invalids (Proust, hiring men to torture rats in his presence), the maniacally narcissistic, vain, jealous, child-tortured (Beethoven, Joyce, Michelangelo), the clipped, snubbed, shunted, but world-relaxed (Mozart, Shakespeare), and

finally, the old tea leaves, broken spars, drifted seaweed, odd
roots and unforeseen shoots that make up, for better and
worse, till death parts one, oneself.

2

Donald Taylor gives a farewell barbecue for himself (he's
off to see his mother in Louisville). He lives in the gate-
house of the princely Gossett estate, more or less watching
the place while the princes Gossett stay in their château
in Normandy. The party takes place in the Orangerie, the
company larger and more menacing than I'd guessed it
would be: Donloubies (triumphant at the confession of
Mrs. Wrightsman, their release from having to depart),
Mullidynes, Krappells, a Count and Countess Czaski, he,
the piano player in the Hotel Biltmore, infinitely more
musical than the musicological jaws. Amazingly enough,
Donald has invited the lower half as well. Davidov is in
evening sandals (over white socks) and a shirt he wore only
twice this week, Patricia is pale but triumphant, her clumsy
beauty contrives a modest slink, to me she is distant,
ridiculous, "How GOOD to see YOU again." (It's like
publishing banns.)

Davidov clumps up darkly, a smiling menace, "Hear you
and Pat had coffee together."

"I don't drink coffee." That golden pump has sprung a
leak. In order to call for home repairs? (Every story is a
minor detail of another story as the librettist of *Walpole's
Love* well knows.)

The moon is like an advertisement for the Orangerie.
It sits low, reddish, almost full, it lacks only a Gossett
gardener to belong exclusively to us. We mill around
bushes carrying glasses of gin and quinine, picking limes
and lemons, Donald, nervous, tinily cyclopean, stuttering,
rallying everywhere with ice bowls, soda, a silver bowl of
caviar and lemon. I turn around a jacaranda tree, smell its
vanilla and honeysuckle bark, think of Walpole at Straw-

berry Hill, his editor, Wilmarth Lewis, Jackie Kennedy's
uncle, in Farmington. Life's princes. *Crack.* Agony in my
ear.

"Lover."

Pat, body shadowed behind the odorous trunk, has
kissed into my ear.

"Cheeeristpat," I yell—under control—in whisper.

"Shhh." Lips on mine. She has on a white dress, sleeve-
less—though the night is cool to chill—cut in the classic
female V so her body dominates everything. In the moonlight, she is the lit-up movie screen.

Sure enough, eye never off her, the smirking, tortured
torturer, Davidov. "Playing games, kiddies?" Mousing over
in sandals.

—Human flesh in moonlight, Bert. You've seen *Figaro.*

"Sloppero," said Davidov. "Why not get out of the cold,
Pattie? They're serving up steaks in the house."

—Scat outta here, Bertie, you make me sick, like some
private eye or somethin', always trailin' me around, Christ.

Behind silver glasses, a dog's low look. Its fury is driven
by his wife's excited beauty, at himself, then at me. "Don't
lick his crumby hide. He can't write his way out of a paper
bag. Derivative, sloppy, and look at him, the ex-chorus boy."

This is a coward who will fight. I am a coward who
almost won't. But am big, even strong, and say with Gary
Cooper-quiet, Bogart-menace, "Be a good idea to cut that
out, Bert. A kiss on the ear isn't a week on Capri. And
I'm a little sensitive about my work. I know you're a great
critic of the art, but I know a little bit myself. I'd just as
soon we saved debate for another time." Or some such
put-off drivel, the speech, as usual, feeding on itself, hardly
related to the heavy breathing, the sense of each of us—
I'm sure—that our hearts were thumping our ribs, dangerous
to all over thirty-five, especially to three running-to-fat types
like us.

Pat, cheated down below, transfers her energy and cracks
Bert's cheek, the sound is a snare drum, *thwack*, over the
garden.

—Hey.

—Wha' was that?

This through the lemon and lime trees. Pat retreats. Bert moaning low, doggily, on his knees, feels for his glasses. I edge away from Pat's exit toward the servants' garden, feeling my way to a plaster cast of Bacchus and Cupid, onto the Old California porch, past pots hanging from its ceiling, into the warm house, where Krappell, mouth pink with blood juice, delivers to Velia, Mullidynes, Donloubies, and the remote, petite Czaskis his old prediction that the Czech film-makers were the harbingers of the Dubček revolution. "The movie-in-the-round, every man in the driver's seat. The psychological anticipation of the end of serfdom."

Old Count Czaski, small, red-faced, a chuckler and man of spirit, says, "Much as I love Charlot, I would have wished they had never brought the cinema to Prague if it had such terrible effects." The Count escaped in 1939, taking out nothing but a pair of dueling pistols whose sale in London enabled him to keep his family for a year. Now he is suing the Polish government for his stables and furniture. The Countess studies law books, writes letter to U Thant, Gomulka, Ambassador Gronowski, Dean Rusk, the Quai d'Orsay. Without a typewriter, on Woolworth stationery which her spidery script dignifies to parchment. She receives no answers. Only Czaski's Biltmore clientele pays attention to him. Mrs. Sears, a cousin of Woodrow Wilson, drinks brandy Alexanders with him every night after "Smoke Gets in Your Eyes" and the E-flat Polonaise. He had complained about the old Baldwin stand-up he was forced to play, and last Christmas, she'd given him a six-thousand-dollar Steinway which he leases to the Biltmore.

Donald's steaks are marvelous. Davidov is vegetarian. One of the world's brutes, he has the habits of a saint. Dark, brooding, he bears his misery into the room, a billboard. Pat creeps after. Thank God for noisy Krappells. Count Czaski tries to immerse Patricia in Polish memories. She says, "Know who Alexander Graham Pucinski is? The first

telephone Pole." The most boorish patron of the Biltmore
has never told the Count a Polish joke.

End of Summer

1

Signs. August 4, summer's height, the sun halfheartedly
(cloudily) sweeping the coastal fog out of the cove and
lawns. I look out the great-glass rectangle of ocean front
and see a single magnolia leaf fall lawnward. Last night,
I heard what I thought was a man's voice saying, "No,
thank you," thought in fury, "Velia's got someone in here,"
turned over, saw it was Velia herself, talking in one of the
strange sleep voices that have for years made the nights
theatrical for me. (Gina, too, is a great sleep talker; many a
night I have laughed to hear, room to room, these fragments of sleep talk, almost dialogue.)

2

Yesterday, Mina, the Golden Triangle, made her first solo
drive on the Freeway, stayed with us, and went out to swim
at midnight with Jeff-U. Skinny two months ago, Jeff-U
has added tan to muscle, his idleness has paid off. He is quite
an admirer of his body, hugs himself, partly to articulate
the muscles, partly to enjoy himself. And tonight he enjoys another body. They go down bare-arse, I watch from
my magnolia-veiled window and almost get charged up
enough myself to wake Velia up for discharge; but don't,
and twenty minutes later, when they return and slip
around to the back lawn, I shift to the kitchen window
and watch them embrace. There is much beautiful mingling,
but despite knee-raising and other somewhat-educated hints

from the Belle Triangle, Jeff-U remains—as far as the not
very good sight of them permits my knowledge—innocent
of the triangle's contents.

All is sign, felt prevision of the end of summer, this easy
absence from Chicago life where I seldom bother to buy
newspapers, have not read The New York *Times* in two
months, listen to the distant noise of politics as bird
gabblings on morning air. What's the difference, I think.
Even that old con man Nixon—whose Cheshire smile
passed right through me at Newark Airport a few months
ago—has been ground into reasonable enough shape by
American life to make him palatable; even the slick little
dollie, Reagan, will speak as many right as wrong answers.
Though could I think long enough, I'd moan here, just two
months from and eighty miles north of the struck-down
Bobby. (Of our house of Atreus with its new patents of
nobility: books, beauty, sailboats, poems, the public weal.
Oh happy oedipal bloom: Ritt has remembered Joseph
Kennedy negotiating for RKO, had seen him with local
beauties while the gracious daughter of Honey Fitz told her
beads and raised the children. Though Lord knows how
well it worked out for us all. Us all?)

On the campaign plane, late April, yet zero weather,
tornado weather in Indiana, Bobby came in after John
Glenn (the pure-eyed astronaut elated by his world tour
for Royal Crown Cola). Blue suit, blue hooded eyes, mouth
latent with smile over squirrel teeth, graceful, dear little
fellow, working the crowds like a medieval jongleur, feeling
every response as new energy for the old themes. That last
day of life, out on Santa Monica beach, an hour south
of this one, diving into waves to scoop a son from the
undertow, banging his head, weary football of the lights and
American noise, which, that night, would be irremediably
punctured. Two months ago today.

Life flies by so quickly, "a field mouse in the grass,"
sped by that hourly communication of event about which
Wordsworth complained in 1800, separating us from every
precious thing in our lives. We are so full of the world,

this great age of wounding and repairing, moving for movement's sake. Hoping feeling will stick.

An almost impossible time for an artist.

At a Contemporary Music Jamboree in Flagstaff, Arizona,
I went to the annual exhibit of Indian arts at the museum.
There among the Hopi sand paintings and Navajo rugs,
pots, jars, and turquoise pins, sat the old men and women
who made them. I elbowed through a sportive crowd to
a silent, pipe-smoking Indian gentleman who sat on a
kitchen chair beside his wooden name plate, smiled, said
how much I admired his work, and then threw in, "It's
not easy being an artist in America."

Perhaps his English was poor, the noise too great. The
question could not mean the same for him (hadn't I asked
it more or less to have an anecdote for the exhibit?).
His look did not differentiate my white-jacketed self from
what it hoped to be distinguished from.

3

Mid-August, our beach shakes with autumnal tides which
strip the sand and expose more and more of the smooth
rocks. In winter, the neighbors tell us, the shore is all rocks.
Even now we spread towels and beach seats behind a
narrowing sand fortress, and still dig out rocks which press
on rear and ribs. Television tells us that Kosygin and
Brezhnev have been summoned from vacation to a full
Presidium meeting, and, that night, the results of the
interruption are announced: troops are marching into
Czechoslovakia. Johnson, enormous face grooved by depths
nothing in his life or reading prepared him for, returns from
a fierce speech to the Veterans of Foreign Wars in Detroit
to confront advisers summoned from their own long weekend in Virginia and Chevy Chase. (Johnson advisers, unlike
Kennedy's, do not, apparently, stray as far as the Vineyard,
though my ex-colleague, Katzenbach, has ventured there, to
be assailed in the local gazette by literary sideswipes from
the off-season editor-writers from New York.)

For the last ten days, we have new neighbors, the Loves, up from Louisiana, father and eight or ten children by three wives (all absent, he's separating from Number Three). The children saturate the length of beach between the felled eucalyptus and the bluff from which it fell. They come in with surfboards, polynesian bikinis, mattresses, rainbow towels. The loveliest of them speaks Cajun French with me, "Que voy que zhe zire, cherie?" and to this cane sugar nineteen-year-old with her flawless Sea and Ski-oiled body, the old music perfesser says, "Que tu m'adorasse, m'belle." She and another of the stepsisters (the tangle of marriages is as complicated as the kelp which meduses the end of the bared tree) are shopping and cooking for the mob of Loves, Williston-Loves, and Freers. "It's lahk the quahtuhmaster caw." Her father, it turns out, owned the beach before Donloubie, was raised in the Villa Leone, and the real-estate advice I've passed him ("The bank buys the property, in five years you sell, pure gold."), he politely lets fly over his head. He stretches, auxiliary bellies mounting to the volcanic navel, and asks if I've read *African Genesis.* I haven't, but concede the events of the day make me think more of sharks defending territory than modern nations. He hasn't heard the news of the Russian move on Prague, nor of the innocently forked address of our President talking of great powers crushing the will of free peoples; he's given up the boob tube's hourly communications.

The sugar cane turns her oiled belly and says, "Daddy, you doan do nothin' but sleepn read."

"Readin' I enjoy, sleep I need," and he tells me, from his Kremlinic isolation, of the good relations down his way between Negroes and Whites. One would think the last years had seen him at a permanent eight thousand feet above the delta.

I tell him our smart black cleaning woman is supporting Wallace because he tells it straight and nasty.

—It's best to know whah you stand.

I agree, though on my other flank the disturbing beauty peeks a smile out from under her lambent arm. She has loved Bobby Kennedy, she can't figgah out that man Nixon, she thinks after leaving Sophie Newcomb she'll fahnd some perfesser to marry and lead a good life goin' different places every summer, she loves travelin', learned maw in Colombia up in the mountains with Indians the terms she was on probation, than she's evah done.

Jeff-U and Gina are part of the Loves' night parties; they swim in the midnight surf. Tonight—I say this for both my flanks—I will swim myself, will risk turning pumpkin, rat, or tubercular; my hope is to draw my sugar-caned left flank down from her party to a strange once-in-a-lifetime moment with the transient perfesser. Why not? Twenty-one years separate us, but in this smorgasbord age of kinky love, what is this but digested bread and water? (In Jeff-U's new *Playboy*, Kinsey's assistant, Pomeroy, tells of a "mild-mannered man" who'd had relations with seventeen members of his immediate family, including father and grand-mother, and had gone on from this good training to most varied experience among the world's flora and fauna. What's your preference?" asked Pomeroy. "Women," was the rapid, surprising answer. "But," reflecting, "the burro is very, very nice.")

That night, the house quiet, I flip on Sackerville's playful outside spotlights and make my way down the sixty-nine stairs. It is dark below the reach of the shore light, I feel along the banister and, on the newel, brush Love's bourbon glass onto a surfboard. It cracks, my big toe steps, is cut, bleeds. I howl, furious, but take off my trunks and run off the pain along the shore. The tide is starting to flow back, but the beach is still wide enough, the lights and waves oil it to lubricity, I run five laps and plunge in. The water is rollicking, warm, intimate. I lie on my back, rock, stare at the starred gauze. The shore outline is a recumbent dragon, no, a turkey. I try not to await, but I await another body on the steps, removing the Polynesian strips from the generous doves and happy wedge. I wait, I roll, I loll, swim, and, by God, I hear hum-bump, hum-bump, and make out a figure on the steps, a girl, the legs buckling in, the hips swaying. I swim up, "Hi," yell I. "Hi thah."

"Who's that?" calls Gina. "Dad? You swimming too?"

Something in the region of my heart dives through something like my intestines, slaps my bare gonads, sinks in my bowels. "No, dear, I'm just cleaning off my rump. Throw me my trunks there from that stump." You clump.

Upstairs, I sit in the—except for the colored-television light—dark and hear that President Svoboda, broadcasting from a hidden radio station, has asked the Russians to release Premier Dubček and leave the country. There has been scattered fighting, the people in Prague, filmed by their television cameras, gather in the squares, sit in front of tanks, the iron muzzles wave over their heads.

While Velia snores I read in a Sackerville anthology Dr. Browne's vaunting cliché that the world he regards is himself, "the Microcosme of mine owne frame . . . my life, which to relate were not a History, but a peece of poetry . . . that masse of flesh that circumscribes me, limits not my mind."

Dumbhead boast.

Gina, back up, watches the late show, one cell of the electronic plasmodium. Some cosmos.

Outside, magnolia leaves and canary-headed flowers on the vine against the window lit by the reading lamp. Beyond, night and ocean, *what lasts*, extinguished by reflections of the room, the electric clock-radio, the sleeping Velia, my work papers, india rubbers, pens and ink cones, the anthology (plasmodium for Dr. Browne), score paper, stylus, my own bulging head, bed, ashtray, cigars, wallet, checkbook, maps, and, source of the reflected deception, the lamp itself.

4

I am to meet Pat at the Safeway parking lot again. The "scene" with Bert has intervened since our rendezvous-making, yet, last night, no signal passed between us, no note of cancellation. We parted without handshake or acknowledgment. But, a man of my word, I will show up on the asphalt, ready, mind and body.

I do. I wait. Ten minutes, twenty. Five minutes more. No Pat. I turn the ignition key. The state is restored, family, morality, ultimate sense. But now, my need is large, pressing. I pull up two parking places from the exit, go change a dollar into dimes, and telephone from a glass booth by the market.

"Hell-O." Bert.

I must hang up, but a lifetime of nonwaste and, yes, straightforwardness inhibits. I cannot even disguise my voice. I but soften it. "Hello."

—Oh, it's you. I suppose you're making a shack-up time with Patty.

—Whatinchrisname you talking about?

—Fuck you. Stumblebums his way through elementary harmony and thinks he can fill every hole in California.

—You miserable dung-heap Davidov. Waddy think your wife's legs are gaping for if you weren't such a hopeless dragass and shitmouth. "Don't hurt me," "don't hurt me," and the next day you're coming on like Mussolini. Christ, I can see why these rubes around here won't give up guns, lice like you rushing around waiting to be crushed.

—You want to try a little crushing there, Wendt? You just wanna try something?

I am blowing sky high. This glass is fogged with my heat. My glasses (I use them for driving but haven't taken them off) are fogged by it. The physiology of rage.

There's another element. At the newsstand, I bought this morning's New York *Times*, thirty cents, flown in the same day. First time this summer, a treat to remember what the great world's about. And what happens? Agony. There's a big We're for McCarthy Ad, painters, writers, musicians, entertainers, the "health professions" (to spare the feelings of dentists and veterinarians), and lo and behold, I, a McCarthy supporter now, haven't been sent it, have been sent an Artists for Humphrey (but that's because they can't get many), but apparently they have enough Musicians for McCarthy not to need me. Half the lousy composers of New York are there, there's even a Wendt I never heard of, probably some stage designer, but me, am I fallen this low, that on a list of a thousand artists, I'm not there? So I sat cramped in the miserable VW, my body steaming for Pat, my head raging at exclusion.

And so stayed in that glass booth by the Safeway market ready to tear Davidov's guts out, wrong though I am. And challenge him. "Here I am, you sac of envy. Creep. Come and get me." Though don't tell him where; nor does he ask. He comes back with throaty gurgles, and I say, "Spit it out, Davidov. Cough it out, you slime."

Three feet away, I see, waving at me, out of some Hal Wallis movie of the thirties, Gus, Davy, Gina, Velia, and Jeff-U. Fog, sweat, my face parboiled. The fish is hooked, cooked, and yet alive. Davidov breaks through his gurgle and splits the phone with a yell. An unearthly yell, they must hear it outside the booth, I have to hold the receiver a foot from my ear. I grind my mouth into the speaker and say, "Davidov, if I see you, I'll turn you over to the De-Lousing Squad. I'm taking to the Public Prints if you ever dare drop your pissy pen on a sheet of paper. I'll expose you to the Chancellor, you watch your step or I'll shoot the guts out of your fat head. Tell your wife to zip your prick to her arse, I have had it with her, I wouldn't touch a cunt you touched with a revolver. Fuck you eternally," and put the receiver gently back, emerge from the glass tank, sweating triumphantly.

"WELL, what was that all about?" asks smart-eyed, rather pretty Velia.

—I forgot to turn in a report on the chamber group it's the deadline I was cussing the secretary for not reminding me I told her fifteen times I needed cigars from the market here I couldn't go up to the Havana Nook. This town heat is killing me!

"It's not hot here," said Velia. "You're just overagitated by little things."

By Bei Wendt

1

September 6.
House empty. I'm orchestrating Scene 7. The sergeant is telling the girl about Walpole and Mary Berry. It is his first sure sense of his own love. Dry recital, but I want caverns of love music under it. There are woodwind choirs, all breathy, then a solo cello breaking into, stopping, breaking into, stopping, and finishing out the declaration. When the girl speaks, I have Miss Berry's music in back of her, but in plucked violins, flute, vibraharp, wood percussions. The sergeant is shadowed by Walpole, by Napoleon (who read the letters to Madame Du Deffand en route to Moscow), yet is held in by commentary music and by the tone-row spine shifted from choir to choir, instrument to instrument.

An hour, two hours, more. I keep lighting and relighting the Muriel blunt, chewing Sour Cherry gum, tossing my neck, working with Jeff-U's wrist-strengthener. My scores are neat. It is a crucial condition of getting played in our time. A slob elsewhere, I am a beautiful scorer, copyist. I love these notes, I make quarter-rests like a cinquecento Flamand, I rule my crescendos into beauteous horns, I rank with the better calligraphers, if not composers, of mid-century.

The telephone. Ignored. It persists. The house must be empty. I've worked long enough.

I answer it. A boy for Gina. I shut up shop, brush the amoebic curls of india rubber into my wastebasket (*Embarkation for Cytheria* in rounded tin), put my pens in the red earthenware jug from Arezzo (bought at the museum there after a joint concert with Dallapiccolo), add my

score sheets to the flat-top snowy mountain. The phone
shoots off again. And again for Gina, Loretta Cropsey. I
tell her Gina's at, I think, the Point, hang up, and hear from
the first floor Gina calling, "Hi."

She comes upstairs, I go to her room with her, deliver
messages, cannot say who the boy was—"Dad, I've asked
you to get the names of callers"—lie on her bed while she
cuts up skirt material and pins it, puts on Aretha Franklin,
"Love Is a See-Saw," a very good singer, the music wretched,
stiff stuff, put Gina's shell ashtray on my bare chest (I have
a convenient cavity), smoke out my Blunt, and listen to her
morning picaresque. Gina gives the lie to Beast City, she
wanders everywhere, speaks to everyone, gets invited for
coffee, tells them easy lies, "I'm from Omaha, my parents are
French, my father's a mechanic, wounded in the war, I'm a
first-year student at UC," and so on. The day's bag is, "I
went to the Point, it was beautiful, I swam, read *Portrait of
a Lady*" (my birthday gift to her, along with the earrings),
"a well-dressed Negro, quite good-looking, about twenty-
five, asked me what I was doing out of school, he was a
truant officer. I told him school hadn't started for me. He
wasn't a truant officer, he recruits people for jobs. He said
he only liked to swim with flippers, and someone had taken
his flippers off his boat, would I have breakfast with him
tomorrow and go swimming," I shaking my head, but with
Gina in front of me, this pure dear fruit of girl, what is there
to say? We are surrounded with rapists, head-crackers, she
wanders on like a nymph in a pastoral. She went into the
enclosure with the Recreation Director, a bored physiology
student, "quite good-looking," he was working on heart
banks, enter a policeman who "asked me if I was a hippie,"
said he hated them, had been at the Convention last week,
he hated Paul Newman, but when Shirley MacLaine had
walked in he'd said, "Come on in, honey," "You sure you're
not a hippie?" She'd played chess with the physiologist, had
been beaten in ten moves, "he was very bright," then ran
into Ollendorf at the Unique and was driven home. "A
great day."

2

Saturday, September 7.

I wake at seven-thirty, eyes amidst the darkening green
of the Tree of Heaven, a trimmable branch of which loops
over the second-floor porch and, in a stiff breeze, scrapes
the window screen. There is no breeze, the day has the pure
deep gleams of an early-fall day here. Shall I put on sneakers
and run in the backyard? Or down toward Dorchester,
dodging the glass bits, the dog-shit, the paper bags and
Seven-Up bottles left by Friday's school lunchers? No.

But I go barefoot downstairs, open the door to the
empty, tree-caverned street. I do ten quick bends in front
of the rubber-banded cylinder that is my day's key, the
Chicago *Sun-Times*.

Inside, I fill the coffee pot with water and Stewart's
Regular Grind, plug in, slide off the rubber band, make a
pitcher of orange juice, and glance at the Cubs (the team's
Methuselah, two-years-younger-than-I Ernie Banks, has hit
his twenty-ninth homer, his biggest total in eight years,
good sign for us oldsters). The first page gives Mayor
Daley's rapid-fire defense of his elegant behavior at the
Democratic Convention, with illustrations of black-widow
spiders, razor-bladed tennis balls, and the dented police
helmets victimized by these occult and more-than-occult
weapons. (Chicago-loving Dick, so monolithic of conviction
he will not grasp that television did not register him as the
sow's ear without some help.) Onto the whirl of yesterday,
I could be reading the Fugger News Letters, the variations
would be in detail only. (*Viva* Detail.)

Two cups of coffee, I weaken during Two and spread
pumpernickel with saltless butter and urinous peach pre-
serves.

Upstairs, Gus and Davy watch Saturday's horror cartoons,
Gina is at Loretta Cropsey's for the night, I wash, shave,
and climb another story to the study, why don't I call it

"workshop"? There sits the pile of worded notes (noted words?). Slag?

Will some twenty-second-century genius, brooding over "the pastoral, thoughtful, tolerant twentieth century," think of Walpole's farewell aria to Miss Berry and hum its pathetic, chromatic, synthetic loveliness as he plugs in the universal music computer and tunes in on the tonal events of Galaxy Scribble?

I proceed with orchestration, do three pages, rather joyfully, working with end-of-spectrum instruments, double bassoon and piccolo, these bearing melodic burdens while strings and brass police the side streets.

Down the hall, Jeff-U's door is shut. Last night I would not let him take the car because the night before he'd gone to Arlington Park, lost money (his affair), and kept the car until two thirty A.M. (mine). I was waking at each sweep of car light down the street and met him in fury at the door. We had harsh words, rare these last weeks.

He is stretched out endlessly in bed, feet and neck out of his blue quilt, just the way my father, grandfather, and I sleep; unblanketable Wendts.

I lift the hand weights ten or twelve times, regarding the musculature—already softened in the two weeks since our return, or so it seems to me. Jeff-U's pants, shirts, underpants, socks, weights, magazines, and papers litter the room. At his graduation last June, I tried to persuade him that high-school essays on the Economy of Chile were not immortal witnesses to his intellectual power, but here they be; his slag. Posters of Einstein and—in color—the Bernini Vatican Plaza dominate two walls, the rest have a Dürer rabbit, an ink sketch of Arezzo by Maniera (which he gave Jeff after I played at the concert in sixty-three, Jeff-U's first appearance at a Wendt concert), and a panel of a Tree of Jesse from either Chartres or Lincoln (stained glass is his forte, not mine).

"Please don' lif' weights here now." Mumble from the bed.

—Sorry.

I sit on his bed and pat his head, a harsh tangle of brown hair. I rub that a bit, his skull is narrow under the hair. He loves to be rubbed and tickled (another Wendtism), and I rub his shoulders. Unblemished, soft-skinned, very strong, tan. The little boy who's spent seventeen-plus years in Wendt houses and in one week leaves for college. Yes, a classic scene, but I surrender to it, I play my part. (We fit into such a small repertory.) Back against the wall, I rub his shoulders. *Der Rosenkavalier* flies up from WFMT below, I stare out, through and above the trees, and remember life with Jeff-U, the frightening announcement by letter from Velia—would we have lasted that first year if it hadn't come?—the room in—was it Cherbourg?—she on her way home, I to stay to finish up with Boulanger, the long birth, twenty-six hours in the American Hospital, the noise of carnival drunks below the window, my first sight of the brilliant bright eyes, the heart-wrenching child, how many thousand hours, playing, reciting Dante, whistling Bach, while I held the bottle for him, teaching him to throw, to bat, to serve, driving with him around Italy and England, with Gina, with Davy and Gus, with Velia, the boy becoming himself, thinning, hardening, his will becoming his own, his lies, his sweetness, swimming in the Neckar, not wanting to go away, staying always with us, no camps, no schools away, reading *I Promessi Sposi*, saving ball cards, climbing in the Dolomites, life, middle-class-American-Wendt life, one of the earth's three billion, one of its hundred million lucky ones, one of my four children, my one and only, unique at least in this, Jeffrey Ulrich Wendt. So long, my dear boy, fare thee well, dear heart. The *Rosenkavalier* dies away, my hand rests on his shoulder, I pat his blanketed rear twice and leave.

—Thanks, *mon père*.

THREE
STORIES

INS AND OUTS

Why not the quite simple effort to touch the other,
to feel the other, to explain the other to myself.
                                                    —F. Fanon

1

Holleb knew the meaning of his respiratory trouble, but
what could he do? For him, outlet was intake. When some
strong reply to the world sailed up to his lips, he drove it
back toward the respiratory tract. Summer, winter, spring,
and fall, Holleb hacked, spat, and blew, He was thought by
most Hyde Parkers to be a drinker. No such high romance.
Their sign, his nose, bulbous, rosy, capillary map agleam,
had been burnished not by Scotch and rye but by a million
handkerchief massages.

"Why Dads blow nosys?" The first remembered question
of son Artie.

The remembered response of May, the ever-yukking wife:
"Brains, Art. Dad's got so much brain, he's got to relieve
the pressure. Why Dad's handkerchiefs"—she let no
routine drop—"have higher I.Q.s than most guy's heads.
There's people running governments today'd swap their
minds for one of Dad's blowers."

If Holleb's inner tract marked repression, May's shimmied
day-in-and-out with that other form of evasion, yuks. Her
big laughs. Wasn't laughter, with tears, the easiest form of
human action?

That her laugh capacity should dwindle, that she would actually get up and do something else, was last year's surprise. A note on the pillow; she had not been up to talking it out with him. "I'm taking off for the Coast. See you in the funny papers."

Amazement, fury, relief, suspicion, jealousy.

The suspicion lit on Kruger, the Grove Press salesman whose rounds seemed to include the tiny Book Nook every other week. Though all salesmen went for her. She'd kept her looks, was taken for his daughter half the time, though she was less than a year younger. Up close, she didn't look so young. The laugh lines had trenched her mouth and eyes. But remoteness, a kind of snoot, kept her from close scrutiny. That and the routines. Still, forty, he'd guess she was taken for thirty.

Apparently it was not Kruger or anyone else. At least when Artie went out to stay with her in July, the only one around the bungalow was the woman she shared it with, a German geneticist at UCLA. "Kind of a lady," reported Artie. "With these thigh-high silver suede boots. And whiskers, real Franz Josef muttonchops. I mean, they were *there*, you could see them. Sideshow stuff."

Sideshow was a category of Artie's mind, though God knows he was a foot, at least, from midget class. Five-one anyway. But height had brought him much misery for years. It was the Great Age for Uglies, but shorties still made out poorly. Holleb, at five-nine, stooped, slouched, sat, and lay low before Artie's sad smallness.

What also surprised him was that Artie didn't stay out on the Coast. May was his favorite, also a shortie, though bigger than Artie. And she'd made Artie a yukker, they amused each other for years. "Give Mom my love," he'd told Artie, expecting not to see him for a long time.

"You got some to spare?" yukked Artie.

In a month, though, he was back in Chicago. Seems the bungalow had a bed and a couch; he'd slept on the floor, using Gisella's boots for pillows. Beverly Glen, called Swinger's Canyon in Westwood, was full of musicians,

starlets, animators, younger technicians, assistant profs from
UCLA, but, said Artie, while music rumbled up and tum-
bled down on them from every side, he, May, and Gisella
sat in front of Johnny Carson and the Late Show night
after night. The talk was whose turn it was to have the
rocker. "Mom wasn't getting too many laughs out there.
It was like living inside a fish." May worked in the UCLA
Library. "The laugh meter there was broken too," said
Artie.

"She probably couldn't adjust to a structured work
environment." The Book Nook's famous charm was chaos.
Holleb had to go in every few months to straighten out the
inventory.

These days, Artie didn't do much laughing himself. In
September he'd started college in Urbana. One semester,
and he was back in Hyde Park. "I can't finish a book. And
those lectures." So he bagged groceries forty-four hours a
week at the Co-op. He had six months of grace before he
turned nineteen and fodder for General Hershey.

His problems were turning him hippie. He had his own
muttonchops, two brown trunks of hair edging toward each
other across his cheeks. And, on top, fuzzy-wuzzy. Perhaps
the intent was not to erase the boundaries between men
and women but between animal and vegetable. In addition,
his chin and what could be seen of his forehead simmered
with boils. Little Artie was a beautiful sight.

Holleb said nothing, did nothing. He felt Artie's misery.

The most expressive part of his son was his room. This
sight hit Holleb each time he left his own. A trash can of
Artie's life, or not a trash can, because that suggested assemblage, a frozen tornado, a planless exhibit of his son's
bafflement. Shirts, shorts, socks, pants, newspapers, letters,
record jackets, crimped tubes of Derma-Sil, cylinders of
Man-Tan, orange rinds, hardened gobbets of toothpaste like
marble droppings—for Artie was an ambulatory tooth-
brusher—what else? Anything. Cans of Fresca and Tab—
though weight was not one of his problems—even soil and
leaves scuffed from his shoe soles.

Unbearable, though Holleb bore it, and then, one day, cleaned it up, hung up the pants, knifed gobs of Gleem from the shag rug, stacked the books and records, piled the garbage into bags, and took the laundry down Fifty-Seventh Street to the Chinese.

If Artie remarked the change, he found no words for it. So, every week or ten days, Holleb cleaned it again. As well, that is, as any room in what May called their "Battered Five" could be cleaned.

Nine years ago they'd sublet the place from Willard Lobz, a singer. Illicitly, for the University, which owned the place, didn't permit extended sublets. Lobz kept it to save storage on his grand piano and record collection while he sang in Europe. The Steinway was tuned twice a year, the collection was locked up in a cedar chest. They took up most of Room Five, Holleb's study.

The rest of the place went to pot. And the University was not to be called when the toilet fell in or wires strayed from the walls. Lobz would "take care of everything." Yes, while he had Puccini up against the wall in Palermo or Bad Nauheim.

Lobz was one of these *beaux laids*, fierce, chesty, full of operatic presence. Leonine, except it was not a lion's head but a monster catfish's, chinless with spears of pale whisker fanning out from enormous lips, nickel-colored eyes, a mat of yellow hair arranged on the great dome in the shape of Florida.

The voice was something terrific. It started below the shoes in a rumble that lasted seconds before words issued. Said May, "We could get the oil-depletion allowance if we bought him." What a diaphragm. What a chest. And an Adam's apple which, said May, he could rent as a box at the opera.

When Lobz appeared in Chicago, Holleb would present him with the latest crisis in plaster or wires. Lobz was an operatic listener. He listened louder than many yelled. The body throbbed with rumble, then moved with gigantesque motion, charged the telephone, dialed with furious strokes

of a thumblike pinkie, and then, a great piece of fortissimo
lip; his technique, the Multiple Threat. "You got a damage
suit on your hands, Simmons. We got hot wires sticking outa
the walls here, one of these kids gets toasted, you've had it.
Ninety-nine to life for you, Simmons. Criminal negligence.
I'll take out full-page ads, your name in a black box. I'm
sitting right here now with a man on the *Herald*. Don't
tell me that, I called you nine times myself, you better get
you a secretary knows something beside Polack. I got me
a lawyer's itching to crack your skull for a jury, we know
what you Mafiosi electrics been givin' the people of
Chicago." Followed some Italian curses, or perhaps *Rigo-
letto*, and the phone was crashed into itself; once Lobz
cracked the casing. "These jaybirds got to feel the color of
your whip, Holleb. Finesse they don't hear. That's why
you're getting no service."

Of course no electrician showed up. Either Lobz had
dialed Weather Report or he underrated the insensitivity
of Simmons Electric; men who service the homes of mid-
century cities were no virgins when it came to abuse.

By the time Holleb got an electrician himself, Lobz was
fighting Donizetti to a draw at the Sud-Deutscher Rundfunk.

He tried deducting it from the rent, but Lobz was a
master of epistolary violence; it wasn't worth his static.
Holleb wrote the repairs off. There were very few cheap
apartments left in Hyde Park, and, for all its defects, the
Battered Five was convenient, steps away from the Book
Nook, a grocery, the laundry, the few restaurants and coffee
houses spared by Urban Renewal. In a dying neighborhood,
the few live coals were here. Besides which, he could walk
to the *Herald* office in ten minutes, it was even closer for
Artie and May to school and work. And what could you
expect in a modern American city anyway, Arcadia?

2

Holleb was the business manager of the neighborhood weekly. He also wrote a column about anything which struck his fancy. Such free-wheeling columns were a Chicago newspaper tradition, from Lardner and Hecht to Mabley, Harris, and Royko. Holleb's dealt with everything from neighborhood gangs to comments on books and University lectures. It was a popular column, Holleb's picture appeared above it, he was a minor neighborhood celebrity.

He was not a bad writer, and though not ambitious, his desk was filled with sketches and notes for longer essays, even books. He'd published one long piece in the *Southwest Review,* an essay on the conventions of newspaper reporting, the subject which interested him more than any other. He had a working title for a book he might write about it, *The Fictions of Journalism.*

Holleb distrusted his profession. May said it was sour grapes because he was at the rim of it, but he didn't think that was the case. The journalistic situation was, if anything, worse on metropolitan dailies. If a neighborhood reporter couldn't get a story about his own neighborhood straight, how could men sent to the four corners of the world without language or social lore come up with anything but bilge? It was hard writing up what one knew. When you wrote up what you didn't know, it was professional insanity. Or so thought Holleb. He went at the subject in frequent columns. One of his favorites was called "Reflections on Malinowski." "What do we learn," it went

from the journal kept by the great anthropologist during his pioneer field work among the Trobrianders? Here he is, the European student of language and customs, living month after month cheek by jowl with his subjects, and what fills his notebooks but reveries of lust and murder. How does he divert himself from "the savages"—as he calls them in one of his gentler references—but by reading detective stories. Mostly he broods on his disgust, nay, his hatred for "the brutes."

Shades of his fellow Pole, the novelist Conrad. But this is a scientist, a super-reporter, a model for anthropologists from Mead and Benedict to Leech, Geertz, Powdermaker, and Fallers.

Can we wonder at the turmoil of the world when men without a tithe of Malinowski's learning or genius are sent to report the political opinions of Asian villagers? Diplomats or reporters, these are the men whose muddled accounts inform the world's decision-makers. (Cf. the Herald column of Sept. 17, '63 on Hughes's Ordeal of Power.)

Is this what Scripture means by Evil Communication?

May especially disliked this column. "More show, less tell, Billy. You sound like the Court of Appeals. Judgments, judgments. Less schmoos, more delivery," with four or five other variations. Hers was the tenacity of old composers; give her a theme, it was mangled for an hour. A pretty woman with such brilliant eyes, most people couldn't remember their color—blue. She had the stiff nostrils and high cheekbones of snoot, yet she was not snooty. If anything, she was the reverse, crawling before anyone classed beneath her in the organization tables she'd grown up with, janitors, Negroes, workers below the craftsman-shopkeeper class. The word, even the concept "class" was alien to her; which, of course, meant her sensitivity was riddled with it.

"It's no joke turning out quality on a deadline."

"You bet your life. I wonder how Lippmann managed." Her voice was rough, thick, from childhood diphtheria before antibiotics made the disease a strep throat. Without that voice, she might have been a Milwaukee cheerleader, married an inspector at Schlitz. Instead, shy, she read and got a scholarship to the University, where they met in freshman, married in junior year. Twenty years, minus the one in Beverly Glen, an easy year for him once the shock had worn off, once he'd stopped dreaming of running her down in a car. It was relief to be away from that tongue which grew rougher each year. In a long marriage, what is unthinkable at the beginning may come to seem a caress. As in any form of human degradation. The first years, his columns might have issued from Olympus; she quoted them to friends. The last years, he was relieved at her attacks; it showed she still read him.

"Lippmann's got top-level sources. And what's he do but hand down judgments?"

Lippmann, though, was Holleb's model, and Holleb knew how much more Lippmann did. He'd had a fortunate lifetime of observation and literary practice, and he'd worked out comprehensive principles. He, Holleb, only scratched at the surface of things. He had not even put together the little he knew.

"If you don't know what a tree is, you can't describe a branch." Holleb had used this reproof of Erasmus to Dürer as epigraph for one of his favorite columns, "The Question of Coherence." It had come out a month or so before May's taking off. "When do we know," it began

that something really counts? When do we know a true conclusion, how differentiate it from a "Fading into the Sunset" convention?

We force events to cohere for us by stuffing them into old containers, old story patterns. Three meals a day, funerals, graduations, how true are these to the life surge? Isn't our very sense of life deformed by such false stages, false expectations, by violated senses of fulfillment?

It ended, "Readers, don't look in next week for the solution. Holleb doesn't know it."

3

A week before the anniversary of May's departure, a cold, late-March day, Holleb, having cleaned Artie's room and cooked himself some liver and onions, was half-dreaming in an armchair by the window, when the doorbell rang.

Through the speaker system, Holleb asked who was there and heard some response about Biafra. People in Hyde Park were always collecting signatures for petitions, money for causes. (Sops for violent Cerberus.) Holleb pressed the admission button and waited by the stairwell.

A young Negro in a blue daishiki came up the stairs. "I'm collecting for Biafra," he said. He had no can for money or clipboard for petition signatures; odd, thought Holleb, but he subdued his uneasiness. In these times, it was a white burgher's obligation to suppress suspicion of Negroes. Of—correcting himself—blacks.

The daishiki was some reassurance. When a man wears what sets him apart—and these tunics were still uncommon in Hyde Park—it means self-consciousness has found an outlet. Such a man is not one of those stymied anonymities who are tranformed by sudden rage into assassins.

"I'll get my wallet. The situation is frightful."

The fellow followed him into the living room; Holleb supposed it was all right. In fact, he was thinking he would offer him a cup of tea—they might have an interesting talk—when the fellow asked, "You got the money?"

That did unsettle Holleb, but again, he calmed himself; manners weren't the man.

The fellow was about twenty. He had a large head, the hair was bushed in the natural style, though the coiffure wasn't natural. The sides were trimmed low, the bush rose only in the middle, a camel effect. The mouth was large, the teeth were big, though Holleb remembered no smile. The skin was almost fair, a dark gold. Holleb remembered thinking there was less melanin in that skin than in that of some Caucasians, strange in view of the hair. This while he drew out his wallet, said cautiously he never had much money around, and handed over a dollar.

It was then the fellow clouted him with his fist, and something more, brass knuckles, coins, something that flashed and caused Holleb to move enough so that he was caught not in the face but the neck. It was terrific, he couldn't breathe, couldn't call. "No," he must have tried, maybe "Help," and the fellow punched him again low in the stomach. The fellow's face was near his, bunched in excitement and cruelty. It was then Holleb must have seen the teeth, heard the heavy breath, smelled and felt a hot, vinegary discharge from the leaping body. He was down, his wallet grabbed, he grabbed for the fellow's shoe, a blue suede, a hush puppy which arced out of his hand and then drove into his chest. It was all Holleb remembered of that.

He came to on the floor. Artie, kneeling and crying, "Dad, Dad, Dad," was putting a washcloth to his face. Holleb rang with ache, so much he could not localize it. It made him distant from the room, from Artie from his, yes, tears, from his strange sideburns, from his voice, "Are you O.K.? You poor, poor Dads. What happened? I called the police. Easy, old Dads."

The apartment, it turned out, had not been so much burgled as assaulted. The man had taken a hammer to Lobz's Steinway, the keys were cracked, the mahogany case was pocked and splintered. Chairs had been knifed, their stuffing bled into the room. Glasses and cups had been smashed and trampled; there was a glass icefall in the dining room.

Holleb spent three days in the hospital, and there looked through thick mug books, page after page of Negroes with records. Local Negroes, local records.

The sergeant, an alert-looking fellow in civvies, eyeglassed, neat, nervous, pointed to pictures as Holleb turned pages. His tone was studious, even loving. "Got this one with a baby carriage full of hardware over on Sixty-Third. Here's a fine one. Dumped lighter fluid on his momma and lit up. This one here hoists Impalas. Only Impalas. Fourteen years old. An Impala's missing, he's on the street, I don't think twice." The pictures which looked so much alike to Holleb were for the sergeant intimately different. "We been hunting this mother a year. His trick's carving initials on girls' cheeks."

Holleb's man was not in the books. At least, he didn't recognize him.

"We'll keep after him." The sergeant got up, a small man with the large books, a C.P.A. checking out company records. "I think we've got a chance. He'll be going up and down the streets with this Biafra. We may well get him. Then, Mr. Holleb, I hope you'll stick with us."

"What do you mean?" Holleb lay in his white hospital wraparound, his sides taped, his face bandaged. With his almost white hair, he looked like a piece of human angel food—but smeared, battered—an odd extension of the antiseptic cubicle with its air of formaldehyde and the terrible histories of the mug books.

"Charge him. See it through the court."

"Of course. Why not?"

"You'd be surprised. People lose their lumps, they lose their interest. They get lazy. Scared. Or, in Hyde Park, they start thinking, 'These poor . . . these guys . . .'—who beat their brains out, remember—'they got no chance in life, why should I make it hard on them?' and so on. You'd be surprised."

"Foolish," said Holleb.

4

Two weeks later, Holleb was more or less back in shape. There were a few welts on his body, he had a small scar on the base of his neck, but he wasn't in pain. The apartment was cleaned up also, except for the piano, about which he hadn't dared write Lobz. At seven he got a call from the sergeant. "Mr. Holleb, we've got a line on your boy. We think he's one of that nest of dopies that hang out in the Riviera Hotel over your way on Dorchester. We're going to go in there about eleven o'clock, eleven-thirty, so your bell rings late, don't be scared. It'll be me with somebody for you to look at. I hope."

Though he usually went to bed after the ten-o'clock news, Holleb waited up in the armchair. Or tried to, for he woke to the humming buzzer. One o'clock. Fuzzy, he put a bathrobe over his shirt and tie and went downstairs.

In front of the glass door, between the sergeant and a patrolman, stood a black man in a violet turtleneck and orange pants, head hung low, regarding his shoes. Holleb, following his look, saw untied shoelaces, strung like lax whips from brilliant black oxfords.

The sergeant motioned Holleb to stay put behind the door, then cupped the man's jaw in his palm and raised it into the hall light. A horsey, huge-eyed face flowered toward Holleb's in terror and imploration.

It was, of course, not his man. This fellow didn't even have a bush, didn't the sergeant remember his description? Besides, the man was his own age, if younger-looking. There was a raw cut on his cheek, a puffy, active, furious rose. In a week he'd have a Heidelberg *Schmiss*. No, not his man.

He shook his head. The face in the palm leaked relief, the eyes closed, the dark flesh sank around the cheekbones. Holleb wasn't thanked, he no longer existed.

Upstairs, unable to sleep, Holleb sat in the dark and watched the whirl light of the patrol car raise blue welts on Fifty-Seventh Street. It was heading off, east. Were they taking the man home, or down to the Twenty-Third Street Station to dig out a congruence between his life and their tally sheets? Search long enough, they should be able to come up with something. That *Schmiss* hadn't been earned at the barber's.

They would, thought Holleb, have to do subtler research to line up his life with their sheets. He too had a *Schmiss*, though it had been earned on the right side of the law. But his own tally sheet was nothing to carve on granite: Marriage: over. Son: miserable. Apartment: in bad shape. Work: third-rate. Books: unwritten. Victimizer: uncaught.

He was able to tabulate it himself, he was at his own immediate disposition, he hadn't inflicted any visible scars, personally. These were his pluses.

Against what, in the morning, he would call better judgment, Holleb suddenly understood and almost forgave his attacker. The daishiki and nutty coiffure hadn't been enough for him. The money wasn't enough for him. Conning wasn't enough. His terrible rage, his fierce sense of himself, had wanted something more. To inflict on a Holleb an unearned pain. To make the secret welts of a Holleb visible.

Holleb knew the weakness of this fatigued exoneration, knew the evasiveness of easy pardon, but tonight, as the sergeant had predicted, he wavered.

Tout comprendre, tout pardonner.

Though who comprendred tout? Of May? Of his victimizer? Holleb had been abandoned without a word by a yukker, he'd been knocked around by a cruel man. Where did they sit on the spectrum of cruelty? With the farcical basso Lobz? With the poison-hearted Malinowski? But Malinowski described his savages, did not stomp them. And Lobz's basso soothed thousands.

If you didn't have the brain of the one, the Adam's apple of the other, weren't you even more obliged to hurt minimally? To bag groceries, grow sideburns, drive rage back to your lungs, and blow your nose the year round?

In this world of opulent expression, where even soup cans were given voice, who was Holleb to advocate self-repression? Were not such chains being struck off in daily celebrations?

It was not clear.

The world, where action was loved beyond truth, beyond the full report, insisted Holleb had to fish or cut bait. He could forgive and forget, remember and pursue. In the great holes between, truth fell through.

It was not clear.

But, as of fuzzed head hitting soft pillow in this early morning, Holleb thought that, yes, if they caught his man, most unlikely, but if they did, he would, yes, probably, reluctantly, see the darn case through.

MILIUS AND MELANIE

1

They were to meet at the Wollman Memorial Rink in Central Park. A stupid idea, his, and in the unbalanced sentiment of reunion, agreed to by her. If they had even heard each other's voices over the phone, they wouldn't have gone through with it, but no, they had transmitted the proposals and confirmations through Tsvević; it had been Tsvević who'd spotted her in his painting, Tsvević who'd told him he must see her again, and Tsvević who had put in the call to Tulsa. "You must transform your emotional *situation*." Tsvević, an intellectual straggler who compensated in ferocity for modishness, was undergoing Sartre; *situation* had nothing to do with its banal English uses; no, it stood for fixity which choice would shatter.

Tsvević gleamed with false wisdom, his dab of nose, popped blue eyes, and ice-colored lips mere service stations for the gray-topped mental apparatus which ran the Language Schools and, for thirty years, no small part of Orlando Milius' life. What counted even more in Tsvević was the maniacally tended flesh whose terrific muscles bulged clothes into second skin. Every morning, in sneakers and sweatpants, Tsvević ran four laps around the Central Park Reservoir, a character known to policemen and taxi drivers going off late shifts, and to the thugs who worked the West Side Eighties and Nineties. None had ever held him up: out for gain, there were nothing but gym clothes and flying feet; out for mischief and violence, there were those

92

muscles. Such confidence muscles gave small intelligence, thought Milius, who, seven inches taller and fifty pounds heavier than Tsvević, was soft, had always been soft, and though not weak, for he walked a lot and lifted furniture at his wife's frequent command, had none of the confidence of size or strength. Milius would never appear in the park after dusk, he crossed streets with caution and swiftness, treasured all uniforms and the pacification they promised. A civic coward. Yet it was he, not Tsvević, who had almost a hero's record in wartime, had worked in the hills with partisans, had, if not shot, been shot at.

But he had not had the confidence to telephone Melanie Booler in Tulsa, Oklahoma. Indeed, lack of confidence had hidden his feelings about her for twenty years, and even now, when he had at least recognized something in his painting, timidity had slurred identification; she had just looked familiar, an ideal woman, too beautiful and wise for him to have known.

Tsvević had spotted her at once, and, great fisher of feeling, had drawn Milius' old longing from him. "That's your Melanie."

Of course it was. Naturally. Melanie. Who else? On the floor in his loft, looking up at the canvas pinned in light, Milius saw her skating inside the smashed cobalt arcs and gorgeous polygonal blots. Once again the pilot had brought him in safely.

Safely, yes, but into harsh country! Up the corridor, Vera's cabbage soup steamed in on little Hannah's flatulent tromboning; and, in Milius' wallet, reposed the villainous paragraph from the *Times Literary Supplement* clipped out by his London publisher, daggered with a red question mark, and airmailed across the Atlantic. It was one of those rare weeks in which Sartrean surgery did not have to go a-begging.

Now, zipped to the neck in his old orange suede jacket, an overturned keel of black lambswool on his gray head, Orlando Milius diverts his nerves from the noon meeting by focusing on the brilliant New York scene. The Skating

Pond blares pink and white; little frozen sea, fleshed over
by sweatered, jacketed, scarfed, and capped New Yorkers
twirling under the stony smiles of the great hotels, Plaza,
Pierre, Essex and Hampshire Houses. Sunday morning, mid-
December, yet a Floridian sun has softened the ice to a
green scurf which permits no skating distinction but
awkwardness: tots skitter, goosey girls shriek, corpulent
swaggerers crumple.

Twenty-four years. She will not know him. Or worse, he
will not know her. The crowds will rush on and off the ice
at noon, and they will be lost in the rush. "To the left of
the gate by the railing" wasn't sufficient direction. Had the
railing even been here? It was surely not where they used
to meet. No, they would walk together from Columbus
Circle, skates around their necks, Melanie darkly golden,
her body, so shy and full, turned military by a thigh-length
leather jacket out of which stuck her beautiful, stubby legs,
black in woolen stocking-pants. Large-eyed, quick, shy, but
never anxious, while he walked in fear that Sophie would
catch them in the Park, righteous in illegitimate possessive-
ness, picking them out with that look which boiled needles
off pine trees.

When Vera, quieter than Sophie, but with a fierceness
disciplined in wartime hills, learned what he had done, the
ice under the skaters' blades would not be cut as often as
his heart.

Learned?

Was he confusing Melanie and the *TLS*?

No, they were of a piece. There was meaning to the con-
vergence. Vera would spot the common treason. Yet her
father, dear old Poppa Murko, would have understood. Did
he not want his turgid, scholar's versions of the Chinese
tales put into clear English prose? Those beautiful chunks
of Ming erotica which he had mined from Zagreb archives.
And which now, for the price of a bottle of aspirin, trans-
muted the amorous encounters of Nebraska salesmen into
sensuous pageants. What had he, Milius, done, after all,
but clean Poppa's Serbian gunk from these Oriental dia-

monds, polish them up and put them into American set-
tings? With no thought of large profits or glory. Just to
make enough for paints and canvas, to keep Poppa's daughter in cabbage soup and his granddaughter in trombone
lessons.

Yet he was not wholly innocent. No, he had made one
mistake: he'd hinted at the Chinese sources of his books,
but had never mentioned Poppa Murko. And perhaps a
second mistake: he'd yielded to Benny Goss and American-
ized the books: Mei-ling Fan had become Dora Trent;
Ch'o Tuan, the eager scholar, was Roderick Peake, the
lascivious topologist. "Now we've got us something," said
Benny Goss. Yes, Benny, a dagger. Any minute the phone
would ring, Benny would see the paragraph clipped from
the *TLS*, and with the rage of the cornered pornographer,
he would throw Milius to the wolves. To Vera.

To Milosovich and Krenk. Twin canines, he remembered
them, sharp, torpid, yet turbulent men, dark and ugly, he
could not distinguish their features, or disentangle them.
Spittle-lickers of Mihailović, they'd sold out to the Ger-
mans, and he, Milius, had had to cut out for the mountains
with Vera and live like a block of ice for a year while
Milosovich and Krenk drank slivovitz in Gradisti. After
the war, they'd surfaced in England with fish in their teeth
(red-brick chairs of Serbian Studies), and now, behind the
anonymous authority of the *TLS*, they did their poisonous
survey of Serbian Oriental studies, straying just far enough
to include "the vulgarized, baroque renditions of Professor
Murko's versions of the *Jou-p'u-t'uan*, the *Ching-P'ing-Mei*
and the *Ko-lien h'ai-ying* made by neither a Serbian nor
an Oriental scholar, but by a third-rate American writer,
O. Milius."

A day, a week, and Vera would learn that he'd stripped
her darling Pop of his rightful possessions, and she would
turn him into soup. Ah, Melanie.

Yes, out of his need, as out of the broken polygons of
his painting, came the dear love of his life, surely that, his
Beatrice, his Laura, his Stella. Yes, noble Sidney's precious

star, he knew those lovely poems: Stella sees the very face
of woe, painted in my clouded face, how she will pity my
disgrace, as though thereof the cause she know, and some
heart-rending, bull's-eye ending, "I am not I, pity the tale
of me." Yes, he was Milius *Pictor*, not Milius *Auctor
Plagiarist Thief.*

Dear God, what the artist had to become in America.
Poor Wilson hiding out from the income-tax men to sip
his champagne in peace, the poets all mad, spiked on their
own dreams, exhibited like Cromwell's head for public
delectation, the painters smashed up in automobiles fleeing
the ravenous curiosity hounds, poor Jackson, dear Joey.
And who flourished but museum directors, gallery owners,
publishers? Business actors all, bearing their expensive
agonies for cocktail-hour inspection, or, lacking the gift of
gab, for fifty-dollar-an-hour confessors. The artists looked
normal, jovial, quiet, only occasionally stabbing a wife or
doping their veins, the only workers left, and what happened? Milosoviches and Krenks. Mindless teeth, snapping
at air, coming up with artist hearts. *O tempora, o mores,
senatus haec intellegit, consul vidit, hic tamen vivint.*
Vivint? They strut in Bedford Square, shine in the *Times*,
these critic-heroes, faggots, full of hatred or wild, mad en-
thusiasm, consumers, editorial powers, dressing themselves
in the snot of kings, rejecting, accepting, declining, apprais-
ing, and we, weak-willed artists, we follow, we succumb, we
bend, we take them at their own worth. Astounding them.
And they eat us. Oh, Milosovich, oh, Krenk, shoot me here,
shoot me.

And Milius, lost, pushed his hand to his head; his hat,
little upturned lambswool boat, scooted to the ice, and a
tiny skater, unable to stop, ground into it, and smashed her
tiny nose on the ice; blood and screams flowed over the
green scurf, and Milius found himself gripped by fierce
hands, shoulders shaken by a ferocious little man yelling
into his face, blissful in his hatred, grateful for his daughter's blood so he could bite the world's throat, and Milius,
trying to shake loose, called out, "Little girl. Darling. I'm

so sorry. Forgive me. How are you? Little sweets, take a
soda with me. At the Zoo Shoppe. Come," and he pushed
his yellow gloves into the wild man's chest and, punched
in the ribs, began to punch back, what was he doing, here
on a Sunday bringing blood out of a child, punching, and
then a stout, gray-haired woman in a cloth coat rushed
between them, picked up the child, thrust her into her
father's arms, stooped for Milius' hat, put it on his head,
and said, "Orlando. Orlando, dear. Are you all right? It's
me. Yes, Melanie."

                                                                2

The Obiitelj, the Family, that was Tsvević's name for the
fifteen, then twenty, then seven or eight of them who met
day in and out at the old Tip-Toe Inn on Eighty-Sixth
and Broadway or in the creaky three-story brownstones of
the upper Eighties and lower nineties of West Side Manhattan. They used the Serbian name, abbreviated to Obiit,
because Tsvević, a Serb, was the organizer. The others
came from all over the Balkans, Willie Eminescu from
Moldavia, Veronica and Leo Micle from Bucharest, the
mathematics student, Panayot Rustchok, from Sofia, and
from Pest, their great success, Belá Finicky, assistant professor of Oriental Studies at Columbia, who introduced his
most confused and beautiful pupil, Melanie Booler, of
Tulsa, Oklahoma. The Americans in the group were usually
transients, pupils in Tsvević's Language school, Tip-Toe
Inn acquaintances or sympathetic types who hung around
the Soldiers-and-Sailors Monument on Riverside Drive.
It was by this classical preface to the mausoleum of General Grant a few miles up the Drive that Tsvević's pupils
met on weekends, here that Milius first saw Melanie. He
had already come to understand that what held and
stamped the Obiit—Balkan core and American accretions
—was failure. Other New York groups, formed at the same
time out of similar drifters, foreign and domestic, some-

how acquired the motor power which drove them through
the Depression and the war into various triumphs, artistic,
theatrical, publishing, and publicity, but the Obiit found-
ered in eccentricity, quixoticism, sheer inability to make
headway. Milius had thought about it many nights. Why
was it? Lack of ambition? No. The Obiit members were full
of schemes, personal, civic, worldly, universal, timeless.
Lack of tenacity? Perhaps, in part. But more, it seemed
that American life wasn't ready to absorb these unassimil-
able bits of the unassimilated Balkans, these fragments of
fragments. The Obiit, like their native lands, were the
shuttlecocks of established powers. You'd think these people, ancestrally alerted to overreaching ambition and top-
pling regimes, could have adjusted to American life. But
no, hardly a handful survived—Tsvević, Eminescu, and
Milius himself. Though he had never been a true part of
them. He'd come to earn a living and stayed for Melanie,
but always, his persistence, insularity, and, yes, hardness,
had held him to his painting, and this in almost complete
isolation from the powerful temperaments already making
themselves known in New York—Pollock, Rothko, Klein,
Hofmann, de Kooning. They were unstoppable, and after
the war, they constituted the field, their critics, friends from
WPA days, preceding them with brilliant manifestos, their
gallery sponsors alert to the importance of abstraction in
the opulence, anxiety, hedonism, and skepticism of postwar life.

By then, the Obiit were scattered beyond reassemblage.
The war had assigned them, fed them, broken them; even
their bodies, oddly enough, had strange chinks through
which certain war and postwar diseases found ready and
fatal admission—hepatitis, lupus, erythremic myelosis. By
1948, ten of them lay in the cemeteries of Queens. Who,
watching the dark, gorgeous, noisy energy held in the corner
booths of the Tip-Toe Inn could have foreseen such deci-
mation?

In 1935, when he first met Tsvević, Milius, aged twenty-

eight, was living in a bedroom-kitchenette apartment with
Sophie Grindel, a severe, sensuous Latin teacher at Stuyvesant High School on Fifteenth Street. Sophie and the
monthly hundred-dollar check from the WPA Arts Section were his support. Sophie had forced him into the
project. "If you couldn't daub a barn, you've as much claim
on the funds as those bums at the Municipal Building."
She got her cousin, Sasha Grindel, a painter by virtue of
talk and possession of an easel, to sign his form. "That
sulky Dutchman dreaming of Ginger Rogers, and that
galoot Hammerslough reading Trotsky while the other
bums swipe at the walls. Roosevelt stands in back of them,
he can stand in back of a real American like you. Talent
or no."

Sophie was no admirer of his painting. He was income
supplement, bedwarmer, audience, and chef. While she
corrected *ferro, ferre, tuli, latus,* Milius broiled carp, made
matzoh-ball soup, tried out pasta dishes. Why not? He
stayed home. He went out only once on a project, drove
Sasha's jalopy through the Holland Tunnel to a New Jersey
post office, and painted what he thought would be a fit
mural for this center of Washington's struggling colonials,
an ocean of English red and black out of which coagulated
shivery red, white, and blue streaks. Up on the ladder, he
bore the catcalls of the Philistine postcard buyers. During
Christmas, he did part-time work dressing Fourteenth
Street department-store windows. Most of the year, he
just painted at home or on the walls of his friends' apartments. Indeed, it was learning to use this diseased skin
of cheap apartments which opened his eyes to his screen
techniques and led him to think out his notions of acci-
dent-proof painting. The apartment walls were his Paris
and his Provence. Smoke and brick dust now, they were
no more durable than the spaghetti alle vongole of some
Tuesday prewar dinner. Less memorable to that great eater,
Sophie. In the morning, when she left, the six square feet
above their bed would be a mean green grime; at four,

she'd return with her quizzes to a thick garden of color, and would barely nod at it. Was this what Cicero, that canny sybarite, had taught her?

Sophie was not harsh or mean, only intense and fierce. Powerful, nervous, silently demanding, Roman-nosed as her authors, her features dominated the narrow flesh of her face, the subtle lips whose underflap was gripped by powerful teeth when he had troubled her, straight hair the color of a Moselle white wine, full of rich gleams, though sparse; and the eyes like hot chocolate, steaming. They'd seen each other first through an Ohrbach's window he was decorating with sugar frost and holly, she checking out a pile of cashmere sweaters with the volatile, chocolate eyes that soon fixed his. Her underlip drew into her teeth, and, behind the glass, in shirtsleeves, Milius had felt a shimmer of heat. That night he'd gone home with her— there was no nonsense anywhere in Sophie—and, the next day, he'd removed his clothes in a paper bag from his brother's Bronx apartment and moved into her two and a half rooms down the dying street from the high school.

Sophie had no friends, and Milius was too absorbed in painting to visit his old friends in the Bronx. They saw almost no one but Tsvević, a substitute German teacher in the school system who, at Stuyvesant, tried to pick Sophie up. When, one day, he succeeded, he found himself brought home to Milius. A shock, but for Tsvević's disciplined system, one activity could substitute for another without noticeable abrasion. Lust stymied, Tsvević orated, planned, organized. He was beginning to roll out schemes of language schools. Urban man was in trouble, flabby in mind, flabby in body. "Tissues feeble, issues trouble." Tsvević's passion that year was Quintilian. "Perfect Man is Man Speaking." Exercise would build up the tissues, recitation of great poems and speeches would do the rest. They'd be no overhead, classes would be in the open air, "*Mens sana in corpore sano*, eh, Miss Grindel?"

Over the next months, they worked out the Scuola Quintiliana; notices were inked on the back of laundry

cardboards and put in windows along Broadway. The first
meeting was to take place on Saturday, March 21, at the
Soldiers-and-Sailors Monument. The day came, but no
pupils. Only Tsvević, Willie Eminescu, and Milius, the
instructors. For forty minutes they shivered in a trough
of Arctic air, then adjourned to the Tip-Toe Inn to re-
group their forces. It was decided to delay the opening for
a month, change the name to the *Mens Sana School,* and
alter the curriculum to instruction in foreign languages beginning with words for parts of the body, words which,
as the new notice had it, "would be riveted in memory by
overt motor activity. $2.45 per week."

3

By the seal pool, an arc of fish flew by their heads. Chow
time. The great commas waddled, honked, panted, dived,
and then such grace, delight, and marvel. Melanie Dube
laughed quietly. The powdered, grandmotherly lumpish-
ness disappeared into smile lines. Under the specs, the peri-
winkle eyes, within the gray hair, deep gold shadows. (Ah,
thought Milius, Melanie in his mind, the seals in water.)

They walked by the wolf cages, the gnus and ostriches,
then north along the chunky feldspar wall which split avenue from park. Melanie talked of Jack, her brilliant son, a
wanderer, guitar player, dropout and C.O., Milius of Vera,
Hannah, and his books, of which she hadn't heard.

Out of breath a bit, yes, but inside, Melanie and Milius
felt musical, joyous. What were years but signs for out-
siders? They were insiders, and, an hour later, over English muffins on a couch in Melanie's room at the Hotel
Bolivar, Milius, awkwardly, but not upset at the awkwardness, took up her unringed left hand and kissed it.

How could it be? Thousands of hours had not dispersed,
but only screened his feelings. Anonymous, cautious, side-
lined, he felt singled out, magnified. Orlando Milius, hero's
name on a coward's heart, oddity cloaked in oddity, he had

not looked into his feelings for thirty years. A painter, his feelings were absorbed by the techniques of appearance. No wonder his paintings were strange. Yet one didn't choose the strange, one fell into it. Like birth. (What to do but breathe, cry, suck?) Or the war. There he was, four thousand feet over the iron river, the ocher shack on the lip of the copse, and Vera, Djovan, little Vuk, and Poppa Murko with his wooden trunk of papers. Alone, he had felt all alone, and there was Vera, intense, tiny, her cartridge belt across her breasts, her black hair clipped under the astrakhan, and old Murko, dear, snaggle-toothed coot, sitting on those Oriental grapes. Ah, it was hard. Old Murko could draw roses from a rock garden. At night, above the icing Sava, he read the manuscripts aloud, and Vera's face, touched by the steaming raka, flushed in the sudden, masculine silence. Yes, Poppa knew his stuff. He had learned plenty from the wily Mings, knew his lungs weren't going to last another winter in the hills; and provided for his manuscripts and his daughter. That was the way life went: Those who knew their hearts arranged the lives of those who didn't. Was it too late? For him? For Melanie?

For Melanie, no. Not from the first minute, seeing Milius punched and hatless, her sweet Orlando, so blotted a mixture of subtlety and confusion, so intricate and awkward. Despite Dube, dear Dube, as far out of the mainstream in his way as Orlando in his. She'd fitted around his oddities all these years, she would not pain him now. But he floated on those depthless oddities, she was only another one along with the white wool socks he wore to bed summer and winter, the collection of snakeskins, the rooster imitation. Poor Dube. His puzzlement underwrote her week in New York.

She had never tried him beyond puzzlement, but she was ready now. Not that she had ever been one to force things. *Wu-wei.* That's what she had learned from Belá Finicky in Chinese Thought. *Let nature take its course.* Sails, not oars; the stirrup, not the whip. It was her nature, as well. Rivers bit away at old beds, and formed new ones. (Did that mean old beds were abandoned?)

Milius walked home through the park at Eighty-Fifth Street. Provence. Purple vineyards, silvered olive trees, Renoir gardens, Monet ponds, Cézanne mountains freaked with jets of gold. Oh such beauty. His hands in the yellow gloves tensed and perspired, he knew the sign, he walked fast, he must get home. At Fifth he hopped a bus over to Second, then ran down the block, stormed up the stairs past Vera's call, "Orlando," and, in the loft dived for his paints.

But Vera's cry was not to be shut off, and guilt amplified it in Milius' ears. He dropped his brush. "It's happened." At last. She's found out. Down the hall she'll come, a pot of steaming water in those partisan's hard hands. Benny Goss, Milosovich, Krenk, Hannah, Sophie, the ghost of Belá Finicky, Poppa Murko, and the lustful Chinese scribes would sup on his souped-down flesh. It was over. Provence? Hah. The butcher's knife. Orlando," called Vera, and then another cry, "Brat. Brat Lando." Another voice: Baritone.

The door whirred. A great slab of man grabbed Milius in his arms as if he were cardboard, whirled him dizzy, kissed his cheeks. Hannah and Vera cooed and leaped at his flanks.

It was Vuk. Cousin Vuk.

He'd flown in today, hadn't Milius been reading the papers? There was to be a reading at Madison Square Garden, the only poet ever to read there. "Not one word publicity, and the house is sold off in two hours. Tickets skulped for fifty smockers."

Vuk the Bard, Tito's greatest export, life's king, subsidized for singing what Djilas was jailed for saying. At eighteen, he had told Stalin to his face he was going out of his mind, and the old iron man, with the Georgian worship of the poet-seer, had taken it deeply to heart. So dissolved the world's miseries in that shark's face with the wise, ice-blue eyes.

Now Vuk was, as usual, suffering. Heartburn, cramps.

He raised his sweater, shirt, and undershirt, put Milius' hand
against his rib cage. "Feel, Lando, feel," and in a loud
whisper to both protect and excite Hannah, "Weemens is
keellink me." Rome, Brussels, London—"incredible"—
Paris, Barcelona—"estupendo"—even Dublin, two, three
a day. And drawing a pack of Gaulois from his corduroys,
"Plus fumigottink mine lunks." The hard, narrow flesh
devoured by little Hannah and Vera till the shirt dropped.
Then, in Milius' ear, "But waddya hell, us Communist
mission is focking capitalists." This the shy rail of a boy
skiing the hills with his bag and shotgun, bringing back
the snipe. Now, in Serbian, he stuffed them with that
great cake which was his life: tiger hunting in Nepal,
swimming with La Cardinale at Porto San Stèfano, stran-
gling a rabid camel in Kabul, debating Rumlï in Vienna,
frugging in a Siberian igloo. And the erotic Niagara roared:
one-legged beauties in the Pescadores, tree-loving in Zambia,
a flowerbath in Oahu, and heart-cracking loves with an
Israeli sergeant, an Amarillo cattleman's wife, a florist's
assistant in Kuala Lumpur.

But Vuk, seismograph as well as earthquake, spotted un-
easiness in Milius' laughter. "Enough. Let's walk, Lando.
I must get some New York gas to my lunks," and took
Milius off to Central Park, where Milius, content to be
Vuk's oyster, opened up his troubles.

For Vuk, though, Milius' troubles were unrecognizable as
troubles. How could sheer possibility, whether for love
or hatred, be anything but good? Vuk was delighted about
Melanie; it looked as if one could go on a long time. For
Vuk, life was a trail of eggshells. That a shell should suddenly churn with new life was a wonder. "And where is
this nymph of yours, dear Lando?" He must see her, this
wonder of sixty-year flesh.

As for Milosovich and Krenk, he would grind them. If
he could face Tito, Stalin, Khrushchev, and Mao, it would
be an eye's blink to crush Serbian scum into nonexistence.
He would read them out of the world in Madison Square
Garden, pop them into dust in Chattanooga, St. Louis,

Winnipeg, and L.A. He would pull them out of literature like decayed teeth, and he could celebrate Orlando's beautiful erotica—though personally he didn't care much for fancy smut—that was no trouble, but first, they must see Melanie, "your neemph."

Vera?

Vera would understand, appreciate, adore his being refreshed for her. "Like dugs, weemens love sneef of other weemens on bones." As for leaving her, well, that was perhaps too much. Life was no coffin, each day a nail, one must move after one's heart, but leaving, leaving was much trouble. He would not dream of leaving his own wife, she was his mother, sister, lover, nurse, why should he leave her, she knew nothing—hah, thought Milius—about his other focking, why should she, she was brilliant, beautiful, had a life of her own, strictly faithful to him, who would need any more? With his shark's smile, insistent, innocent, powerful.

At the Bolivar, Melanie was celebrating reunion with Tsvević.

Reunion?

Tsvević was putting it on the existential line: Hot coffee and cold turkey. In detail. (Serious advice could not be capsular, look at *Being and Nothingness*, look at *Saint-Genêt*.) He had hardly warmed up, did not relish the entrance of Milius, let alone Vuk. That a Tito stooge, a ninth-rate versifier, a publicity-gorger and narcissist should preempt his platform was a bit much. Seldom calm, Tsvević grew into a frenzy of calm. His sentences lengthened, his face grew polelike under constraint, the madly exercised body quivered inside the grimy tweed. He was disturbed, yes, dismayed by their indecision. Life called to them, the very earth suspended its course so that they could come together again, yet here they were, locked in bourgeois fears, corpses of life.

Ah, well, perhaps, but not that afternoon, that dusk, that evening.

For Milius and Melanie are in the Paris Theater swept

by the love story of a racing-car driver and a widowed
script girl, melting as the difficulties of the thirty-year-old
French beauties blot into their own.

While Vuk—at Madison Square Garden—dedicates his
reading to that great artist in prose and paint, his old friend
and comrade-in-arms, Orlando Milius, assailed on the left
by vicious Serbian cannibals, on the right by silence and
poverty.

And while Vera Murko Milius lies on a velvet ottoman,
head aburst with Leo Tsvević's story.

Tsvević stands in front of her, a sword, vague eye on a
print above her reeling head, a Byzantine Christ whose head
lies shipwrecked on its reef of shoulder. "Serbian agony,"
he growls. "Smash these icons."

"Darling Poppa."

"No regrets, Vera. No bitterness. Bourgeois gloom saps
vitality. Look up at Leo, darling." Vera looks up. "Liberate
Orlando. And you liberate Vera." An iron hand grabs hers,
draws her up, they are nose to nose. "You have camouflaged
une mauvaise situation, chère Vera." His great eyes swim
in the red-veined net.

Milius and Melanie drink Cherry Heering in the Bolivar
Room, go upstairs, and, in the dark, take off their clothes.
Sympathy performs its magic fusion. The clumsy, creaky
bodies understand; they are lovers once again.

Ten-thirty, and Milius takes the crosstown bus, in his
hand a cellophane sack of chocolate kisses from Whelan's.

In the tiny living room, Vera Milius rises, fierce and silent.
The chocolate obols are laid on the ottoman. Minutes eat
silence. Then Vera begins, quietly: the historical introduction, the Balkan histories of treason, epic stories, the
long fight for national freedom, the wars, the Bulgars, Turks,
Austrians, and Huns, the traitors, Djuleks and Mihailovićs,
who dog Serbian history. She should have been alert to
treason. She should know the grain of the world. Like
Milos and Brankovic, Orlando is infected. That her darling
father had seen him as a son, that she should have been
his prize was spice on the legend. Yes, even as she was, the

years of her fullness given to him, Ganelon, Djulek the Bimbasa, Judas. Robbery. He had robbed his only heir. What price was it to come into the world the child of Milius? Sixty-two years of age, treason took a new turn here. And with what? A sugar babe? A gold digger? A baby doll? No. No, beauty she could understand, flesh she understood, but such treason, no. To salt his treason, his rebuke, he took a woman older than his wife, a rag discarded years ago, a western American woman, with dental plates, white hair, hard of hearing. Was this the madness of abstract artists? That they had no touch with life, the world? Was this the meaning of his treason, that it went against the grain of flesh as well as family? If he'd brought a filthy nag, yes, literally, a horse into his bed, she would have only more clearly seen the insanity of his treason. My God. And he brings me sweets, chocolates, Judas kisses.

Vera, small, dark, blunt-nosed, solid, pours her survey on his head. Powerful, analytic, a great moment, and in English, her second language, her father would have been so proud. Justice, intelligence, wisdom, passion employed to describe, correct, chasten. She ended in a great breath, rose, as high as a small woman could, he imagined her with the bandoliers across her breasts, the fur hat, the knitted gloves in the mountain ice, Vera, the great soup-maker, enduring here his few dollars, making her own world amidst the aliens, back now alone on her mountains, a heroine of family life, out of the sagas. And he, a swine, thief, two-timer.

Milius sat alone in the parlor, heard the toilet flush— Vera allowed herself the privileges of being natural—he crushed a piece of candy, the stain was beautiful, he would put it on canvas. He sat brooding, and then, bored, and tired; but there was only the other side of their bed. Did he dare?

Yes.

He went in. She was, of course, awake. (Could pain advertise itself in sleep?) He took her breaths as whips, undressed, ashamed of his body's ease, put on his pajamas,

did not dare empty his bowels, only allowed himself to
urinate, ashamed even here of relief, brushed his teeth so
his breath would not add offense, crept around to the other
side of the bed, undid his pajama string for more ease, slid
under the quilt. "Forgive me, please, dear Vera. I'm so weak
a man. Please forgive me."

She had often rebuked him for ease of sleep while her
ears seined the city's riot. He tried not to sleep before she
did, but once again, his body triumphed, and he snored,
terribly. Vera then could sleep herself, certified by the
criminality of his noise.

4

The next morning brought great changes. Via a telephone
call at six-thirty. A reporter, then another, then the Yugo-
slav Embassy, then the State Department.

It was Vuk. But by mischance. Life had caught up with
him. The cake had its worms. He was in Lenox Hill
Hospital, skull crushed, sure of recovery, but in a bad way.
Reporters were chronicling his New York day. The feature
seemed to be one Orlando C. Milius, American painter
and author, whom Vuk had visited in the afternoon and
extolled at Madison Square Garden a couple of hours before
he had been mugged, slugged, robbed, and left for dead.

For most of the day Milius smoked in the blaze of
contemporary publicity. Pen, mike, and camera elicited
every available piece of his body, every cent of his income,
every stage of his life. By noon he had watched himself on
television and read about himself in the early editions with
the happy puzzlement of a child seeing a drop of water
under a microscope. "So this is Milius, this mass of warts,
this lump of crystals, this strange being who has been
given my name." He was described as "handsome and
distinguished," "faded and undistinguished," "a youthful
sixty," "an elderly man," "a famous painter," "an unknown
poet," "a war hero and scholar," "an unemployed language

teacher." He could not wait to cart his new lives over to
Melanie.

She, unaware of his fame, had sat all day at her window,
watching a veil of cobalt sleet lift from the city, seeing the
dendrite ache of Central Park trees, daydreaming the strange
turn in her life. Orlando, my dearest, no sleet with you.
Our autumn is harvest time in dear New York, sweet
nature's town.

Milius, arriving at six, was almost an intruder. She had to
shake herself from the day's cocoon, face up to his excitement and great news. The Willeth Gallery had made over-
tures, his first show in a major gallery; Benny Goss, voice
full of gold instead of rage, had planned new editions,
translations, campaigns for awards, critical conferences, the
literary works.

Night edged dusk, Orlando wore down. Too much. The
variety and speed were too much. Their embrace was static,
the amorous focus blurred. "We must go out," he said.
They studied the movie section. *Blow-Up* had just opened
at the Plaza. "That's our dish."

In his fine chesterfield, bought years ago in the Gramercy
Thrift Shop, riding downtown beside his lovely Melanie,
holding a newspaper which carried his own picture, Milius
felt like a man whose rich personal life was of public con-
cern.

In the dark of the Plaza, watching the two chippies
wrestle each other naked on the purple backdrop paper,
Milius had an erection. And simultaneously, a tremendous
idea. He would paint screenlessly. He would lay clear, intricate blocks of space events directly on canvas. No subtle
schemes of indirection, only direct interrogations of matter,
unambiguous shafts through surface forms.

What joy.

He turned Melanie's head toward his and, in the dark,
kissed her lips. Nature had its seven ages, yes, but each
generation altered their dynamics and duration. He and
Melanie were vanguardists of the sexagenarian revival.

Yet, an hour later, eating at a Second Avenue steakhouse,

there was another relapse. The peppered vodka-and-bouillon drinks, the adolescent hamburgers and onion, the noisy, gaseous, prinked-out night of Second Avenue, were not the backdrop for resurrected feelings or revolutionary passion.

At the Bolivar once again, holding each other, eyes closed against the sad circumstance of their bodies, loving but spent, half-querulous, half-amused, Milius and Melanie separated in the labyrinth of desire.

5

Artists, Milius knew, were hypersensitive to their cycles, emotional and social, intellectual and sexual. According to Françoise Gillot, Picasso had a daily rise and fall: her job was weaning him from noon blues to the two-o'clock assault on canvas. Milius' friend Praeger, the poet-obstetrician, had a yearly cycle: a fine, productive spring; a frenzied, coruscating summer; then an autumn and winter of uncheckable misery. He himself, thought Milius, had an elephantine cycle: his works took years to come to anything; his passions were lethargic as glaciers, his discoveries immense, but molasseslike in realization. The discovery in the Plaza Theater had led to a week's thick-headed absorption in paints. Now, his insight come to almost nothing, he surfaced for air. Melanie was gone, gone and he'd hardly noticed. His last hours with her were more nostalgic than amorous, scarcely a backdrop for his painting. For a moment, he couldn't remember if he had taken her to the plane. He hadn't. He had moled it in the attic, refusing phone calls, not speaking to Vera or Hannah, forgetful that he had been, unaware that he was no longer, a public figure. Now fog throttled dawn light at his attic's glass wimple. Worn-out, stained hands on his long face, Milius was carved by his ache for Melanie. Seven-thirty. He'd been up since six.

He put on his chesterfield and astrakhan, kept on the lumberman's boots in which he painted, and went out. He

walked by the great, silent museum which showed no
Milius, into Central Park, up and down the unshaven little
hills, across the empty bridle paths, between great rocks
befogged into Rhenish ruins. He walked northwest to the
reservoir and waited. A runner passed, another, and then,
chugging slowly, lined, gray, pullover limp over his knick-
ers, Tsvević. "Leo," called Milius softly.

Tsvević stopped, took breath, stared in fright. "Who?
Where? What's up? Oh, you, Lando." He jogged in place,
panting, eyes popped and veined. "Something wrong?"

"I'm so restless. I had to get outside."

"All right. I'm finished. Let's go home."

For years Tsvević had had a woman friend who cleaned
his apartment. She'd died a year ago, and Tsvević had not
touched a broom or picked up a newspaper since. The
place was clogged with candy wrappers, socks, shoe rags,
empty tubes of Bufferin, exhausted inhalators, copies of
Horoscope and the Balkan News-Letter; the rugs were plots
of dust; months of burned toast and bacon fat hung in the
light motes.

It was a little better in the kitchen. Tsvević brewed tea,
cleared the table, poured into clean blue cups. They sat
at the window which gave on a coppery well of light in the
apartment-house courtyard. Tsvević regained confidence.
"It's worked out badly, Lando. Who would have guessed
that Titoist monkey would turn you into a public freak?"

"A freak? The picture in the paper? That was nothing,
Leo."

"You're wrong. It was everything. Kings have lost thrones
with less exposure. You're fortunate you lost only Melanie."

"Melanie didn't leave because my picture was on television."

"Your picture was on television because of the disloca-
tion in your life."

"What are you saying, Leo? Make sense. Don't talk like
a foolish mystic."

"Mystic? We mustn't be so quickly contemptuous, Orlando. The world has mysteries beyond the scope of J.-P.

Sartre. Have you not read Teilhard? Matter has its mysteries, and the spirit is not insensible. All conditions are enchantments, Orlando. The mistake may have been in forcing the situation. Acceptance, Orlando. Our lot is good." He tossed his soaked teabag toward a garbage pail; it missed and spread its tiny leaves against the porcelain side of the stove.

Nine-thirty. Milius walks across the park as he had come. The Queens factories have sent their fumes into the risen mist; café au lait. The rocks are lit in the hollows where the crystals mass. At Madison, Milius goes into the drugstore and changes ten dollars into quarters.

In Tulsa, it is only seven-forty. Dube answers the phone. "Hell-o." Milius' throat fills, his heart thuds on his ribs, he can't speak. "What's this?" says the voice. "Jack? Trouble?"

Milius tries to say, "Wrong number," but can manage only phlegmatic clearance. He hangs up, wipes the perspiration off his forehead with the sleeve of the chesterfield.

Two weeks ago, the failure would have thrown him off for a month, if not permanently. Not now. Now he will wait two hours and phone again, person to person. The operator will get Melanie to the phone, then he, Milius, will manage the rest.

EAST, WEST . . . MIDWEST

Alas, we Mongols are brought up from childhood to shoot arrows . . . Such a habit is not easy to lay aside.
—Chinghis-Khan, March, 1223

a small thing, lightly killed
—Agamemnon, line 1326

Bidwell, a man, like many, woefully incomplete and woefully ignorant of it, was, this Christmas Day, worse off than usual. Hong Kong flu. "The latest installment," as his usually quiet, usually uncomplaining wife put it, "of Asian vengeance." Bidwell's single scholarly contribution to her domestic arsenal: an essay on the Pendulum of Revenge which had swung between East and West since the thirteenth century.

"One more trip up these stairs"—carting iced grape juice to his bedside—"and your Genghis can notch up another casualty."

"Chinghis," corrected Bidwell, part-time historian of the Mongols. Their second-oldest exchange.

"Historian, journalist, translator," as he listed himself in *Who's Who in the Midwest*, Bidwell was functioning in none of these roles when Miss Cameron called that Christmas afternoon four years to the hour since she'd first shown herself to be what she'd had to be put away for. Not up to Chinghis, not up to Christmas games, and cer-

tainly not up to Miss Cameron, he was reading old letters in
bed when the phone rang at his elbow.

He identified the dead voice between "Mis" and "ter."

"Mr. Bidwell?"

"Speaking."

"This is Freddy Cameron."

"Miss Cameron. Goodness me. How are you?"

"Better."

"I'm so glad."

"How are you?"

"Not too great. Got the flu. Can't shake it. Been in and
out of bed for two weeks. You get it, you get over it, and
you get it again. They call it the camelback."

"I'm sorry." And oddly, the voice, rising from death, was
full of sorrow, no formula. Bidwell had her narrow, foal's
head in mind, could see it narrowing more in genuine,
illegitimately genuine sorrow. He was still the unwilling
usurper of feeling which belonged to those who had denied
her. These victims of deniers. How many millions had suffered for that cangue the fifteen-year-old Chinghis-Khan,
Temüjin then, had dragged from yurt to yurt month after
month. "Thank you."

"I wanted to talk to you."

"Yes."

"I mean." The pause which asked him to say her piece;
but only the wronged dead could make such wordless
demands. "See you."

"Would that be right, Miss Cameron?"

"I don't know."

"Mightn't it trouble you again?"

"Yes."

"Shouldn't you ask your doctor?"

"All right. If it's all right with him, will it be all right
with you?"

"I think so. Soon as I shake this flu. Though it looks like
a bad bet. You're up, you're down, you're up, you're down."

"Thank you. When?"

"When?"

"When can I call you about it?"

"I should be O.K. in a week or ten days. Maybe two weeks. Say three. You can call me at *Midland.*"

"I'm sorry I called you at home."

"Tsall right. I'm glad to know you're better. And while we're at it, Merry Christmas, Miss Cameron."

"Yes. You too."

"So long, then."

"Yes. So long."

Thirty feet up on the third floor of the old brick house, Bidwell opened window and storm window, scooped snow from the cottonwood branch he'd failed to trim that fall, and brought it to his boiled forehead. Could all relief be so simple.

This Christmas week, the astronauts Anders, Borman, and Lovell were looping the moon in Apollo Eight, but down here, thought Bidwell, down here, even the fish are begging us to let up. Featured in Sunday's *Midland,* the coho salmon loaded with the DDT washed from its plant-louse-killing jobs in Indiana and Illinois. The pendulum of ecological revenge. Oil, bled from underwater shale, burst its iron veins and ruined the shores where the stockholders of Gulf and Humble lay on their dividends. Pigs and cattle, murdered for their chops, loosed lethal fat into the arteries of their eaters. Chicago, named by a smell-shocked Ojibway sniffing the wild-onion tracts, stank with the sulfurous coal palmed off in arm-twisting contracts. The air, the lake, where a trillion silver skeletons rotted forty miles of shore-line (the starved alewives washed in with the opening of the locked interior by the St. Lawrence Seaway). Out Bidwell's windows, north, south, west, the locked slums, leaking vengeance on those who'd locked them there. "A fifth of American color television sets are dangerously radioactive." Last Sunday's feature in *Midland,* and there, sucking poison into their cells with Garfield Goose, his little boys, Josh and Petey. In fury, Bidwell called Sears, threatened them with a follow-up story in *Midland,* and in two hours, a red-headed engineer, Swanson, zoomed up from the Loop, in hand two thousand-dollar boxes, scintillators whose needles reported his boys safe. Safe, that is, said Swanson, until the gaseous regulator tube broke down, and the voltage soared to transmit reds, greens, and blues.

The classic hang-ups of the twentieth-century burgher, and they were Bidwell's; in spades, for they were also the staff of his Sunday supplement's life.

And now, his very own pestilence, Miss Cameron. Obsessed, frenzied, the great mechanism of perception wild with unreality. A pair of legs, a pair of ears, a pair—he supposed—of breasts, all the paraphernalia of a reasonable woman, and then, above the neck, behind the eyes, between the ears, a loose nut. Back to the factory. But no, the factory turned her loose, and now so did the repair shop, and once more she was after him who had nothing, next to nothing, to do with her.

This Christmas week, between bouts of chills and fever, Bidwell worked on the Christmas Day of 1241, when Batu, Chinghis-Khan's grandson, crossed the iced Danube and battered the town of Eszterzom. Europe, a small island of feudal civility, hung by a thread. Batu's armies had wiped out Kiev, Ryazan, Moscow, Bolgan, Vladimir, and Pest. There was nothing to stop them but the immobile, tank-like knights of Hungary. Then, Christmas Day, Batu got the news his uncle Ögödei, the Khakhan, had died, and back he turned. Europe was saved, as it would be saved by such threads for three centuries, until its sea power flanked the masters of the Eurasian landmass and began that great rise of the West, which, this very Christmas week of 1968—as its feet were chilled by Eastern threat—reached the moon itself. A distance which should annul the old divisiveness of the world. A great story.

For years Bidwell had published bits of it in the *Harvard Journal of Asiatic Studies*, the *Abhandlung für die Kunde des Morgenlandes*, and the *Journal asiatique*. Austere, careful studies, but Bidwell had literary ambition, and in mind a fine book like Mattingly's on the Armada or Runciman's on the Sicilian Vespers, a work Josh and Petey would see

on general reading lists, not merely in footnotes. This ambition went against the grain of his graduate training, but
there it was, a desire to shape data into coherent stories
which would serve men who counted as models and guides.
All right, such stories were formed by fashion and lived
by style, but they were what deepened life. Didn't Chinghis,
didn't all heroes, live and die by them?

Sweat poured into the blue clocks of his flannel pajamas;
he pulled the great quilt about his chilled bones. Mind
adrift between the Mongols and Apollo Eight, Bidwell felt
the Great Divide in things. The lunar odyssey had its
elegant technology and its political-commercial hoopla.
Its heroes were no Hectors, no Chinghises, only burghers
like himself, bolstered by exercise and the great American
confidence in mechanic triumph.

Where did he, Bidwell, stand with these Moon Loopers?

They were the stuff his sort made sense of, the titles of
books his sort wrote. Their risks were somatic, his mental;
they moved in space, he time.

They lived like finely tooled nuts in a great machine.
And how would they die? They had no choice. Bidwell's
subject, Chinghis-Khan, had constructed his death, had
planned the extermination of the Tanguts, chosen his successor, and then moved north of the Wei to the cool air
of the Kansu mountains. No wonder the Mongol bards rose
to their great epic; Chinghis had worked his life out as a
poem.

Yet the astronauts too were controlled by story. Christmas
Eve, they read Genesis to earth as sunlight poured on the
lunar crust. Bidwell, fever rising, back troubled by a mattress button he was too weak to rip off or shift away from,
felt their voices fuse with the racket of his children.

Human buzz.

What did human enterprise come to, great or small?

Commotion.

The fever drifted him, Bidwell scraped bottom, felt himself buzzing off like an old bulb.

They were all going to have to make it on their own.

Ethel, Batu, Chinghis, Josh, Petey, Shiffrin (his boss at
Midland).

They'd feel the void he left. Yes, but then augment their
own emotional capital with it. Functioning men wasted
nothing. What could be more ornamental than young
widowhood, the loss of a father, a friend?

Sig Schlein would look through his manuscripts, decide
what could be salvaged for articles, and wrap up his biblio-
graphical life with an elegiac paragraph in the *HJAS*. A few
sheets of paper, a few feet of earth, a few real, a few crocodile tears, and Farewell Bidwell.

And for years, maybe, Farewell Batu and the other
Mongol chiefs whose ghosts he'd animated. Though they
could take it better than he. Their bloody deeds were on
record, his own lay mostly hidden, some in his boy's heads,
to be disinterred on couches fifteen years from now (if
people were still buying that paregoric). "My descend-
ants will wear gold cloth, feed on tender meat, ride
proud horses, press the most beautiful young women in
their arms . . . and they will have forgotten to whom
they owe it all." August 18, 1227: Farewell Chinghis.
"Buzz" and bitter lemons. December 24, 1968: Farewell
Bidwell.

A bad night.

But somehow, by morning, he'd outflanked the flu-
dazed grip on his life. A silver band showed beneath the
shade. Christmas morning. "Time, Daddy."

Weak, but clear-headed, Bidwell in his sweat-damp
clocked pajamas, led Ethel and the boys toward the Scotch
pine on their green *tayga* of carpet, where lay, scattered like
Chinghis's victims, packages of every color and shape.

The geometry of burgher dreams.

2

Back in 1964, Bidwell was translating extracts from the
Secret History of the Mongols for the University of Min-

nesota Press. The *Midland* typing pool sent up a girl who
did extra work at home.

Miss Cameron. Five and a half feet of long-faced timidity, hands crossed before her parts, eyes down, though
sneaking up when she thought his weren't. Yes, she did
extra typing, she would be happy to do his manuscript.

He gave her a short section about the kidnapping of
Temüjin's wife Börte by the Merkit warrior who impregnated her. Miss Cameron brought it back the next day, a
fine job. He gave her the rest of the manuscript, about a
hundred pages.

A week, ten days, two weeks, and there was no word from
her. The typing pool said she hadn't called in and, further-
more, had no telephone. They assumed she was sick. She
lived on the edge of the Lawndale ghetto. The Friday before Christmas, Bidwell drove fearfully on the shattered
rim of the slum and rang the doorbell of her apartment.

She came downstairs, and when she saw him through
the glass, a small hand went to her small chest. "I'm very
sorry," she said opening up. "I've been sick."

He told her not to worry, he'd been concerned about her
as well as his manuscript.

A smile showed a half-second on raw lips. Physics had
cloud chambers for such short-lived states. What self-dis-
trust killed such smiles? Miss Cameron's long hair, a dull
red, shook about her narrow shoulders. Cold? Fear? Nega-
tion? "I'm almost done with it. Do you want what I
have?"

In her dead voice, these words hung all sorts of interroga-
tion before Bidwell. He wanted nothing from Miss Cameron but what he'd paid for.

"I'll wait till you finish. Can I bring you anything? Food?
Medicine?" There was a deep barrenness in the stairwell.
Miss Cameron was as stranded as the old moon. "No,
thanks," she had everything. "Good-bye," and sorry she
caused him so much worry. "I can't remember why I didn't
call. I didn't know so much time had passed."

Monday she brought in the typescript. There were hundreds of mistakes in it, omitted paragraphs, garbled sentences. He had the whole thing redone by another girl in the pool, but said nothing to Miss Cameron, only thanked and paid her.

That Christmas afternoon, he answered the phone.

"Why did you?" asked the dead voice.

"Excuse me."

"You had no right."

"Miss Cameron?"

"You shouldn't have done it."

"Please tell me what's wrong."

"You know." Sly and accusatory, new sound in the monotone. "You know."

"Look," said Bidwell, "let me get a doctor for you. You're not in good shape."

"No." A wail. "No. Tell me why you stood at the window. Naked you were. Pudgy you are. Yet had your way. With me." Then fiercely, "It's you should see a doctor." The phone banged.

Bidwell rang up his analyst neighbor, Spitzer, told him what happened, asked if the girl sounded suicidal or homicidal.

"Probably not," said Spitzer. "She's having an episode. Happens frequently on Christmas. Or Sundays. The routine's broken, there's nothing to intrude on the fantasy. Can you get hold of her parents? Or some relative?"

Bidwell knew nothing about her, he'd have to wait till the office opened in two days, then he could check with Personnel.

"You could call the police," said Spitzer, "but I don't advise it. The girl's called you because she's got it into her head that you're important to her. If you bring the police, it'll confirm the worst of her fears. Don't worry. She won't hurt anyone. And she won't throw herself out the window."

(False prophet Spitzer. Though it was four years off.)

That night, the phone jangled him from sleep.

"St. Stephen's Day, Mr. Bidwell."

"Oh, Lord. Miss Cameron. What?"

"I must see you. You came again. The scale fell from you. Devil. At the window. Yet it can't be. I'm so, so, so mixed up. Please see me?"

St. Stephen's Day. Every year they went to Sig Schlein's Boxing Day party. "Today?"

"Please."

"Where? Not at your place. Wouldn't be right."

She would come uptown, they could meet at Pixley and Ehler's on Randolph opposite the public library. It would save him miles.

This was rational, she was aware of him. All right, he'd be there at ten-thirty. Pixley and Ehler's. How did she pick it? Chicago's Olympus of the radical thirties. His boyhood. Thick buns frosting in the windows, bums mixing with scholars from the Crerar Library upstairs, the filthy classic hulk of the Chicago Public Library across the street.

At ten-thirty there was no one at the round tables but a bum dipping a cruller into coffee.

Bidwell waited at one of the tables with a pot of tea till Miss Cameron swung open the doors. In a cloth coat which didn't seem up to stopping frost, hardly enough to contain her, and hatless, the red hair like thread laid over a counter to be woven for something more useful than itself. The long face, beak-nosed, chapped, pale, eyes a clouded blue and looking as if stuck in at the last moment, full of haste and hurt. Her progress to his table was a drift. Then, arriving, head down, she said, "Thank you."

For coming? For existing? For not being something contrived by her brain and found nowhere else?

"Miss Cameron, I came to persuade you to let me take you to a hospital."

The raw face slapped against her palm. "God," it said. She sat down.

"Miss Cameron. Tell me what I can do for you."

The face faltered, thickened, grew inward, the eyes

cleared, lit with what he had not seen there before. "Have you not killed the devil's warrior for my bed, Temüjin? What a question."

Wednesday morning. Chicago. Nineteen-sixty-four. Women pouring out of the IC tunnel where Capone had had Jake Lingle, the diamond-belted go-between, shot to death, the news dealers calling out Johnson's Christmas menu on the ranch, the bum lapping his cruller, and here this frail cup of girl's flesh thought itself the bride of Chinghis-Khan, eight hundred years and fifteen thousand miles away.

"It's just me, Bidwell, Miss Cameron. It's nineteen-sixty-four, and you're Miss Cameron, somewhat unwell, and you typed the manuscript about Chinghis and Börte for me, and I think it's confused you."

Her face blinked. Bidwell could make out the present taking over her face, a hard march through swamps, but she made it, she nodded. Up and down went the foal's head. "I know," and as he was about to welcome this with "Good," the face blinked again, the smashed eyes said, "But he told me."

"What?"

"At the window," she said with her small wail. "He said you'd take me back, though Jaghatay was in my belly. Here," and a thin hand came from her lap to the brown middle of the coat to show the unlikely presence of Börte's son.

Bidwell, a weight of misery in his own stomach, found nothing to say. Her head rose and fell, his went from side to side.

"Yes," she said, the face blinking again. "I know it's in my head." Which now pendulumed like his.

Bidwell, knowing, even as he did it, that a risk was in it, covered her small hand with his gloved one.

"Gawd," she moaned. The head twisted away from its stem, her body, rising, followed it. Before Bidwell could get his bearings, she was into Randolph Street, red head down, ramming the cold air.

3

By the time he'd gotten her personnel file and located a
mother who lived in Evanston, she'd called to apologize and
request another meeting.

"All right," he said, his campaign formed. "At the same
place."

Where, not Bidwell, but mother and mother's priest came
with a car. Miss Cameron was wrapped up and taken to
the Sisters of Mercy in Milwaukee, "not," said Spitzer,
"a great center of treatment, but they'll be kind to her,
and she'll be off the streets."

Eight months later, Bidwell received a letter in green ink.

Dear Mr. Bidwell,

*I know I caused you trouble. My mind troubled. The
man at the window—was it not you? I would say it was
real, though I know you could not have been at such a
place. But did you not mean it for me? Sitting there with
your glasses, so kindly, why not? The world thinks Genghis
a monster, but you showed me how in bad times, he drank
his saliva and ate his gums, slept on his elbow and saved
his Börte. Did you not mean me to know I was to you what
Börte was to him? I cannot quite straiten it out. But remain*

VERY TRULY YOURS,
(MISS) FREDERICK CAMERON

4

Monday, January 15, 1968, three weeks to the day after
she'd called, Miss Cameron rang him at *Midland*. He was
having his weekly fight with Shiffrin, the editor. His junior
by ten years, a classic Chicago newsman out of the City
News Bureau and the *American*, Shiffrin had married meat
money and put some of it into the sinking *Midland*. Hard,

thin, a board of a man, Bidwell called him Giacometti. "A face like a cheese knife," he said to Ethel. "When it comes at you, you think it'll slice you in half. And his ideas are narrower than his face."

Shiffrin was on top of whatever was on top, but for him that meant what appeared in the newspapers of St. Louis, Milwaukee, Minneapolis, and Chicago, with dollops of *Time* and *Newsweek* for intellectual debauches. "You should be reading the tech and business mags," Bidwell told him the first week, but Shiffrin was unable to detach the text from the ads in *Aviation Week*, and besides, the mere sight of a technical word blanked him out of consciousness.

When Miss Cameron's call came, they were having a shouting match about a piece on the students. Bidwell had listed twenty different issues raised by the world's students, the lighting system at Prague Tech., the language question at Louvain and Calcutta, football at Grambling, political issues at Hamburg and Berkeley. To this he'd attached a tail of explanations from commentators, Aron, Howe, Feuer, McLuhan, and a handful of college presidents. A rapid, agitated surface, but it covered lots of ground and let the pancake-sodden readers of the supplement get an idea of the complexity of the matter.

To Shiffrin, it was Bidwell's usual academic glop which turned every second piece he touched "into the *Britannica*."

Of course, he was right, was always right. To most of their readers, Joey Bishop was Einstein, the amount of information that could be ladled out in any one story should not exceed a recipe for French toast. If Bidwell hadn't been there since the Year One, and if he didn't do good rewrite jobs, Shiffrin would have bounced him.

"Look, find some little spade chick on the Circle campus, let her yack away half a column, then get some yid prof to yack up the other half, a few pictures, and we got our story. Save this truckload of cobwebs for the *Atlantic Monthly*." Which is more or less the way it would work out, and another issue would be ready to wrap Monday's fish.

Bidwell took the call from the switchboard in mid-dispute. "Mr. Bidwell?"

The whirl in the office subsided, hung. "Oh, yes, Miss Cameron. How are you?"

"I'm fine. You said I could call you."

"That's right."

Shiffrin's black eyes bounced off his cruel nose and moved skyward. Then finger-snapping.

"I'm afraid it's not a good time, though. I'm in conference."

"Finish up," said Shiffrin. "Nail the nookie, and let's get shaking. It's sixteen to press," meaning sixteen hours till their press roll.

"Call in half an hour," said Bidwell and hung up. "If you had nookie like that, you'd turn monk."

Shiffrin's wife weighed in at a hundred and sixty pounds, all vocal, he ran through the secretarial staff with his agitated wand, overpromising, underperforming, he understood women trouble. "Professors like you working me to the grave, I'm ape now."

This last week, Bidwell had been writing up Ye-lü Ch'u-ts'ai's revelation to Chinghis that it would be better to regard towns as resources rather than pools of infection, a great moment of generous truth in the Mongol world and the never-ending education of the Khan. All right, he, Bidwell, would make the best of Shiffrin.

He arranged to meet Miss Cameron in Pixley and Ehler's.

Four years later, the Crerar was gone to I.I.T., but the buns and the bums were still there. And Miss Cameron too, about the same, the long face bent over two cups. No smile to meet his, but her look was relaxed, even intimate.

He shook hands, his bare, hers gloved. Their flesh had still not touched. Which Bidwell knew counted, though not how. "And," weeks later, "what could I have done?"

"Thank you for coming."

"You're looking well."

Which brought blush and smile. The body gets simpler

near the surface. Its economy there offers small variety to
register the terrific feelings beneath. Bidwell could but guess
the recrudescent girlishness of Miss Cameron's smile, not
coyness, no, only simple pleasure in the situation which
the inner time of derangement had kept from the years.
"You haven't changed," he said, meaning the standard
compliment.

"I hope I have." A remark in clock time, and its own
evidence. "It's why I wanted to see you. To show you I understand how wild I was."

Was this all?

He sat down to a cup of tea, continuation of the cup
he'd drunk four years before, but bought by her for whom
his taste was absolute.

Bidwell, fleshy head given jots of youth by the frost,
civil tonsure indulged at the sides and back in concession
to style and barber's prices, had now a vagueness of feeling,
seeing in this half-smiling, pale person not only an old
trouble but also a not-bad, if thin woman's body.

"Your trouble seems to be over."

"Mostly over."

"Still have bad times?"

"Now and then. I don't drink now."

"I didn't know you did that."

"Once a week, I'd really lush up. Now I sit tight."

Bidwell eased off his overcoat, stuck his scarf in his sleeve.
Like most Pixley customers, Miss Cameron kept on what
she'd come in with. Who knew when quick hands would
grab? He should have seen this as trouble.

"What can I do for you?"

"You are," said Miss Cameron. "Seeing you. That's all.
Just this. And to talk to you every once in a while."

The strange creep of human feeling. Unable to stay put.
Could he find pleasure on that thin chest? What would
pass between Pudgy and Miss Giacometti?

"I suppose that's all right, Miss Cameron. It's not a
hard way to help someone."

"You're a good person."

"Not really. It's habit. Laziness. Though, you know, I probably can't see you once a week. But we can certainly talk on the phone. Maybe on Thursdays. That's an easy day at the office. Then, every once in a while, we can meet here."

Which created her schedule, her life.

Every Thursday after he came back from lunch, Bidwell would answer the phone and talk with Miss Cameron about her health, her work—she did part-time secretarial work at Northwestern—and her reading—she was going through Will Durant, had been in *The Oriental Heritage* since the day after their first meeting. Once a month, they met in Pixley and Ehler's at five o'clock and drank tea for an hour.

The Thursday after their fourth and last meeting, the telephone did not ring. Bidwell waited uncomfortably, felt its silence, felt the absence of that dead—though somewhat revived—voice. Ah, well, she was out of town, sick, at a movie, or, true revival, she'd faced down her madness, seen through the old delusion.

The next day's *Sun-Times*, though, showed something else. At the time of her usual call, Miss Cameron was jumping out of the tenth-floor window of the Playboy Building on North Michigan Avenue. The first such occurrence there, clearly a dramatic one, for Miss Cameron had, as far as was known, no business in the building. Other than the melancholy one therein reported. She'd been seen by an elevator operator at lunchtime, "While most came down, she went up," and then, when the rest came up, she took the quick route down.

The famous owner of the building couldn't be reached for comment, but a spokesman said the girl was a mental patient, perhaps the building was chosen as a deranged protest or symbol, but, of course, there was nothing to be done about that. Most of the building's windows didn't even open; the woman had found a janitor's storeroom and even then had to climb up on a trash can and smash the window with the nozzle of a fire extinguisher.

A small thing, lightly killed.

   Bidwell was, of course, very upset, but the week passed,
he worked on Chinghis-Khan's eradication of the Tanguts
and did not think of Miss Cameron; except the next
Thursday, when the silence of the telephone stirred him,
and that night, when the garage door shut behind his
Pontiac and he was alone the usual few seconds in the
dark.

   What a death the poor narrow thing had constructed for
herself. No campaign, no successor, no trip to the cool
mountains, only an elevator ride, a smashed window, an
untelephoned farewell: "This is it. I can't ask you anymore.
Let alone by phone."

AN URBAN IDYLL

O happy hearse
—Spenser, *"November Eclogue"*

IDYLLS OF
DUGAN AND STRUNK

1

On a hunch, Strunk took the check over to Dugan in the hospital. "Is this your baby?"

Dugan's head is mummified, chin to scalp; the cola-colored eyes peer over damaged cheeks. "Lire. The rat." He passes the check to Prudence, sitting in the armchair.

She reads. "Six-point-seven billion. Who's this princely Corradi?"

"A Beinfresser holding company. What is it, a million?" Strunk says he makes it a million-two. "No lagniappe."

"Not from your aunt," growls Dugan.

Beinfresser was his discovery, he'd been after him over a year, and though he'd worked harder and come up goose eggs, he'd never wanted to open a prospect more than this one. Ten days ago Strunk's girl had shown him how. Well, this was only first blood. The Beinfresser Library. The Beinfresser Student Village. But lire. "If computers fell in love, I'd call it an accident."

"Maybe that's the way the Holy Ghost dishes it out." The check was drawn on the Banco di Santo Spirito.

Early spring light off the Midway. April 12. Roosevelt's Death Day in Dugan's calendar. Lucky it wasn't his own. *University Aide, Ex-White House Assistant, Casualty of King Riots.* He was stupid, but maybe now, after a terrible year, he was getting lucky. He had Beinfresser's first in-

stallment, he had Prudence—who could also be charged up
to Beinfresser—and he was going to walk out of here more
or less as he was a week ago.

But was Beinfresser pulling something? Lire didn't leave
Italy. Maybe he was just thrashing around—angry that
Dugan cornered him—twisting an arm to make a nickel,
making the University pay for conversion of his spare
lire.

The glooms and twists of fund-raising. Strunk had laid
it out for him the first day, three years ago. "Philanthropy's
a Circe. Makes brutes."

Dugan had spent four years shepherding fifty midwestern
congressmen through three hundred billion dollars of ap-
propriation; he did not take to the chickenfeed of university donors. "They don't have to give."

Younger, gloomier, kinder, an endless generalizer, Strunk
said, "They smell our interest in their death. Makes 'em
mulish. It's not like plucking taxes from Topeka. You're
head-to-head with these dollars."

Which was so.

Donors were coaxed over soufflés, in swimming pools.
One studied their habits, wishes, connections. One knew
one's rivals, strayed sons, forgotten cousins, Boy Scouts,
Heart Fund, Ba'hai. One learned the seasons of donation:
seeding, watering, bloom, the stems of resistance turning
brittle, dropping into the basket. Even then it wasn't over.
In three years Dugan had already been ambushed by de-
vious wills, consumptive litigation.

Meanwhile, despite his pride at taking no guff, he ran
errands, commiserated sniffles, confiscatory taxes, the
moneyed nature of things itself.

His first year, he'd gone once a month to the Cliffhanger's
Club for cheese soufflé, apple pie, and the discourse of
Lynch, the bond man.

Out of the Georgia scratch country into the Chicago
grain market, then, after the First World War, sensing the
shift in Chicago big money from goods to paper, Lynch
started the first great bond house west of Manhattan. A

bachelor without apparent ties, a fund-raiser's dream, he
was worth at least seventy million. Gray, froggy, his vague
eyes hung from a large, warty head; a real beaut. Subtle,
cold, autodidact and pedant, he was mad for discourse and
learning. Yet never bought a book. University fund-raisers
borrowed requested titles from the University library and
read them, preparing for the lunches.

In Dugan's time, Lynch was wound up in violence.
Carlyle, Sorel, Lenin, Sartre, Fanon, the *Iliad*, and the
Old Testament piled by gold spores of soufflé to be grabbed,
leafed through, quoted in refutation. "Got you, Dugan."

Dugan lost himself in dispute and took no guff. A New
York street battler, a wounded Korean vet, he had authority
in the old bond man's eyes. "Not that your rutting dog
fights changed the world that counts."

What counted was dedicated violence, the violence of
purification, a strike, Watts, Algeria. "I bring not peace."
Lynch was wild about Stokely Carmichael, "a new Lenin,"
and was driven up to the University to hear him. His
Negro chauffeur, Henry, sat beside him "so you can hear
what a great black man sounds like." But Stokely's cold
rage roused old cracker blood, Lynch wrote out a question
and told Henry to ask it: "Spose, suh, that rev-ole-oosh-n-
erries is moh crupt den ex-ploiders?" Bird's-head jeweled
with sweat, Carmichael ran sad eyes up and down the
little chauffeur. "You're wearing our master's livery, and you
ask me such a question. Who wrote that out for you
brother?"

"Answer the question," croaked Lynch. He meant Carmichael, but Henry pointed to his right and said, "He did."

The *Tribune* photographer took a picture, the only time
Lynch's face appeared in a Chicago newspaper. This "out-
rageous impropriety" was his excuse when Dugan popped
the long-suspended bubble of his philanthropic intentions.
"You see what happens when I stick out my neck. I get
smeared all over the newspapers. Can't afford that kind
of thing. I'm the diocesan financial adviser. Imagine what
the Cardinal thinks. You'll have to wait."

Dugan's complexion was curd white, the pallor of repressed fury. The old man, scared, blinked, then covered, asking if they could try Carlyle's *Frederick the Great* next time. "Hitler's favorite book. Goebbels read it to him in the bunker."

"We'd better cool it awhile, Mr. L." Dugan would eat no more soufflés.

A step, which, back at the University, he double-checked with his boss, Erwin Seligman, the Provost. "Absolutely. Tell him to shove it." Intense, elegant, baldly handsome, a tongue-holder and aristocrat. "I'd rather go under than dangle from that fourflusher's whims."

Said Strunk, "It's the beast of flirtatiousness. They dangle their dough under your nose like Elizabeth dangled her stuff for the ambassadors. The whole universe is a come-on. Djever see a two-month-old kid tug a blanket over his eyes?" The bachelor talking to the father, the ex-father. "My God, even flowers do it. Folding with the sun. And rocks. Those winking crystals. The Principle of Uncertainty. Sheer flirtation."

They worked facing each other, their desks by the trilobed, iron-ribbed Gothic window, one of hundreds in the educational Carcassonne along the Midway. "Americans live in an historical rummage sale." Strunk's blue-shirted, gorilla arm waved at the useless crenellations, culverts, contreforts. "Midway Gothic. And jungle," the arm over the slum-miles under the University's architectural eyebrow. "Mies glass, Saarinen concrete, Pevsner topology. And behind, the American behind. With our rejecta. And here," the great arm over their slanting nook, "our little museum."

Sure enough. Back of Strunk's head was Dugan's two-dollar Pissarro print, woods, sky, fishermen, tow path, a pond doubling and confusing the rest. Behind his head, *Playboy*'s Miss March, "lasagna-loving, sitar-strumming Lisa Joy Sackerman, M.A. in Slav. Lit." Tacked beside Miss Sackerman's pale watermelons was Strunk's own graphic, a swollen-winged moth, *The Thoracic Viscera*, the wings, lungs, the central clutter, the muscular baggage of the heart, the screw-ribbed pole on top, the trachea, the crewel-stitched pole beneath, the descending aorta.

On their Indiana maple desks, amidst bank reports, Olivetti and Dutch Royale typewriters, Florentine blotters, Swedish letter openers, were Dugan's souvenirs, the quartz chip from a Mayan palace, pink limestone from the tower where Roland had supposedly blown out his warning and his brains, a conglomerate sliver from Injon which, with a quarter-inch of Pekinese steel, had been removed from Dugan's left elbow in 1951.

"Fossils, sediment, souvenirs, imports, hand-me-downs. Historical junkshop. And what am I doing now? Setting up a transatlantic telecast on genes with Crick, Perutz, Watson, and Burkle. Those little human museums." He meant the genes.

Dugan was on Strunk's wavelength, liked him immensely, and though he seldom saw him outside the working day, knew he was the one he'd call in a pinch, had, in fact, after his son's death and his wife's breakdown.

They sat across from each other day after day, never quarreled, seldom felt disparity, though Dugan was fifteen years older, a hard-noser, athlete, fighter, a little man, and Strunk was huge, soft, a pacifist and do-gooder, a fantasist who wanted to alter the world and make himself heard doing it.

Strunk's reveries were violent, formed out of Eric Ambler and James Bond. He daydreamed himself in Park Lane tweeds carrying lethal pencils through chancellory gates, kidnapping presidential grandchildren to force changes in policy (infantile fingers mailed, one a day, with menacing but high-minded notes), organizing guerrilla wars on Burmese borders, convening world revolutionaries, himself and the late Guevara the only white men. Then, tanned and hardened, converting twelve-year-old Thai maidens into sexual H-bombs, riding herd on the aligned golden backsides of Santa Monica, sipping at the True Beloved's clitoral brim.

In daylight, Strunk outlined salvationary schemes, discerned threats to civic harmony, leaky valves, closed doors,

defects in thought and state which he called to the attention
of congressman, policy-maker, theoretician, and physician
in newspapers, magazines, letters. A new, unknown Voltaire, demi-poet, demi-artist, urban dreamer, reader, raised
in Manhattan, educated in Chicago, a bachelor who'd not
been east of Long Island or west of Oak Park, M.A. in Eng.
Lit., University functionary and one-course-a-year lecturer
in the English Department.

Whereas Dugan, born in La Guardia's New York fifteen
years earlier and two miles southwest of Strunk's birth-
house on West Eighty-Second Street, fighter, traveler, ex-
father, ex-husband, daydreamed pastorals. His life as violent as a legal, urban, burgher life could be, Dugan had no
utopian thoughts. The University was the closest waking life
he'd come to his reveries, and he believed this even after his
fourteen-year-old son was stabbed to death on a Hyde Park
street.

Dugan celebrated his fortieth birthday in October, 1967,
"the two-hundred-eighth anniversary of Georges Jacques
Danton, French revolutionary figure's birth," said the All-
News Station WNUS. WNUS remembered Danton, no
one remembered Dugan. Burkle, the Development Office's
hope for the next Nobel, told him that after thirty-five, fifty
thousand brain cells a year were irreplaceably destroyed.
"Not a large fraction of ten billion," but, at forty, Dugan
figured a quarter of a million lost cells no joke.

He'd birthday-treated himself to a color television set.
Feet up on the old black-and-white one, drinking his
nightly bottle of dollar German wine, he watched the shift-
ing Renoirs of the Cronkite News. A scientist found that
plants registered human antipathy. Hooked to a polygraph,
they sweated anxiety when threatened. What next? Rocks?
Matter itself? Unneutral neutrons, shocked electrons? The
whole universe a sensorium?

So why not gloom for Dugan? Fifty trillion cells fired into
feeling by ten billion (minus a quarter-million) neutral
triggers. "Enough neural combinations," said Burkle, "to
register everything in the universe." Let alone Dugan's

troubles: the war, the gripping stink of sulfurous air through the window, the cells dying in his four-decade-old head, his stubborn prospects, the birthday without his son, his wife cracked-up in Oswego.

2

What other woman would unerringly find the wrong manhole, and falling, fallen, be saved, and how but by "dese tings." Her "bosoms." There in the middle of Clyde and Diversey, he, Strunk, and the Burkles walking to the restaurant, and no Lena, or only her head, which was screaming, "Omigawd." A black-matted cauliflower yelling in the manhole. Unlikely. (As it had been from the first day in the Amsterdam Avenue Library. "Scuse me, mister, could I take a look at that book you got there? I never in my life seen such a big book.") Hauled out of the manhole, groaning, she ate her way through clams, ribs, and shortcake, now and then hefting her bruised beauties, "Omigawd." Scene Ten Million of Lena's Theater.

Pain or pleasure, it never ended: chasing rock-throwers off the fence, "Don't gimme that racial shit, boy, you're a rat, black or green. Toss another of them rocks and you get it right inna mouth"; piling the Appalachians' mattresses into the Rambler ("Miz Dugan, you one fiuhn person"), shouting at the Sub-Committee Hearing, "He's a goddamn liar, Senator. Don't tell me, Smalley. I moved you in them five rooms myself, what you givin' these senators that shit for?" With Javits saying, "Now, look here, let's keep it calm, please, Miss." "Miss! There's ninety pounds of son out of this Miss, Senator. This man is lying. I moved him in myself. He is just milking you guys. Right, Smalley?" "Hell, Miz Dugan, ahm jis tryin' to git these senators tuh see the kiuhnd of thing, ya know," and Kennedy said, "O.K., Van, take down what this woman has to say."

Those first weeks in New York, she was the country mouse, no question, up from Simsbury, Ohio, nine hundred people, five Italian families who got together every month to sing opera, the kids taking parts, the factory money going into the pizzas and red wine from her father's *'storante*, people driving over the bridge from West Virginia or even the mystical sixty miles over the hills from Pittsburgh. (When someone had to go up there for X-rays, the families would see him off as if to the moon, he'd return with stories of the terrible roads, the turns, the black fog.)

It was from Pittsburgh their troubles came, Domenico Buccafazzi with the gold watch to be raffled for the Poor Widow with Seven Children Whose Husband Drowned in the Oak Grove Brook, and next month Papa asked him, "Who won the watch?" and it was someone over in Branchtown, and a month later, it was another watch, and this time it was won by a Mrs. DiBaccio, a Crippled Lady in Oak Grove, and Papa said, "I don' believe," and drove the pickup over the hills, and there was no Mrs. DiBaccio in Oak Grove. And one day Luccio, the fruit man, came in the house and told the kids to get under the beds, and said to Mama, "Don't go downstairs, whatever." In the street was a black Imperial with curtains down on the windows, and they all knew only They could own such a car, and Papa went into it, and was gone three days, they thought he was never coming back, and Mama said to Luccio, "I'm going to the FBI, I'm an American," but Papa came back that night; though not the same inside.

At night, the old people sat in the room with red wine, she would close her eyes on the couch and would hear how the little Oak Grove vegetable man, Cucciadifreddi, who'd Brought Over his sister's son and taken him into the store, had been forced by Them to Show the Sign and shot the boy himself and threw him into the river. She had gone to the funeral with Mama, and when people wondered how such a good swimmer could have drowned, she had said, "But, Mama, he was shot," and Mama had stuffed the rosary beads in her mouth and said, "Where you hear

that? Who tell you that? Milena, please don't say tings like
that."

In Tampa, staying with Cousin Franco, who ran a club
on the Gulf, she'd gone to a party, there were racks of fur
coats, and the ladies' heads jerked toward them every other
minute (as they had been gotten, so could they be got),
and Franco came not with Cousin Mary, but with a pile of
hair-mink-and-diamonds, Margarita, who invited Milena for
a sail on her boat, till Cousin Franco said, "She don' visit."
She had helped out at the tables, serving whatever it was
that passed for Cutty Sark or Johnnie Walker, when the
ladies started grabbing their coats, and there by the dance-
floor palms, like a George Raft movie, stood the iron-eyed
men with guns out, cursing.

Her brother Louie whizzed through law school and the
bar exam. Every week, he'd be taken to New York or
Chicago, and lapped it up, thinking what a card he must be.
He hadn't finished the exams a month when a man whose
picture she later saw at the Kefauver hearings showed him a
list which said, "Louis Masiotti, Judge of the Circuit
Court," and Papa said, "We're moving," and they'd gone
north, but one day the man showed up and asked Papa,
"What happened to that son of yours? I showed him the
list. Is he crazy?" And Papa said, "You know kids, he went
on the bum. He is a restless kid."

Lena's cousins from Oak Park invited them to a party,
Milena and the Irish husband who'd worked for President
Kennedy. They were jeweled and furred and talked about
their children. One of the cousins had blue streaks on her
face. Two weeks before, her husband had been gunned to
death in his bed, the blue marks were powder burns, and
she was drinking with the wife of the man who'd made
them.

Dugan told Strunk, who said, "Sure, but they're getting
these guys now. Giancana has to live in Mexico, Genovese
is in the can. With this immunity thing, they can't take
the Fifth. Anyway, television is killing it. The kids don't

care about the furs and nightclubs and fixing horse races.
Watch. In fifteen years, there'll be no Mafia," but when
they found Mikey bled to death in the street, though it
was the Apostles that stabbed him, no question of that,
Strunk believed it was the Mafia and wanted to have all
of Lena's relatives hauled in till one of them broke down
and confessed.

But by then, she'd started to break; one look at her face
zipped Strunk's mouth, and he took care of the coffin, the
service, the grave, the newspapermen, got Lena into the
hospital, and sat with Dugan till he could manage by himself.

Though, thought Dugan, in a way Strunk was right, the
Mafia was guilty, for wasn't it that crazy theater in her
blood that not only made her heroic but made her force
Mikey into the squad car and ride up and down the
streets fingering the boys who'd forced the white boys to
climb the ropes in gym and push them off? And wasn't it
in Mafia towns, Tampa, Newark, Buffalo, Youngstown,
Chicago, that government rotted and ghettos burned?

But Dugan's misery had fogged his mind. What did the
cause of it matter? The kid was dead, one of the best ever,
the only thing he'd come close to being lost in with love.

And the second thing, Lena, was as good as dead.

In the cold-temperature lab, Dugan had watched a professor dip chrysanthemums into super-chilled nitrogen. Out
they came, apparently the same, but crystalline. So Lena
went through the funeral, apparently unaltered, only slightly
abstracted, but within, the motion was gone. Strunk took
her to Billings, and from there she went to Oswego.

3

Dugan discovered Beinfresser in the Periodical Room. Once
a month he speed-read through thirty or forty periodicals
in four or five languages. The gift of tongues, found out on
Ninth Avenue among Puerto Ricans and Poles, developed

in Brooklyn College, Korea, Washington. In *Der Spiegel's* series on "The New Breed of Tycoons," he learned Beinfresser had not only gone to the University, but regarded himself as a "true offshoot [*ein echter Sprössling*] of Chancellor Tatum's reforms." It was during the Depression ("a moneymaker's good times are other people's bad times"), he'd cornered the dormitory coal and laundry concessions, made twelve thousand Depression dollars a year, and won a special farewell from Chancellor Tatum at the graduation ceremony: "You're the model of the student this University exists to eliminate."

In 1946, out of the OSS, he showed up in civilian clothes in Frankfurt/Main with enough of a stake to pick up the war's usable junk: tires, rifles, messkits, soap, iodine, antibiotics, boots, condoms, airplanes. He had a work force made up of DPs, deserters, cripples, quislings, Staatlosen, Krupp foremen, Undenazifiables. They peddled his goods door-to-door, unfroze the assets in widow's mattresses, socks of gold sovereigns, wedding silver, unworked pig farms. Twenty years later, "this great coiner" ["*dieser grosse Münzer*"] was "the Dedalus, Ariadne, Theseus, and Minotaur of the largest corporate labyrinth in Europe." *Der Spiegel* listed "a small fraction" of the companies, "Uganda Ores, Buttenwieser Computations, Banque Nationale de Ruande, Walsh Construction Toys, Fahnweiler, Peyton Shoes, Tucson Metals, Weymouth Investment and Mutual Fund, Corradi, Sempler, Cie., Montevideo Freight and Shipping, Foulke-Arabo Petroleum Products, Meysterdam, Wrench Ltd., the Hamburg *Presse-Zeitung*, the Nord-Suabische Rundfunk, and *Peep, A Weekly*."

With the help of Alfred Somerstadt and Jean Docker of the Business School, Dugan followed the Beinfresser trail. Section 60-735A of the 1959 Internal Revenue Code was called by the author of *The Great Treasury Raid*, "the Beinfresser Provision," tailored by Beinfresser lawyers to his mutual-fund operations and inserted in the bill by Representative Templeton (R.-Ariz.) "without opposition." Mrs. Docker had done a dissertation on mutual-fund ma-

nipulations, but Beinfresser's were beyond her grasp. "He's
just another social tapeworm."

   Somerstadt was more useful. A jolly, little fellow, tycoons
enchanted him. He'd written a three-volume work on Diesel,
Heinkel, and Bosch; these were the true forces of German
history. "Hitler," said Alfred. "What is that *Schwein* but
an economic splinter." Beinfresser was something else.
Each day Alfred discovered some other refinement in the
corporate geometry. "This fellow's an artist. Not a Bosch—
he's no scientist—but money. Money he understands."

   "Does he have money to give?"

   Alfred's generous lip puffed out that absurd irrelevance.
"What's that going to do him? He wouldn't give a quarter
to a daughter."

   "He's got a daughter?"

   "Of course not. Can you see him putting *Geld* into baby
shoes? This man is pure. An economic saint."

   Dugan had enough of the celebrant's mass. He needed a
lead-in, but didn't spot one till Tatum showed up in
Chicago for a speech to Midwest Philologists.

4

The ex-chancellor was a man who relished distant views
and noises—droning, humming—the genuflection of furniture, all heights, pulpits, platforms, theater boxes. He
was built to be looked up to. Tall, muscular, his face loomed
with northern contrasts, salt-white hair combed into waves,
blue eyes deep in deep sockets, cheeks red at the bone
points, and creviced with years of public sufferance of fools.
His voice was rough, scraped, his hands thick-veined, a
farmer's except for the nails, small reflectors which, as he
talked, mooned around for emphasis.

   Dugan, a sniffer of snow jobs, had to fight off a giant one.
Tatum, like a great clown, made himself life's butt. He told
Dugan how FDR had seen through him. "Ickes and I were
after the Vice-Presidency. Roosevelt handled us like counter-

feit fives." He went back to Chicago, defeat in his face. Failure was infectious. Soon he couldn't handle trustees, other university presidents, the faculty. "Those opera tenors did me in."

The eyes stayed on Dugan's, a weight of assessment. For *Harper's*, he'd written, "Kennedy's death scattered a flock of loyalists over the country, rough Irish trade that cleared the trail of his political flop and called it gold dust."

"Good fighters only remember their losses, Mr. Tatum. That's the way with you. And probably that billionaire graduate of ours, Beinfresser. He's always talking about you."

"Oh? What's he say?" Tatum never objected to hearing himself quoted. Though he had a fine clipping service and had seen the piece in *Der Spiegel*.

"He mentions what you said about the University existing to eliminate types like him. Yet, you know, he thinks of himself as your disciple. You're probably one of the few living people he's showing off for."

"Absurd. Except for an annual Christmas card, atheist Jew to atheist Baptist, I don't hear from him. Just an annual touch of spiritualist Esperanto."

"Maybe," said Dugan, sticking in, "but types like him are after some kind of championship. What they need is someone to crown 'em. Like Napoleon needed the Pope. I think it's why he sends you Christmas cards, makes references to you. I'm convinced all he needs to know is you're still behind the University. One letter from you, and I'd bet in a year or less there'd be money for a building. Named after you. The Tatum Cryogenics Laboratory."

Said Tatum, "I thought whatever the University was like now, it had good technicians. As usual, I'm wrong. The technicians are just romantic poets. Mr. Dugan, this man wouldn't notice if my corpse were left in his bathtub. As for the University, it wouldn't name a baboon's toilet after me. I enjoy a bit of Celtic twilight, Dugan, but at eleven o'clock in the morning, even my eyes are usually on the objects in front of them."

"You know your powers better than anyone, Mr. T."

Something went on in Tatum's face, a small anxiety. "Power is something men understand very differently. I've been around too many sorts to reconcile them."

"Some sorts are unquestionable, aren't they? Something comes off, or it doesn't. In public life or private. I was around Washington for two Cuban crises. I know the difference between bringing something off and not bringing it off. You can tell the difference in people's walks, the way they eat, when they joke, how they go to bed."

"Public failure intensifies private relationships, Mr. Dugan."

"Not mine, Mr. T. I can't operate anywhere with failure in my system."

"I think you'll come to feel differently. Even about the relative failures of your Mr. Kennedy. I think he was a fairly strong man after the Bay of Pigs. The admission of stupidity is strength. As for that Missile-so-called-Crisis, that was a sporting event, whipped up for personal redemption. Those silver calendars, JFK to RSM or whatever, they were boys' trophies. Banana-state dramatizing. Look at the Sorensen book, with all its theater talk, 'roles,' 'postures,' 'antagonists.' Crisis was just drama for your sportive ex-bosses. They'd burn up the world for a good show.

"I say the hell with all these strutters. Everyone quotes Acton's maxim, but how many believe it? I do. Stay in power long, and the concrete turns to smoke. You can't handle it. You can't tolerate opposition. And you exhaust your own aides. Look at the married life of a powerful man's subordinates. They're emasculated by him. He sets the schedules, tells them when they can go home to their wives. And if he wants, the wives will sleep with him. In their dreams, half of them do.

"I'm not speaking out of inexperience, Mr. Dugan. I stayed much too long at the University and nearly ruined it. And I was one of the few in America who knew what it was all about, knew, for better or worse—and you know it's worse—it was going to be the center of action.

"The best-intentioned become posers and tyrants. You
don't want a letter from me, Dugan. You know the rich.
You don't pat them at a distance. They want the dogs to
come to their hand for the bone. I've got enough trouble
finding a little meat for myself."

"That old queen," Dugan told Strunk back at the office.
"One lousy letter. I should have beaten it out of him."

5

Leonard Strunk had bad luck with girls. This after an
adolescence that, as that tunnel of horrors went, was a
tunnel of love. From fifteen to eighteen, Strunk was almost
continuously in love, and although he did not "lose his
cherry"—as the touching expression of those years went—
till his junior year at college, the body-hugging, tongue-kiss-
ing, and digital probation of a good lot of pretty New York
and Chicago girls fed masturbatory pleasure, sometimes,
blissfully, on the unclothed belly of whomever he'd brought
up to his room to tune in on Amorous Brahms. Now, in his
late twenties, masturbation remained Strunk's chief sexual
relief.

As a good part of Strunk's life was determined by what
he read, any shame about masturbation was allayed by
select readings in twentieth-century novelists. When a
Norman Mailer condemned it, Strunk sulked. "Why," he
complained to Dugan, "the writer who strokes himself
more publicly than any writer since Whitman should have
this terrible bug about the most economical of pleasures,
this old economist knoweth not."

Dugan disliked such subjects, had to force hearty interest.
"When a man's work is done to corral nookie, and Mailer
must get plenty, he's naturally going to crow over poor
lugs like you beating their lonely meat to Judy Collins. If
he ate shit, he'd be knocking hamburgers."

"It's more complicated than that. The guy hates solipsism. That's masturbation. It's why he had to give up fiction,

how he saved himself from the loony bin by reportage. See that piece on the Pentagon in *Harper's*. Mailer's our Henry Adams. Explaining America's sewers and cathedrals for the East Hampton feebles."

Masturbation wasn't Strunk's unique source of sexual joy. There was also Mrs. Babette Preester, a thick, sometimes ardent divorcée, secretary to the Committee on New Nations, who shared herself with Strunk three or four times a month after a suitable dinner and what she called "downtown entertainment." (Shows, movies, concerts, good or bad, as long as they got her into the Loop.)

In addition, a student sometimes brought her problems to him in such a way that his fear of endangering a small hold on the English Department was overcome, and, at least for the duration of the term, he enjoyed more or less steady sexual joy. There were occasional windfalls elsewhere: a hat-check girl at the Astor Towers had, to his delighted surprise, winked at him over Babette's low forehead, he'd made an engagement with her when retrieving his coat, and she'd come to his place on Dorchester a few times, though it was clearer than it was with Babette that she and Leonard shared nothing but each other's parts, clearer that long-term interests could not be realized or envisaged in Leonard's bare-floored, scarcely furnished, book-and-paper-laden bedroom-kitchenette.

Much of Strunk's spare time was spent concocting schemes, plans, suggestions, and criticisms, which were written up in letter form and sent to people of appropriate authority and influence. More and more, the correspondence absorbed his spare time and channeled his large energies. Sometimes, though, he thought his letters might be the static of a mind that was otherwise not getting through. Weren't letters a substitute for real writing? Toil without test? Yet how else be effective? It was better than writing on toilet walls. Though, God knows, more expensive.

Strunk bought stamps by the hundred sheet, and when postal rates were upped he suffered an economic crisis. In addition, he used fine stationery, Pott-sized, creamy rag paper

with his signature, O. Leonard Strunk, engraved in six-
point golden Mauritius off left center, his home address,
in smaller script, off right.

He wasn't vain about his correspondence, nor did he
consider it in capital letters as a life's work of commentary
and reportage in the manner of Walpole and Grimm.
Strunk thought of himself as a small conduit of serious
ideas and humane complaints, a Voltaire without genius.
Unlike Voltaire, he wrote no intimate letters, no mere expressions of wit, gallantry, or poetic gloom. He wrote to
aldermen about potholes in the street, to the Bundy and
Rostow brothers about Southeast Asia, to thinkers and
scholars about their discoveries and specialties, and, after
Christmas, wrote to the foreign artists who'd painted the
finest UNESCO cards. He exchanged letters in French
with Papa Ibrahim Tall about the problems of African
carpet-makers, in German with Willie Fenstermacher, the
concretist poet of Lech-am-Arlberg, and in English with
Vuk Murkovich, the poet, about the bards of Montenegro.

In addition to corresponding with Private Persons, as
his account book labeled them, Strunk wrote to newspapers
and magazines over the world. His account book was covered
with red dirks for Unacknowledged and blue skulls for
Unprinted letters, but it was a bad year that saw fewer than
a hundred in American newspapers alone. The Chicago
Sun-Times, the Des Moines *Register*, and the Santa Barbara
News-Press regarded Strunk as a Steady, and their Letters
column was instructed to use one Strunk a month.

In the spring of 1966 Strunk began writing to someone
who became his single most important correspondent. Miss
Elizabeth Schultz had been a student in his "Lyric from
Wyatt to Berryman," and was now a researcher for *Newsweek*. She had begun the correspondence by writing Strunk
what she said she'd meant to tell him after the course, that
it was one of the finest she'd taken at the University. Strunk
had replied in grateful acknowledgment, but, as his epistolary impluse was not so easily slaked, he wrote a longish
response. What would interest her? He couldn't remember

Miss Schultz by looks or intellect (though his record book
showed he'd graded her A). He settled on a disquisition
about the functions of news magazines, the perils of their
simultaneous obligation to entertainment and comprehensive authority. To his pleased surprise, Miss Schultz wrote
back an account of the transformation of her research (she
worked in the Business Section) by the editorial and writing
staffs, and related this to those fashions and conventions in
lyric which were, "as you showed us in class," the key to
many of the finest poems in the language. So delighted was
Strunk that he wrote back an account of structural trans-
formations in neurosis, kinship, language, and religion as
he had intertwined them from pages of Lévi-Strauss, R.
Barthes, J. Lacan, and N. Chomsky. Miss Schultz replied,
after a week "spent on the texts," and her answer generated
a full-scale epistle on the relationship of PERT ("Program
Evaluation Review Techniques") to such other "self-gener-
ating systems as musical scales." Miss Schultz slid by this
epistolary iceberg, waited ten days, and discussed the attempts by Wright and Breuer to overcome the "tyranny of
New York property rectangles, perhaps another system of
self-generation." Her gentle caution evoked in Strunk a
tender flow of ideas which, in a few days, found epistolary
form in a discussion of the relationship of basic forms to
basic concepts. ("Is not the triangle inevitability, the pentagon authority?")

In short, Miss Schultz became Strunk's Interdisciplinary
Recipient, his steadiest pen pal. In a year and a half, they
exchanged more than fifty letters.

Strunk began to wonder more and more about her. One
August day he decided he would take his pre-fall-quarter
vacation in New York, but the afternoon mail brought him
Elizabeth's reflections on Mini-Art and the Warhol Strategy,
with a postscript which said that she was about to spend
two weeks with her parents on their farm south of Little
Rock. It was the first personal note since Letter One. His
Interdisciplinary Recipient was a farmer's daughter. She,
a daughter, could have a daughter. Not now—she was a

Miss and no East Village hippie-mama—but the potency
was more than likely there.

That evening Strunk reread the letter and felt the grip
of loneliness. What to do? He telephoned Mrs. Preester,
but was told by a baby-sitter she wasn't expected till late.

He put on his summer suit, a pale gabardine he'd bought
five years ago in Field's basement, and went over to the
Oxford Lounge, from which, three or four times, he'd extracted a girl for a horizontal hour in his apartment. Tonight, however, the Kansas City Athletics were at the hotel
across the street, and there were no spare girls.

Strunk walked to Fifty-Fifth Street, east to Jackson Park,
and through the underpass to the lake. Out on the Promon-
tory, black girls in bikinis stomped and curled to the
isolating music of flutes and bongo drums. Coals under
hibachis, beer bottles and cans shivered with fire and moonlight. From the vaporous green lake rose Elizabeth Schultz,
long and softly ropy. Each nude tendon, each sweet transit
from curve to curve, sped him to her. "Open, open," begged
Strunk.

The next day, he wrote to Arkansas.

Dear Elizabeth,

The study of autism (Mahler, Fuère, Bettelheim) reveals
the connection between excrement and the sense of self. The
autistic child identifies with her excrement; a throwaway,
she becomes excremental to save the last vestige of her self.

Elizabeth, I must interrupt the train of thought. It is
warm here. Mercilessly. Perhaps it is time to bring up (not
as ejecta, let alone excreta) a matter long on my mind. I
have been in hopes that you and I might be able to enrich
our epistolary mutuality. It would, I mean, be a great
pleasure for me to see you. To spend some time talking with
you.

I had thought of going to New York now, but you are
not there. Before the beginning of the autumn quarter
here—that is on Oct. 1—I have several free days. Would
you perhaps consider reserving a room for me at a hotel not

far from your apartment? Yours is no longer a neighborhood
I know well. In my boyhood, it was one to be shunned in
fear or approached in trembling. At any rate, perhaps you
will think of this proposal and decide what is best. I sign
off, then,

> In cordial hope, in hopeful
> expectancy, but, in any case,
> immer dein,

Leonard S.

Post scriptum: Please forgive rude brevity. Much to tell you
anon re. cultures which prize excreta (Shakes's father;
post-Mongol Near East—cf. treatise of Ibn-al-Wahdwa);
sewage, drainage-ex-aquaria (Med. Lat. sewaria, sluice of
millponds), thoughts of Rome and Knossos, the Austro-
Germany of outcast (excretum) Freud, Protestantism
(cf. N. Brown on Swift, Luther), money as dreck in 11th-
century Europe. But, dear Elizabeth, all this can perhaps
save till we come together, hopefully, dare I say, in new
phase of our relat.   Y,

L.

6

The Thursday before his flight to New York, Strunk was
too skittery to write any letters at all, couldn't read, couldn't
do more than pack and repack, deciding which two of four
suits he should take, and which of the two pack, which
wear. Strunk shopped with the finesse of tornadoes, in with
a head-low rip, hand riffling Forty-Two Longs (though his
arboreal trunk and arms needed Extra Long), then choice,
change, fit, and out. He had one tailor-made suit. In July,
1967, a Lebanese tailor from the Loop, in deep water after
the Arab-Israeli war, took his stuff up to the Windermere
Hotel and offered bargains to Hyde Parkers. Strunk dis-
gorged a rare hundred and fifty dollars and emerged with a

"Mediterranean blue-green double-vent glen plaid" that made him look like an Aegean Island. Said Mr. Dalah toward the Strunk-filled ballroom mirror, "Downtown you wouldn't walk out of here for under three-fifty."

The plaid was cut too squarely for Strunk's hulking shoulders, and Mr. Dalah had surrendered too soon to his extensive rear, but the suit was still Strunk's best, and thus hung over the closet door for Elizabeth's first sight of him.

That morning he took twenty minutes passing the electric razor over his face, inspecting and practicing expressions, trying for leanness in his generous cheeks, for depth in his puddle-colored eyes, length in his too apish jaw.

No beauty, Strunk, but after all, Elizabeth knew what he looked like, he had not put on more than ten pounds in the years since she'd been in his class, there were still elements of good looks that could be assembled by good will. And her letters bore no sign that Manhattan had raised her standards of masculine beauty beyond Strunkish reach; he might pass, especially in these days when even monsters were thought beautiful.

He ran in place, shoulders back, stomach in, great legs high. The razor cord twisted around the faucet, the razor pulled out of his pumping arm and crashed on the sink. The white plastic cracked, the buzz castrated into whine. Twenty-six dollars.

"Vanity," he told Dugan later. "There I was metamorphosing into Gregory Peck, and Matter Itself rose up against me. I ought to tear this up." His ticket.

Dugan said any woman who passed up a hunk of male glory like O. L. Strunk would be too thick to penetrate with human weapons. He drove him to O'Hare for a final buck-up. "I expect to see you back totally unhumped. An April carpet."

"Poor thing's probably in a wheel chair."

New York.

When he was a boy, Third Avenue was bums, pawnshops, bars. Lexington was the limit of the habitable world. You crossed to Third with fear. Now it was a gold-flecked pleasure tent converging downtown in fifty-story glitter. Here, at Elizabeth's corner, were restaurants, antique shops, tailors, cigar stores, butchers, a mailbox. The box which held Elizabeth's letters. No hand behind any light but one could write those letters.

She lived two doors east of Third above a frame shop, closed but lit. Ten names on the mail slots, girls from Teaneck, Hartford, Greensboro, and Mason City who came down the old steps for buses and taxis to ad agencies, dental offices, brokerages, Newsweek. Strunk pressed E. Schultz, 3C.

Telling Dugan as much as he wanted to a week later, Strunk confessed that the first look was a shocker. Here was this girl of questing intellect, of voice liquid with kindness, and, at the doorway, greeting her admired instructor, her mind's correspondent, her future lover, there was . . . Slob. Sheer Slob. And not even the Slob of Inattention— mind elsewhere on difficult matter, Thales tripping on the dungheap—but Conscientious Career Slob. Blond hair wild, hip-huggers uncomplimentary to big bottom, shirt stained, middle buttons misbuttoned so hole showed torn brassiere (a bit of tug there). She wore black glasses, had a yolk-tinged smile. What, he had wondered, was this self-presentation supposed to mean?

The place was not quite in motion, but looked as if the order of creation had just been sent in. Clearly the elements had not been able to get into shape on their own. Skirts, newspapers, New Statesmen, bridge scores, glasses, packaged-gravy envelopes, cracker cylinders, toothpaste caps, stockings, record jackets, manila envelopes, socks, panties, exhausted ball-points, piles of anything.

"It's a little crowded here." Said easily, liquidly. "I don't know what to throw out. My consumer mind. But here you are. The best item in the place." With an arm-shove, clearing a wounded couch. Then opened a labelless bottle of soybean-colored liquid and poured into glasses which many, less fastidious than Strunk, would have refused to touch. "I tell you, Dugan, at that point, I thought the old leaning tower would fall. Yet, I dunno. Somehow, in the room, she had that wine at her mouth, and there was this sweetness in her smile. Terrific. And she had the loveliest, clear jawline. I love jawlines. And an out-of-this-universe cream-and-fruit complexion. I tell you, she just came together for me. In that sewer of a room. Maybe that was the reason for it. A dung setting for the queen pearl. So I stayed. The whole week. The bedroom wasn't bad. And she's a heartbreaker. I recommend letters."

7

In Geneva, where the Rhone debouches into the Lake by the Quai du Mont Blanc is the Hôtel de Pologne, eight stories of angelfood-cake limestone, its lakefront windows shaded by purple awnings which, from the excursion boats docked below, appear the proper regal flourish of this most republican town.

Barney Beinfresser occupies the top three floors of the hotel. Six years before, plaster walls were knocked down, and, in the tripled spaces, walls of mirror and satin put up. Persian beds, Murano chandeliers, Roman chests, Empire beds, Brussels tapestries, French fusils, Danish desks, and American business machines were lifted by exterior cables and installed through dismantled windows. Fifty of the prettiest girls in the canton followed to answer phones and press buttons.

As is well known since the rise of capitalism, money will give a cripple legs, a bald man hair, a faded woman skin of rose and silk. Barney Beinfresser's money put gloss in his monk's crescent of black hair, exercised and massaged his flab into muscle, tanned his short body (and, in shoes, subtly elevated it), shaped his face away from his persimmon nose, educated sideburns over his great ears, and polished

the very air around him. Girls genuinely lusted for Barney
and told themselves—as well as him—that for richer or
poorer they would be his.

Barney had horses and Barney had planes, Barney had
assistants whose assistants had horses and his assistants had
planes. And all this he had earned himself.

After a couple of head-bashing years in which he'd used up
the stake he'd accumulated as a student-businessman at
Chicago, Barney converted small Yiddish into German and
became a denazifier for the OSS, a role which had him, a
sergeant, outranking colonels. He worked out a technique
for uncovering concentration-camp guards masquerading as
inmates: a key question, a five-hundred-watt spotlight in the
eyes and a punch under them; his confession rate was
tremendous. He lived in a Rhine castle, commandeered
cars, concerts, wine, and girls.

Meanwhile, he prepared.

He crated gargoyles off cathedrals (some fallen, some
helped to fall), picked up dinner services of Meissen and
Rosenthal china for cigarettes, and trafficked heavily in
enemy souvenirs.

He had an OSS colleague, Corporal Vincenzo, who was
attached to the Committee of National Liberation for
North Italy. Vincenzo was in the Piazzale Loreto on April
29 when the bodies of Mussolini and Claretta Petacci
were hauled in from the hills. Before they were strung up,
Vincenzo cut off a few square feet of their bloodied gar-
ments and took pictures of the excisions. These, cut into
square inches and mounted on inscribed plastic with the
demarcated picture attached to the bottom, brought in
fifty thousand dollars from collectors in New York, Paris,
and Beirut. On May 1, Vincenzo and Beinfresser just
missed a ride into Berlin, where they hoped to convert the
remains of Hitler into inventory. It was one of their few
failures.

In June they drove their crates in half-ton trucks into a
Dolomite village and laid low till October. Vincenzo
caught pneumonia, Beinfresser confused the antibiotic

dosage, and Vincenzo died. Barney dug him a deep grave.

Two weeks later, Barney had his first office, a cellar room in the bombed-out Röhmer section of Frankfurt/Main.

8

March, 1968.

Beads of mist from Mont Blanc hang across the Petit Saleve over the beautiful lake and the gray Old Town. Strunk would have shivered with historic delight, but Dugan is too busy to shift historic furniture. His quarry is very present-tense indeed, hairy-wristed, claw-eyed, clumped with terrific force, empty of courtesy.

Dugan and Beinfresser. They sit in an anteroom of an office Dugan will never see. Dugan is sure every word here is taped, there's probably a camera in the gold doorknob.

He has opened up with a conclusion: Beinfresser is a distinguished graduate of the University, his wealth is reputed to be considerable, he, Dugan, wishes him to become a permanent part of one of the great institutions of the world. "What endures at universities is the contributions of the faculty and its graduates. And what houses them. Everything else is transient. We hope a Beinfresser Library or Laboratory will be a fixture of the scene."

"I'm not much on sarcophagi."

Beinfresser's hands are at ease. Only small movements in the arms under the tan cloth suggest that he is not just waiting for Dugan, that he too is heading for something.

"If the next century's Shakespeare and Einstein walk out of the Beinfresser Library, nobody would call it a sarcophagus."

Beinfresser is annoyed at Dugan's shoes heeling his ten-thousand-dollar carpet. Nineteen-dollar shoes. The universities better get with it. They send men after money who look as if they don't know what it is. But Dugan seems a tough cookie. Why is he hung up with a third-rate enterprise? What's lax in him? Where's he been broken? He tells him a new Shakespeare won't need a new library. "Electronics is making an oral culture. Tribal. Nobody ahead of anybody else. Nobody storing it up in files or banks."

What a nerve, thinks Dugan. The *ancien régime* keeping the farmers down on the farm. "Anyway, I'm not thinking about plays I'll never see, Mr. Dugan. I'm only at the *Titus Andronicus* stage of my own life. Shakespeare worked with stories, I with money. I can't bury what I work with. You're not talking to the old Rockefeller now. He was," and Beinfresser pointed a thumb past his ear toward the old city, "a Calvinist. 'Money is the sign God knows I've acted right.' Pretty notion, but sheer balls. I may have been a lousy student, but in Tatum's day, even mules like me found out how to read old rocks. I'm no Calvinist. Money isn't sacred to me in any way. It's just what I work with. Not for. With."

Dugan held back from anything but a look of absorption.

"If I give money, it has nothing to do with Band-Aids. When I give it, it works for me directly or indirectly. It buys me something, or it puts odor-of-rose instead of wolf in someone's nostrils."

Dugan gave him a cold nod, old man to naughty boy; such a big bad wolf playing Machiavelli.

"I don't hide much, what's the point? I'm not even beating around your little bush. You got in here because I have a feeling. That's all now. A feeling the University and I may have something in common besides my degree. It may be certain studies that can be done that I'd, as it were, pay for. Or some property we both can use. I don't need to tell you the University has a tax advantage over even a well-lawyered businessman. Mostly, it's information I need. Maps. I want to know what's going to happen. And I don't want my maps to change too much.

"The universities are making all sorts of excitement. They're spilling over their containers. That changes the maps. My notion is you've got to get better containers.

Things change, but rational men must see how they'll change.

"I've operated in junk heaps and ruins. Better than most. But that's over. I'm miles away from that part of my life. I don't want my factories in smoke. I've had that. I was booted out of Iraq last year without an ashtray. I don't like that. I want to get out before the pot boils. A good university's an information center. Maybe even a generator. I might be willing to pay for a plug-in.

"But don't expect anything by next Tuesday. Don't expect anything at all. And don't dun me. I don't forget. You're on my docket. There's a fair chance you'll profit the way you want to profit. But, let me, as they say, do the calling. This isn't a brush-off, Mr. Dugan." He was up. Dugan, in rage, followed.

"I can't have lunch with you. But there's a delightful girl, Mlle. Quelquechose, who said you caught her eye as you came in. She would enjoy your company. And there's always an excellent lunch for people with whom I do business.

"It's been a pleasure, Mr. Dugan."

9

Living as he had for three years in a place where most people systematically deformed their appearance in the interest of that higher appeal which disregards it, Dugan was exceptionally pleased by those who looked as if they'd studied how to look splendid. So the girl who sat on one of the gold couches of the lounge which spooned off the corridor of Beinfresser's anteroom converted the weight of the moneyman's assault into air. Mlle. Quelquechose was quite something.

A small girl, a pert beauty, hair cut boyishly like Mia Farrow's, a nose that started for blueblood hauteur, then buttoned off, blue eyes clear in liquid brightness, a small chin, nectarine cheeks. A miniature beauty, but then, for surprise, for erotic drama, within the red-sweatered suit, an almost-Lena-like affluence of breast, and, out of it, what Dugan especially treasured, splendid legs, longer than the shortish body promised, the length emphasized by the nyloned inches north of knee to red mini-skirt. The legs pointed his way, crossed like a man's at the red pumps, and an almost male, a gruff little voice came from the red-corollaed throat, "I'm Prudence Rosenstock, Mr. Dugan."

Beinfresser combed more than the Swiss cantons for his flowers. Prudence was Miss Western Michigan, 1962, a model for the Sears Roebuck catalog who'd saved to try it with Galitzine in Italy, hadn't lasted, and had been found by a Beinfresser man in the Milan Galleria cadging emergency income.

The autobiography unrolled in a Fiat 125, "a nervous car," said the Hertz girl, herself a likely enough candidate for the Beinfresser offices. Beinfresser allowed the girls a thousand Swiss francs, and a couple of hundred miles. Prudence suggested they drive into the mountains. Dugan, surveying the map, lit on Vezelay. He'd never been there, never been in Burgundy, and the idea of having the rest of his three days in Europe with Prudence, Burgundian cuisine, and medieval marvels was a powerful draw. Each expectation advanced the other. In fact, allowed it. Dugan was not the sort to enroll in Beinfresser's Fuck-Now, Kneel-Later business. He had to have at least the illusion Prudence was part of a Larger Scheme of Pleasure. He would not even let her charge the Fiat to Beinfresser.

It turned out he could discuss it with Prudence. "I may be semi-professional, but it sure doesn't suit me. I'm like a nun there. I mean, I live in the hotel," she pronounced this charmingly in Dugan's ears, HOE-tel, "and I go up-stairs to the office, and when there's no work, I go shopping with the girls or fix my hair or read, which is O.K., I love to read, but," and she tipped around in the corner to coax Dugan's look from the terrible twists of the Jura roads, a marvelous, novel animal in her round beaver collar and toque, a fur bloom on the red suitcoat. "I mean, where's

159 **Idylls of Dugan and Strunk**

the Struc-ture of my life? I mean, what does it lead to?"

She got lots of good advice from her business acquaintances. Lying, bare, in the Gritti or the Paris Ritz, looking out the windows at the Salute or the Place Vendôme, she'd posed the problem many a time, and had received numerous if unvaried solutions. "Flowers shouldn't worry about their future." Occasionally a job offer. "Sure, more reception whoring, and I had a year at Olivet, bet you never heard of it, but it's a good school." An occasional marriage proposal, "but I'm only twenty-four, my looks are the type that last, if you don't drive us over the cliffs. I didn't have it as a fashion model. You know they want these pieces of pipe that can fold themselves up six or eight times and still come out taller than me. I used to tie ice cubes against my cheeks. A girl told me if you did that long enough it would make them look as if they had caves in them. These big houses love those caved-in cheeks. The more money you spend, the more starved you're supposed to look. You're thin, you're spiritual. I mean, the human body has so few variations, people go after any crazy detail. Next year they'll be looking for girls with hair on the lower lip."

They ate a lunch in Beaune that was so regal in detail and strength, they decided to take a room in the hotel, and there, after half an hour to digest and play with each other, they snoozed, alternately cozying each other's backsides in their semi-laps.

That night, after hours in town and a dinner served like a mass, Dugan told Prudence *his* troubles. Troublemaking was a fine superstructure for love. The tongue was an eloquent penis, the ears generous receptors. Trouble-telling preceded every deep relationship, as trouble itself deepened, then ended it. The resistance of flesh to flesh, earth to cultivation, donor to beggar, fact to system, this was proper scene for the few great human moments. Dugan lay beside the soft beauty in the lumpy bed in the Hôtel de la Poste, muttering his wounds, salving them in her soft bowls, her soft hills.

The next day, in Vezelay, he bought a postcard of the

most beautiful of the church's capitals, a dreamy stone man pouring stone grain into a stone mill, an amazed stone man holding a stone bag to receive the stone flour. The Guide Book explained: Moses pouring the Old Law into Christ, Saint Paul receiving the purified text. "Like experience," said Prudence. "You go through the mill, so next time you do better."

Thought Dugan, Beinfresser has poured this crude beauty my way, but what we have done together has refined her into what I won't do without. There she curled in the Fiat, gob of American melting pot, white German, white Celt, taught letters in a PWA high school, love-making by a second-string guard, Western Civ. by a nail-biting doctoral candidate from Ann Arbor, ambition by movie magazines and the Tonight show, found useful by Beinfresser and now found crucial by Dugan.

10

The day's letter from Leonard was hardly more than telegram length, and then that evening, his telegram arrived with more or less the same message, but spelling out which plane she should get on this Thursday.

Ever since Elizabeth had read *Allegory of Love* and found out that love, like the spinning jenny, was an invention, she'd felt reborn, for if love was something patented in eleventh-century Provence, then so was every other conventional feeling somewhere or other patented. In Bi. Sci. 2, she'd read in Darwin's *Expression of the Emotions in Man and Animals* that musculature developed for one purpose was used by evolved creatures for another: hair-bristling to frighten enemies, became, in men, expression of their own fright. Thus she could make the motions of love without being in love. (By 1967, every urban girl in the world knew that.) But more, you could think without having to accomplish anything with thought, could run without going anywhere. You could do anything without having the reasons you were supposed to have when you were first told to do it. Wasn't this what existentialism was all about?

She'd come to define her life by accident as much as anything. The apartment mess which Leonard hadn't caught on to at all, hadn't started that way. She'd been a more or less automatic tidier, as, in adolescence, she'd been an automatic slob, but one day she'd buzzed up to the apartment a guy in a daishiki who'd tied her up, and went through the place like Sherman through Georgia. He didn't get a nickel till he'd raped her. Not unpleasantly, and she naturally took Enovid the way Englishmen take their brollies. A runty, thick-headed, white brute, he asked where the money was. Right in her purse, which she took from the icebox, and handed him one of the two fives. He laughed and left, a handyman paid after a good job. She started to pick up the mess, but stopped. No. There was no point. Who decided what was a Mess and what Order? Let her chips fall.

In a month, the habit of old order was gone; she'd disciplined herself to disorder.

For Leonard, she'd actually compromised. Compromising was something like accepting disorder. Don't buck it. Born a farmer's daughter, with old attachments to natural order, there was no point in making life a series of funerals over old habits. Disorder could include a few of these. Another stage of liberation.

When, in college, she'd spotted her prototype spelled out in novels (the Marquise de Merteuil, Lamiel, Hendricks), she realized her contribution to the new woman could be softness. There was no need to be hard about altering woman's fate. She didn't often feel hard, or mean, hadn't been pushed around enough to be resentful or vengeful. Searching her own feelings, she decided that her independence would be unaggressive, unlike her fictional ancestors', and if not consciously benevolent, at least along her own reasonably gentle grain.

As for Leonard, he cared about everything. He cared who ran for President, he cared who won. He cared for her and he cared for going to bed with her. Old-line, he needed to put the two together; or, at least, didn't bother thinking that they didn't have to go together. He "wanted children," but couldn't separate the curiosity and egoism of having his own from the pleasures of having pretty human minia- tures about the house. She said, "I'm for solving popula- tion problems by adopting my kids." Which annoyed him.

Which annoyed her. For she didn't like to annoy any- body much, certainly not a dear old wise-foolish boob-brain like Leonard. But she had no curiosity at all about seeing what her genes came up with. They weren't her invention anyway. She was just another transient hostess. It would be a grace to retire them. Now that the world's submerged were poking their noses out of the swamps, there'd be genius enough around to pester the whole universe, let alone this planetary crumb. Such, at least, was the view of E. Schultz.

She checked with United, and telegraphed Leonard she'd be at O'Hare at six-forty-six—he was queer for numbers. She had a present to bring him from the Newsweek morgue about this Beinfresser he and his pal Dugan were after. The researchers hadn't been able to check this item and hadn't used it, but as a student of medieval literature she'd lit up at it. The source—an Italian World War II partisan—claimed Beinfresser got his start by selling relics of "Fascist saints" to American soldiers in occupied Germany. He'd gotten Mussolini's death suit, cut it into bloody strips, and sold them for a hundred dollars apiece. He had likewise— claimed the source—disposed of a suit of Hitler's under- wear and Goebbels' clubfoot shoe. Whatever ghoulish use Leonard could make of this exemplary anality, she didn't know, but, if nothing else, he could see her ease of living as relief from it.

She also brought a bottle of the wine he built his courage with. If the gifts didn't stem from love, at least they came

from thoughtfulness and caring. Shouldn't that serve even
so antiquated a dear as Strunk?

The friendly skies of United buckled in the thermal
troughs of early spring. In addition to which, the friendly
plane was more than woman's flesh could bear, computer
salesmen, grandmothers, rusting hostesses trying to enlist
you if they were under twenty, eyeing you out of existence if
you spotted them a few years. And the anal supper plates,
subdivided by Cornell engineers, packaged by Michigan
State. The eggs laid, the hatching skinnerized, the feathers
plucked, the feet sliced by orderly metals, the contentment
quotients laid out on statistical maps. Elizabeth hated airplanes.

Leonard's freighted little head rose half a foot above five
other greeters. He was working to diminish his grin. She
leaned over the rail and kissed it. "Cheers, love." Two hundred pounds of smiling butter.

He drove Dugan's Dodge, badly, a form of disorder she
didn't relish. "I hate cars."

Was it the reason he didn't watch the others? Eyes on
the pop-pop flashes of northbound lights. The Loop huffed
up, the traffic narrowed, slowed.

Leonard aimed for and missed the Ohio Street cutoff,
went onto Congress Street at thirty miles per, ignoring
horns, glares, fuck-you gestures out the windows. On the
Outer Drive, relief. It was the only stretch of road he drove
easily, the Magikist lips, the Standard sign, the Donnelly
plant, the lit-up Douglas pillar, the Drive motels. Relaxed,
he waxed. "It took the eighteen-twelve war to warm Jeffer-
son to cities."

Liz, liquidly: "Why so?"

"Saw the country couldn't depend on Europe for manu-
factures. The anti-city strain is deep in America."

" 'Our alabaster cities gleam undimmed by human
tears.' "

Leonard turned off the Drive at Forty-Seventh, drove past the wasteland fringe of the Southside slum, braked by a field of cinders, and kissed her. "I love your learning, Elizabeth."

Less than most men was Leonard made for automobile loving. Nor did Elizabeth relish the Dodge's mechanic breath, the double-parking yards off the express drive. How much dumbness could go with so much doll? "Preserve it then," pointing at cars screeching around them.

He got his hands on the wheel, started off, gears clashing. (If you can't find it, grind it.) "The Vedas are anti-urban, but the city's made for love."

"They do all right in the country. Sometimes with corncobs." Liquidly.

They drove around the highrise twins islanded in Fifty-Fifth Street, turned up Dorchester without pausing for the stop sign, taking horn fire at the rear.

"The Vedas didn't have urban prescriptions. Buddha did. Like Jesus. The preaching was to the cities. And city people got him in the end."

They were not upstairs ten minutes when the phone rang. Prudence, Dugan's new girl, calling to ask them over for a drink.

Odd foursome of love.

11

In the fall of 1964 Dugan campaigned in California, half for the President, half for Pierre. Nothing big, answering phones, pushing noses out of keyholes, pacifying, procuring, buttering, counting, but it got him out of shepherding his congressmen, and his boss, Bronson Kraus, said he could gather the index figures and feed them to the President once a week.

Which he did, taking a day to gather them, and five minutes to show them to the President and listen to him repeat them without looking at the sheet of paper.

One day, after the session, Dugan told him that he'd been thinking about a guaranteed national income and would like to do something about it.

The huge executive forefinger rammed Dugan's breast-bone. "When I need a shoeshine, Dugan, I'll git me the shoeshine boy."

Dugan was transferred to a closet in the Executive Office Building. Kraus found a place for him with the Archives Division declassifying material for release. Dull work for Dugan, who hated everything about history but making it. In three weeks a Chicago congressman had steered him to an opening at the University; there he flew, and there he stayed.

But Dugan's three weeks in Archives had traced a few grooves in his memory. When he and Prudence drank Bloody Marys with Strunk and his pleasant, ham-flanked, not unbeautiful Slob, Elizabeth, her little Beinfresser item ticked into the groove of an Italian Front cable about one Corporal Henry Vincenzo of the CIC, who, after being seen and photographed in the Piazzale Loreto the morning of Mussolini's death, had disappeared and not been heard from since.

As the others drank, Dugan's groove deepened and widened. Then he leaped up and wrote a letter which released the grip of fury Beinfresser had held him in since he had gone to see Chancellor Tatum at the Drake. The letter, most of it based on Dugan's infuriated guess-work, went as follows:

Dear Mr. Beinfresser:

I want to thank you again for the fascinating talk. I will respect your wishes about not mentioning the subject I broached to you in Geneva. I only wish to tell you that the description of your possible relations to the University Campaign Fund is one which I understand.

I write primarily of another matter which has come to my attention. I've recently been interested in the case of a Corporal Henry Vincenzo of the Counter-Intelligence group which worked with the Liberation Front of Northern Italy (Audisio et al.). There is some evidence that Vincenzo played a somewhat amusing but discomforting role back there. It had to do with the acquisition and sale of some Fascist relics. I need not bother you with the details. What interests me is that the corporal disappeared in May, 1945 and has not been heard from since. His family assumed he had been killed by German sentries in the last days of the war, then stripped of his identification and buried somewhere. It occurred to me to write a number of men such as yourself who were in various Counter-Intelligence groups and might have gotten to know Corporal Vincenzo. If something about his habits were learned, it might lead authorities to him so that his family could be comforted about his last days (if such they indeed were). Did you perhaps know the corporal?

Chicago is on the edge of spring. My neighbor's tulip shoots are making their debut.

Miss Rosenstock, one of your former employees, joins me in sending regards.

Sincerely yours

Hugh Dugan
University Development Office

12

By the time Beinfresser's response came, Dugan was in the hospital. Another consequence of his unhistoric regard for perturbation. For it was he who suggested that they go, the afternoon of Martin Luther King's funeral, to Sixty-Third Street; worse, he who had misinterpreted an informative gesture as a belligerent one, had let rage blot out his good sense, and had waged bitter struggle in the street.

It would be too much to blame him for not knowing that Beinfresser's donation had as much to do with these same events as with his clever letter, for Dugan is an old-fashioned man. That Beinfresser is ever-alert to those perturbations which alter the values of property and chattel is something Dugan knows only theoretically. (The Beinfresser Computer Center, built largely of federal funds—and supplied by Buttonwiese for Computations—began rising on Sixty-Second Street in 1969.) But our idyll does not really care for finance, only Dugan and Strunk, and the girls with whom they will spend years. Beinfresser may make huge gains in Southside property, but Dugan and Strunk prosper in other ways.

This is an idyll.

A final section, then, about the troubled days after the murder of Martin Luther King in Memphis, which occurred the evening after Elizabeth came to Chicago for her first visit with Leonard Strunk.

13

In the monkish beauty of Strunk's apartment, Elizabeth woke. What was that ahead, Notre Dame? No. Slant light transmuting a window shaft of a Mies highrise into a medieval tower.

Behind her, in the three-quarter bed of which he took two-thirds, her good monk, who, last night, had labored so sweetly in their common cause.

No common cause held together the troubled city of Chicago. Rumors burned, and then blocks.

Sunday, she and Strunk, Dugan and Prudence, drove downtown. At Madison Street, beyond the yellow police barricades, clouds of flame-edged smoke swelled, buckled, and broke.

That night the National Guard came into the city. The four lovers watched them—on television—land in planes, take to jeeps and half-ton trucks, then, driving into the city, saw them posted on avenues where stores were shuttered with iron X's, where other windows showed stalactite jags of glass. Smoke from dying fires snaked,

flattened, and floated against the ancient walls, less than
fifty years of age, but older than Pompeii if measured by
cumulative degradation.

Again on television they watched concentrations of violence that made what they had seen even more desperate:
a sibling conflagration in Washington, Robert Kennedy
talking in a Cincinnati ghetto about his brother's assassination, grieving men who had been with King, the Memphis
motel and the room where the unknown assassin fired.
Black leaders spoke direfully, bleakly, menacingly, the President read a hasty message. He had not had a week of
martyr's pleasure after his great moment of renunciation.
Undercut, as always, by the world's K's.

Sunday passed, and Elizabeth changed her reservation.
She called her office Monday, said she'd be in Tuesday;
but Tuesday saw her head in Leonard's lap, watching
King's funeral on Dugan's color television set. Strunk had
a Xeroxed copy of King's dissertation on Paul Tillich.
"God in the streets," he described it. "Mad the way these
myths won't stop. You can see King spotting his death in
the stories, but how does Judas know he must take the
part?" Great nose and lips gilded with the weird light of
the set, the rest of the upside-down head obscure to her.

Dugan, in a chair, hand on Prudence's head, feet up
on the green casing of his discarded black-and-white set,
pointed to Rockefeller in the packed church rising from a
seat to stand with Mayor Lindsay of New York against the
wall. The Rockefellers, said their instant historian Strunk,
were quick learners. "And probably the only white Baptists
in the church." The sermons, the hymns, the mourners in
white ("an African carry-over," said Strunk), the smallest
King girl asleep against the veiled mother, a bored Senator
McCarthy high over his rival, Kennedy, candidate Nixon
leaning over to gab with Mrs. John Kennedy, getting
frozen, beating quick retreat into difficult self-absorption:
the white-power reef in the mahogany bay within the
Ebenezer Baptist Church.

When the casket was put on the mule cart, the lovers

went into the kitchen for hamburgers, which Prudence in-
cinerated on the frying platter. "Two weeks, and I can't get
the hang of it."

Dugan suggested they go see what was happening on
Sixty-Third Street.

Strunk thought it would be dangerous, though there'd
been comparatively little activity on Sixty-Third after Saturday night.

They got in the Dodge and drove down Cottage Grove
by the smashed acres of urban clearance. "Better put the
headlights on, Hughie": Prudence. Dugan pulled them on.
South of Sixtieth Street, every car's lights shone against
the sun.

Elizabeth said she thought the soldiers would be out in
force. At Sixty-Third, under the filthy iron of the elevated,
they waited to turn left. A clot of teenagers looked across
the iron-pillared, El-shadowed street. The light changed,
Dugan went forward and waited for the northbound cars to
make his turn. Behind him, a horn sounded, and kept
sounding. They looked around. "We allowed to turn here?"
asked Prudence.

"Why not."

The horn yowled on, they made the turn, and Dugan
looked around. A black man of thirty or so, leaned out of
the window of a scarred Pontiac and yelled something.

Dugan felt his old street fighter's click. Perhaps it had
to do with the misery of his last year. Who will say? He
stuck his fist out, and yelled back, "Who the hell you
think you ARE?" And pulled up, front wheels to the curb.

"Jesus," said Strunk. Prudence and Elizabeth could not
speak, could hardly breathe, their mental preparation nothing in the dark of this stupid minute.

The Pontiac stopped in mid-street, cars pulled around it,
the driver got out, Dugan's size, a lean man in a green
sport shirt. Strunk could see a block down the pillared
cavern. Guardsmen in olive green, spread ten yards apart,
holding their rifles. A comfort, but Dugan was out of the
car, in the middle of the street, flecks of light coming

through the crossed rails, the teen-age boys moving off the boarded stores through the smashed glass on the sidewalks. They circled Dugan and the other driver. While the girls called Noes, Strunk got himself out of the car. Dugan and his new enemy faced each other, arms raising into pincers, faces stiff with rage. "No," yelled Strunk. "No more." The Pontiac driver stared at the white whale Strunk. Veins split his neck. Then, oddly, astonishingly, his head snapped toward the iron el tracks, and he yelled.

Terror.

Dugan, a statue, absolute marble in the brown street, shook loose, and then, madly, struck out. And was swarmed over, windmilled. Strunk, fear and terror drowned by necessity, called, "Soldiers. Police." Dugan was standing, slugging; six or seven others were slugging, kneeling, there was flash, teeth, blood. And then, from everywhere, people, women, girls, ululating, and the soldiers, up the long street, running, bayonets out. And Strunk was hit in the back, the head, the side, oh God, his insides, his skin, arm, chest, nose, he covered up, the soldiers were there, cars were moving, cars were stopping, and then crashes, smashes, glass, a tavern window, bottles, boys were linked, running up the street, and there were rocks and bottles in the air smashing against cars and pillars, and a low boom, and a flower of fire grew from the smashed store, and then a thick twist of smoke, and the street was a blur, though oddly, Strunk, leaning on the car, his shirt out, face bloody, saw over his arm a small girl and boy, hand in hand, eyes chill with fear, still as flowers on the sidewalk, the sidewalks themselves a frieze, noise turned off, and then sirens and blue whirllights and black policemen and two jeeps and a half-ton truck with soldiers and men and women flooding east and west in the flare-spiked shade, and the fire bloomed, glass shivered, and a thin, old, bearded black man in a burnoose raised his arms, and Dugan, face broken, body filthy, welted, stained, and bloody, was picked up and put in a jeep and was gone, and the old man said in Strunk's ear, "Better git, mister," and then a rifle butt bent his side, and Strunk saw the scared-and-scary face of a blue-eyed Guardsman behind the gun, and got to the driver's seat in front of a whimpering, shrunk Elizabeth and a collapsed, unmodeled Prudence and with unepistolary uncontrol drove wildly through the iron cavern, dodging the pillars, turning north— wrong—on Drexel, winging by glaring incarcerated eyes toward the light, toward the open green and light of the Midway, toward the gray university towers.

TWO
SLIGHT STORIES
OF ABUSE

GAPS

*Thus we see that we can never arrive at the true
nature of things from without.*
   —Schopenhauer, *The World as Will and Idea*

When a gentleman is out of sympathy with the times, he
drifts with the wind. So Lao-tzu is supposed to have told
Confucius, who sought instruction in the rites from him.
"Rid yourself of your arrogance and your lustfulness," con-
tinued the sage, "your ingratiating manners and your ex-
cessive ambition. They are all detrimental to your person."
   William McCoshan, a gentleman out of sympathy with
the times, had no such guidance. And though he did not
exactly drift with the wind, he was a travel agent. (Who
had never traveled.) He descended from a New England
aristocracy whose authority had disintegrated in the rise
of an urbanism and federal power managed by the sons
of immigrants. William had not taken the aristocratic
option of waiting on the side lines until the rulers invited
him into a decorative spot. Instead, he sank slowly until
he found a level which supported him. That is, he left the
University of Connecticut in his sophomore year and took
a job with the American Express Company in Hartford. Six
years later, he transferred to the Dayton office, where for
fifteen years he was the assistant manager of the Travel
Department. He married his landlady's niece and fathered
a daughter.

What William appeared to care about was schedules. From Dayton, "the cradle of aviation," he sent out fellow citizens to Lima and Melbourne, Portugal and Paris, working out for them intricate fusions of tour and pocketbook.

At home, to Elsa, his life's only confidante, he exposed the deeper side of his nature. William, the schedule maker, distrusted the apparent order of things. Beyond human contrivance lay terrible blanks. Planetary schedules and galactic shifts, these bubbles of human dream could pop in a blink. The world's Newtons and Einsteins, convinced they'd uncovered threads of the Real Fabric of Things, were, for William, life's prime dupes. Nothing he'd read infuriated him more than Einstein's remark that God was not malevolent but subtle. If God—whatever that meant—were so subtle, how could such a piece of mathematized dust dare to believe it could touch the least of His contrivances. Closer to William's view of the true Grain of Things was Einstein's wife, also an Elsa, who carried the ashes of her cremated daughter in a sack next to her heart until forced by her husband to give them up. William's own day-to-day truce with Appearance was unmarked by fetish, but such confessional gestures of human incompetence gratified his heart. The world's vacancies had to be stuffed with bilge. The human job was to see bilge as itself, not wisdom.

His Elsa was a true listener, no debater, no echo. Space probes, Korea, cancer, revolution, civil rights, civil riots, William uncovered for his wife the terrible configurations beneath the newspaper facts. The wars of the Chinese periphery were the conversions of peasant societies into industrial markets at the hidden service of the same force that destroyed a thousand of every thousand-and-one eel eggs. As for industry, it was a less conspicuous form of the diversion he provided his customers; Chartres and automobiles were made to stop people from thinking about actualities. "People start thinking about the way things really are, the only manufacturers who'll stay in the black will be the rope- knife- and gun-makers." The Birchers,

Minute Men, Mafia, Neo-Nazis, and the NRA were far more useful than the planners, utopians, and think-tankers. Why? "Because they take care of civil roughage. They're the national excretory system."

William's breakfast seminars came to an end one winter day when Elsa drove their 1961 Pontiac into a low retaining wall and was decapitated by the windshield.

This death, whatever it was, pricked bubble, discharged synapse in some monster's bloody brain, whatever, drove William's fears into the depths of misery. Almost, almost, he had Elsa's ashes saved for his own heart, but no, that was naked unreason. There was no decent human option left but that animal reason which brought food to mouth, head to pillow.

William had never been close to his daughter, Winnie. Elsa had absorbed all the feeling he had in him. Winnie grew, was hugged, grew more, and found her own life. Yet in the months after the funeral, they spent time together, cooking, doing dishes, cleaning the apartment. One day, a propos of nothing, out of the blue, he mentioned to her the possibility of a vacation in Europe, then, on her birthday, reaffirmed it with the gift of a suitcase.

So they drifted into a three-week European excursion.

In July, Winnie and William flew to Milan, and took the train to Rome. The idea was to stay in Rome a week, then fly to Nice, hire a car, and drive west along the southern coast as far as Spain. In Rome, though, Winnie ran into one of William's customers, the boy friend of her best girl friend, and with the flirtatious power of adolescent treason, encouraged him. In two days they felt themselves in love. Winnie begged William to let her stay alone in Rome while he went off to France.

At first it seemed out of the question. The very fact that months of closeness had not brought him truly closer to her increased William's feeling of paternal responsibility and simultaneously deepened habitual fears about her safety. (Whatever *that* really meant beyond scheduled change.)

Yet, after all, she was not his type, their lives depended on becoming increasingly separate; true responsibility would be to give her her wish.

"All right," he said.

But anxiety dominated the night before his takeoff. He went to his daughter's hot little room and studied her curled in regression, legs around the stuffed cylinder which misserves Europeans for pillows. Her breasts, oddly full, glazed with silver sweat, rose and sank in her nightie. Looked at quickly, she seemed like Elsa, but the temperament was a sport. This was a passionate little girl, fed on wild rock music, on the pointless violence and anarchic farce of American pop culture. He forced himself to touch her forehead. "No," she said loudly, though not to him. "No, no." Her life wasn't his.

At breakfast William gave copies of his itinerary to Winnie and Robert, her friend, told them how to place an Emergency Traveler's Notice in *Figaro*, cautioned them to eat sensibly, not stay out late, and remember they were being treated as mature young people.

A Roman summer day. Tufa walls sweated orange dust, the heat close enough to feel internal. William took off in a bus for Fiumicino. For France.

Twenty years of reading had prepared him for it. But had also prepared him to show no excitement, prepared him not to expect and not to be disappointed. In the plane, he read *Le Monde*, drank Seven-Up, and ignored the pilot's invitation to look down at Corsica and Sardinia.

At Nice, a blue Citroën waited for him in the lot.

Two P.M.

William made for Saint-Tropez. Why not? Since Bardot's first films, he'd dispatched hundreds of Daytonians there; he himself was not averse to seeing such things. Who knows?

But what a route. Travel photographers must hang from clouds. How else omit the snack bars, gas stations, motels, bulldozers, house frames, the wads of hotel cement pasted into the hills. Though, now and then the sea showed up between cypress trees and one understood what had brought people here for three thousand years.

At Fréjus he ran into an endless spine of cars. Four o'clock. With this mob heading down the peninsula, he'd never get a room. He broke from the line, made a U-turn, took a side road, and drove southeast for four kilometers.

A chunk of glass and cement rose out of a pine grove. He circled a floral driveway, entered a lobby, and for eighty francs, thirty more than he'd planned to spend, got a room with a terrace, overlooking a slope of pine backed with marine glitter. The bed was large, it had normal pillows instead of the murderous cylinders, and the bathtub was good-sized, important to William, who was six feet and liked to loll.

He stripped, ran in place in front of a closet mirror, breathed deep to force an outline of ribs and broaden his narrow shoulders. God knows, he was no body fetishist, he didn't even care about being in good shape, but why should a man provide comic relief on a beach? Why offend? He took a bath, wrapped himself in a towel, and snoozed. When he awoke, the room was filled with an emerald light. France.

2

Next to the hotel was a small *brasserie* with four tables outside under a string of unlit bulbs. A woman, barefoot, pushed a little girl in a swing. There were no diners, apparently no other staff. William went over and asked the woman if one could order dinner. Yes, indeed, though the cuisine was a simple extension of what they themselves ate. What would he like?

The woman was about thirty, high-browed, her flesh a gold tan, her eyes deep blue, large, and set back, her nose narrow, straight, full-nostrilled, her mouth full. She talked beautiful French, her manner that ease one thinks to find

only in the rich and usually finds only in the beautiful. He
proposed *potage* an *omelette fines herbes,* and wine, but
his unsieved thought was, "You."

William was used to driving such spasms of desire out
of mind, but this innkeeping princess going off to cook his
meal stayed there, the gravity of rump in a green mini-skirt,
the length of neck where the hair parted into braids at
the nape, the solidity of her legs.

It had been six months since he had been with Elsa, and
there had been no one else. His dreams, his reveries, his
sheets bore the marks of abstinence. Yes, there was another
side of the pretty world. The age boasted liberation, but
millions were chained by need, could scarcely admit it even
to themselves. And to break out wasn't easy. Firstly, it
might involve one with tenacious, ignorant people who
could permanently infect tranquillity. Still, one knew there
were millions of fine women, needy as oneself, waiting as
one waited. Every other story was about them.

But he didn't know them, nor even how to meet them.
Dayton was a place like another, bigger than most, there
were stylish women there, long-legged, sympathetic. But
not in his life.

And now this young Frenchwoman who carried his
tureen of soup and extracted the cork from a bottle of
wine with a smile that nipped the tan base of her cheeks,
this woman, if widowed, divorced, separated, if somehow
available, he could surrender himself to devouring.

The mental consumption enriched the soup, the omelet,
the agitating wine.

William constructed a French approach and two or three
contingent follow-ups, and was, perhaps, on the point of
resolve when a black hound loped out of the restaurant
followed by the little girl running and waving to a vegetable
truck bumping up the road, around the driveway, into a
space in the pines. A squat little fellow got out, flicked a
switch which lit the colored bulbs above the tables, lifted
the little girl, cuffed the hound, nodded to William, and

went in. In a minute William heard the rage of family argument.

Life's harsh ecology.

In his room William read the news magazine, *L'Express*: De Gaulle, *Roi de Quebec*; Castro and Stokely Carmichael in Havana; the Pope in Turkey at the Virgin Mary's death house; the film director Godard married to the granddaughter of Mauriac; the death of a ninety-one-year-old poet named Birot, inventor of the word "surrealism." Yes, exactly. The human bubble glistened like a maniac's dream.

The next morning William was on the road at seven, tearing along as if he had a mission. A second's decision brought him past the turnoff for Saint-Tropez. Why break his stride?

There were lots of hitchhikers, and at Cogolin, he stopped to pick one up, a girl who waited motionless with a rucksack at her bare feet. She stuck her head in the window. "Toulon?" Young, perhaps sixteen, with a long, horsey face, yet pretty in a stupid way.

"Yes," said William. "To Marseilles. Maybe farther."

She threw her rucksack in the back on his suitcase and got in. She had on tight, grass-green pants and a yellow sweater. Very well built.

—You going to Toulon or farther?

—Béziers.

—Where's that?

For response, she made an expression he believed peculiar to French girls. The chin went forward, the mouth dropped, the eyes widened. It signified, "Beyond me."

—Maybe you're on the wrong road.

The expression was modified by a shrug and pouted lips: "Could be." He handed her the Esso map of Provence. After a minute she said, "It may be after Montpellier."

—I might not get that far.

This didn't even call for a shrug. Well, she was no orator.

Or perhaps questions violated the hitchhiker's code. Still
he persisted, he'd picked her up for company.

—You visiting people in Béziers?

The facial telegraphy signaled the unseen hitchhikers of
the world that she had been picked up by a real lulu, but
as William sustained his air of expectancy, she said, "My
aunt."

—How far have you come?

—Antwerp.

—Are you Flemish?

A shrug, as much "Perhaps" as "Yes."

—My name's William. What's yours?

Another telegraphic Waterloo, then, "Christine."

Did she like music?

She supposed she did.

Who?

Armstrong. The Beatles.

No, she did not know the names Monk, Miles, or
Ornette, nor did he say from whose album covers he knew
the names.

Did she read?

No time.

Hobbies?

No time.

Did she swim?

Yes, it was why she came to the Riviera.

—If we spot a beach, we can take a dip.

The telegraphy went wild.

In Marseilles William pulled up before a wall on which
was scrawled in charcoal, "*U.S. Assassins. Viet-Cong vain-
cra. Johnson =* 猪." He reached for his Instamatic and
asked Christine if she'd pose in front of that, he needed
a foreground object. She made a bovine facial shrug, but
got out and stood in front of the yellow cement. William
studied her through the lens. She was large, very well developed, though her feet were those of an adolescent, soft,
large, tan, the toenails faintly silvered. "Frown," he said.
"I want to show how America is detested." The Flemish

droop hardened into a tiny smile. Well, they were a bit slow in Wallonia, but they came around.

They went to Montpellier, had a sandwich and a glass of wine in a snack bar, then drove south toward Béziers. The country turned to scrub and then dunes. The Gulf of Lions opened at their left, a piece of blue plate touched with crumbs of white sail and foam. Long, spiky, wild grass bearded the road's edge, and every mile or two, paths sliced through it to the water.

William pulled up on the edge near a path, and said it was hot, he was going to take a swim. Christine's eyes, little blue fish, scooted around in suspicion.

Still, while he changed in the car, she took off her pants and sweater in the high grass.

When he got out in his trunks, she was in a bikini. "I had it on underneath."

She was terrific.

Between the grass and the great basin of water were a few yards of brown sand. From it, Christine hung a probing foot, then dived shallowly and swam a full-armed crawl fifteen yards out. William flexed himself and walked in. The bottom was marshy, the water warm. He swam in her direction.

She stood, the water line at her breasts. William tried to think of something to say, to do, but settled for a smile, which he directed at her till her eyes opened and became part of her answering smile. "I'll race you," he said. She made her "beyond-me" shrug but plunged off, swimming hard. He followed, caught up, and when she kept on, followed again and caught her ankles. She kicked loose and stood up, her eyes bluely puzzled, afraid, excited. He smiled doubly wide, and splashed her gently. She flicked water back at him, he splashed her face, she turned on her stomach and kicked water at his. He dived, his nose an inch from the marsh bottom, turned, and came up under her, his chest touching hers and his legs her kicking legs. She was still a second, then pushed off from his shoulders and swam. William, very excited, swam after her. "Surrender?" His voice cracked between embarrassment and desire.

She stood, blushed, smiled, and for want of something to say, splashed him. At which point he came up to her gently, and, without lifting his arms, kissed her mouth. Only for a second. Her mouth stayed open, her eyes shut. When she opened them again, William put his arms around her, kissed her very hard, and felt her kissing him back. They fell into the water. With his right arm around her bare waist, they crawled to the sand.

She was virgin, there was enough obstacle to cause William to discharge on her stomach. Pained, pleasured, absorbed, she turned over, a hand reaching back for his. They lay this way for a few minutes, then William leaned into the water, washed the dried seed from her stomach, and handed her the bikini, the little flag of sexual liberty. "Don't worry about anything. There's nothing inside you."

She shrugged, not a girlish shrug, and followed him through the spiky grass up the slope.

The outskirts of Béziers are blocks of factories and apartment buildings. He needn't drive into the center, said Christine, she could take a bus to her aunt's. He stopped on the corner she indicated and said, "I wish we could stay together for a while, but it's best not to."

She shook her head. "It doesn't matter. Thank you for the ride." She hoisted the rucksack to her shoulders and walked off.

William found the route to Narbonne and drove very fast, relaxed and happy. Ahead, off the road, a truck lay on its side with a line of police around it. Cars slowed to a cortege for half a mile, then spread and zoomed. *Christine,* thought William. The tight grass-green pants walking down the granular white street in Béziers. Why couldn't two human beings with common needs and common culture (Armstrong, French, swimming) service each other in such a countryside?

But that long bent head walking away down the sidewalk out of sight forever. Out of eyesight.

There was something at the edge of his mind, a buzz of sorts, but not in his mind as much as his chest, a hum of feeling—what was it?

Christine did not walk off with his stuff in her, but her body held what was not just air, not in the clownish human treasury. He, William, was part of her wherever she would go, whatever do. And she, of him.

He thought he might make it to Perpignan, but when the Narbonne signs multiplied, he felt his fatigue and turned in to *Centre de Ville*, past walls of aperitif posters into a polygonal fortressed heart of rose and silver, then past shops to a canal flanked with plane trees. He pulled up by a hotel and got a room.

Oddly, for the first time in Europe, he felt like going to a museum. In Rome he'd gone only to the Campidoglio, but the gigantesque marble feet in the courtyard only confirmed a harsh view of what survived. In museums, William wanted something else—the antique nostalgia.

The *patronne* directed him to the medieval polygon he'd passed on the way in, he walked over, found a courtyard full of Roman fragments, hesitated, then rang a bell for the guard, followed him up a stone screw of stairs into a huge half-frescoed hall with tiny medieval windows and case after case of museum stuff: Neolithic potsherds, Volgae statuettes, Gallic shields incised with boars, "the oldest Roman inscription on French soil" commemorating the victory of Ahenobarbus at Valadium, and then, what William might have been looking for, a bust of Mark Antony, governor of the Narbonne province after Caesar's death.

Antony's tiny bronze forehead wrinkled with puzzlement. The bronze leaked stupidity. This was the soldier to whom Cleopatra, dolled up as Venus, had come in the barge with purple sails, the fellow who'd laughed at Cicero's severed head. This world-shaker was a dope. William's heart trembled with renewed confirmation.

The guard was already asleep, chin on his sternum, huge

key in his fist: the new Frenchman, descendant of the men
who'd carved the shields and broken the pots, who knows,
container of genes that had passed through Cleopatra's
royal corridors. The old stupidity, Gaul to De Gaulle.
William put a silver franc on the inert knee.

At dusk, by the plane trees, William drinks light beer
and smokes a twist of black tobacco barely as thick as its
smoke. The wind in the gleaming trees stirs up odd clicks.
Mysterious telegraphy. The Canal Robine quivers in its
pilings. William thinks vaguely of a grand French dinner,
*pâté, saucissons, moules, mouton, petits pois, fraises, vin
de pays.* It will be in his body by nine. Then, alone, he will
do what he has sometimes done in Dayton, walk the
streets, go into bars, looking quietly for someone with a
face unenameled by commercial fury. As usual, he will go
to bed alone.

A woman at the next table is handing a dish of brandy
to a Pomeranian. William finds himself saying, "I should
be glad to take nourishment from such hands, Mademoi-
selle."

The woman looks up. She is fat-nosed, scraped; what had
seemed blond hair is silver. "Were you addressing me,
Monsieur?"

"I too have a dog." He puts six francs on the table. "Au
revoir, Madame."

Tomorrow.

Tomorrow he will drive back to Béziers, will cruise the
streets. At a corner, around a turn, by an alley, he will spot
the grass-green pants, the rucksack, the lowered head.

But the next morning, William drives back to Marseilles,
turns in the car at the airport, and flies to Rome.

It is four when he reaches the hotel. Signorina Mc-

Coshan is out. He waits by the window. At six there is talk outside the door, then a knock. It is Winnie, and beside her, a flushing Robert.

—What a surprise, Dad. Something wrong?

She raises her face painfully for a kiss. William cannot put his lips there. He smells an unscheduled knowledge.

"I felt I was running out on you," he manages, glaring at them, at their blushes.

GIFTS

I was not come to do any harm but actually gave
presents of my own substance.
—Hernando Cortez, September 3, 1526

Williams had allowed himself six hundred dollars for a
Mexican week, five days in Mexico City, two in Yucatán.

Round-trip to Merida was two hundred and twenty dollars, the hotels ran him about sixty pesos a day—he pre-
ferred third class—meals were cheap, and that gave him
a few hundred dollars for special pleasures. He usually
spent fifty on presents for his wife and his son, Charley.
It took him lots of time to find decent presents, but he
didn't write it off. It was one of his inroads into Mexican
life. Which was one of the objects of his annual excursions
—cultural, historic, and scenic accumulation. And then,
whatever came in the way of pleasure.

It invariably came in the same way.

On each of his little annual trips, Williams ran into someone who counted for him, sometimes intensely enough to
involve months of further contact (usually epistolary),
sometimes only in the imaginative transfiguration of his
wife.

"That's the way it goes," said Williams to his eighteen-
year-old son, his only confidant. "I don't advocate it, but
that's my way. You make your life, I'll make mine."

Years ago Charley had overcome uneasiness at his father's confidences. It was odd, but there it was, he was his father's closest friend.

The Mexican confidence, however, did him in. Giving ear wasn't giving absolution.

Apparently the business had begun as usual. At the University's Olympic swimming pool, where Williams—in excellent shape for a forty-year-old—had picked up a girl guide, Rufelia, an Indian girl working for a doctorate in economics, "bright as a fish, heavy-thighed, thin-armed, beautifully torsoed," and so on, his father filled in detail en route. A mestizo from Yucatán, she hadn't been back to see her family in two years and jumped at Williams' offer, full fare and expenses to Merida in return for two days' companionship. *Muy bien.*

September's the rainy season. In the capital this meant a fat cloud sailing in front of the sun at four-thirty, then breaking into rain for five minutes. In Merida the cloud arrived on schedule but flooded the town, turned the streets into canals, with garbage instead of gondolas. The lights and fan went off in the pathetic little hotel they stayed in three blocks off the *zócalo,* they were "forced inside," and had gone at it in the heat, debilitating despite "rather exceptional joys." (This was about as far as father went with son.)

The girl hadn't been a virgin since thirteen, had had a child at fourteen who was raised by her mother's sister in Campeche. The child regarded Rufelia as a mysterious relative wafted by supernatural gifts to the capital, there to work out reforms for family and *pueblo.*

Rufelia did not regret, indeed felt herself steeled by this early history. She saw herself as another stage of the revolution, the feminine liberation that had been in Cárdenas' original plan.

The village had tried to break Rufelia at thirteen, but the revolution had made her literate, and modernity had dripped in through French and American novels and films to soften the bondage of class and sex. A national scholarship did the rest. When the students had rioted in the spring against Rector Chavez, Rufelia had whacked off the bronze head of Fra Miguel and been awarded its metal ears.

This history became part of Williams's. On the plane ride from Mexico City, her story, its blunted English beveled and angled by Spanish insertions, took the weight from her nose, cheeks, and jaw, lit the raw black eyes, and turned her, in his expert view, into one of the love goddesses who queened it in the Anthropological Museum. That miracle world of collection and instruction culminated in this fine-breasted, small-smiling talker, on, under, and beside him in the Hotel San Luis. And yet, in the unfanned woolen air, with the sweat flooding the harsh sheet, and his heart slipping beats, Williams felt he'd been forced into wolfing his pleasure, felt unusual indigestion, and then, in a most gloomy postcoital gloom, felt that he'd had all that this Indian girl would ever give him.

Never had he been so divided from one of his intimacies.

It was partially language, for Rufelia's intelligence could not vault her limited English and his more primitive Spanish, but more, he felt he was playing parts in her story: He was the childhood rapist, the purchasing *yanqui gringo*, the bargain-maker who never lost. In the hot room, forty hours more in hand, despite the revival that would surely come in several of these, Williams began preparing the cultural pleasure that might ease this indigestion.

The night was the fifteenth, Independence Day. No accident, of course, for Williams' intention had been to see the Mexican President hail the anniversary in Mexico City; now he would do with the provincial version.

The water had seeped into the earth; by dinnertime only a few streets were impassable. He and Rufelia walked the white-walled streets to the green square ringed by the colonial church and the yellow mansions. The square was filled with more than the usual taxi drivers, kids, and loafers; the band was there, Indian ancients in blue caps and the beautifully pleated white shirts of Yucatán. He and Rufelia ate in an air-cooled box in the loggia, papayas and mole, tacos and fried eggs, four beers and coffee, and then walked the market streets, loud with preholiday pitch. Williams bought a fake antique (a two inch clay goiter-sufferer), a three-dollar watch inside a gleaming Swiss face, and, for ten pesos, a bejeweled bug held by a chain to a perforated perisphere, "for you, Charley, if it didn't crawl out of my coat."

At the square, a blue, winy night relaxed the heat grip, the soft gold of the church and administrative palace leaked over palms and pepper trees. The band worked toward a few of the same notes, singers ground out local specialties, the benches were filled, couples strutted, minute children peddled Chiclets, grizzled Indians allowed themselves annual shoeshines, and soldiers set off fireworks from the palace roof. The apparatus of small-town excitement.

The mass of Indian faces, the lucent shoddiness of festival, brass bleats and tropic momentum, a whirl of sensuous information in Williams' head that altered the fatigued ease in his legs and groin, the capillary strain in his rear, the slight, coronary hop in his chest.

In his fifth slow round of the square with Rufelia, he saw in the eyes they met that they'd become a couple, memorable, identifiable. He belonged, he could notch Mexico into his life.

Eleven o'clock. The mayor would repeat Fra Hidalgo's cry at midnight, the bells and Catherine wheels would tip the celebration.

"Let's go to bed," said Williams.

Around the corner from their room was a ten-by-twelve-foot swimming pool, open to the sky and ringed by live trees and vines. They got into bathing suits, the way they'd first seen each other the day before. Alone, they swam back and forth in the hot pool, brushing each other's bodies, working up for the amorous nightcap.

In their room the fan, a great-winged adjustable bat, revived. They dried off naked beneath it. Rufelia's cherry-tinted body gleamed from shards of street light broken by the shutters.

—You been often in hotels with men, Rufelia?

—*Jamás.*

—Come on, now. You didn't learn everything at the University.

"Never in hotel." Unembarrassed, though not at ease.

Williams was the sort who asks whores their history. More, he almost never failed to love the women he stayed with, one night or twenty. This meant their story was important, and not only their body's story. He wished to know thoughts, hopes, pains, how they met what seemed to him one of the world's three great problems (that of subjugated woman, the others being the population mess and the earth's relationship to the universe). He was a writer for a business newsletter, he relished the trends and numbers of manufacture; nights, he stayed up speculating over Beacon, Anchor, and University Press lists.

Williams never finished any books but novels, yet he regarded himself as the equivalent of a Ph.D. in several subjects. Without ambition, hating little but other men's, he threaded his burgher ease with these annual weeks of experience, drawing on them to translate his nighttime reveries into the facts of flesh.

He lifted Rufelia, no easy matter, onto the great double bed. They lay, arms coursing each other's sides.

The account, at this point, veered for Charley into a realm that seemed at least in part formed by fantasy or by some symbolic fiction. His father, long-headed, the burned brown hair grizzling to silver at tips and clutches, framed his full smile into a mockery of meditative remembrance. Or was it all tale-teller's contrivance? Was the mockery in the facts or the telling? Was its motive pain or boast?

Charley heard about the next day's trip, the narrow road razoring the flat, furzy fields, the hills, the thatched *pueblitos*, the doors open to the filthy yards, the hammocks, the chickens, the bony black cows, the spurts of mangrove jungle, the asparagus-thin roots tangling with each other into million-legged beasts, the maize and *henequén* fields asleep in the rising dew, the sun jeweling them while the dusty

Studebaker whanged along at sixty, his father wordless, working out some connection between the simmering Indian girl beside him and what he was about to see, the empty priest-state in the limestone hills.

"Took us an hour or so," a wonderful trip, though the country didn't change, just the harsh grass and the fronds with their glass-sharp fringe, boring terrain with the villages plopped every now and then along the road, surely the way they'd been for fifteen hundred years. "God knows none of these big-hatted farmers had ever come within any but market distance of Uxmal."

Uxmal now was palaces, pyramids, gorgeous nunneries and temples, gray and pink magnificence, mathematical and masonic genius, "what carving, what symmetry. And it was absolutely still. We were alone. The guard slept at the table, we didn't even buy a ticket, just left the car and walked over a ragged path to the Governor's Palace, built on one of these scary staircases, not so tall, but steep, and eighty feet long, the entrances trapezoidal cuts, all scored with these stone mouths and twists." They heard odd noises, scurfing, scurrying, then saw the iguanas' little dragon-tails whisking into cracks in the stones. In the air, red flies pecked at their sweat. "Just the two of us, the animals, and this dead city."

The girl climbed the staircase and stood in front of the frieze, arms akimbo, while Williams sat at the bottom below her summoning face. "The place turned you into an actor." Her hair fell back, "the blackest black in nature," and the full, Chinese eyes, "You can see how the Indians came across the Bering Strait," her fine, solid legs like mangrove roots, "leguminous," a dark Indian remembrance of hierarchical glory, "and I remembered some miserable book about sacrifice to the knife and blood redemption, and, kind of joking, I climbed up to her like a victim. The white god Quetzalcoatl, though a bit unplumed"—hand touching the bald inlet to the burned, grizzled hair—"crazy, you know, but we act all the time, the place called for it." On the plane from the capital, she'd recited a Mayan poem about the body's gift to the furious god. "Yet a human being looked mighty good in that dead city, even if she was only imagining a razor blade tonguing your heart."

So Williams mounted the stairs, receptive, and then, at the top of the flight, not quite kidding, Rufelia pushed at his chest. "I grabbed at her arms, we pulled and wrestled around, sex in it, but fight too, and maybe some of what had gone before us. I was excited, I tell you, scared and excited, and full of love-hate for that crazy little Indian."

Which confused fooling led to her rolling down twenty stone steps.

When Williams got to her, an army, "literally, an army of ants in two columns, twenty feet long, black ants with scouts and generals and ordering sergeants, was crawling over her thighs. There were lakes of blood from her knees. And she couldn't move, her arm was bent over, the nose looked broken, there was blood in her mouth and her eyes, her face was glued into hysteria, and there I was, knowing you can't move a broken person. Scared out of my head."

And had left her there.

For the next batch of tourists or the guide or whoever. Had torn off in the Studebaker and, back in Merida, had paid his bill, and left a note for her with her ticket, an envelope of pesos, and instructions to see the doctor as soon as possible, forgive him, and adiós.

"Which is how come I got back yesterday instead of tomorrow."

"Whew."

"Whew is right."

"I hope she's all right," said Charley. "Can you get in trouble?" Though his mind was sunk in the ugliness of it.

"They know my address. I guess I'd hear if anything happened."

"Maybe you should call the hotel down there, see if she picked up the ticket."

Williams regarded this pared-down replica of himself sitting up on the bed, and rubbed its hair.

He went to his study and telephoned, and was back

twenty minutes later carrying the jeweled bug chained to the
perisphere. "The manager said she'd only broken her arm.
What luck. I forgot to give you this."

"Alive?"

"Sure it's alive. It eats those leaves there."

Charley thanked him, and accepted thanks for his advice.

It was, however, the last advice he was going to give his
father. And, if he could manage it, he had heard the man's
last confession.

TRADE
NOTES

STORY-MAKING

Story-making?
No.
Notes for a story. ("The 'I' Colder than a Lens.")
Instead of a return address, the envelope said, "I suppose you've heard Jean L.'s been killed in an auto accident."
I hadn't.
At forty, the death of friends is new enough to thrill as well as grind. Jean wasn't much of a friend, ever, but she was the lead role in friend Al's comic serial, and I'd been around in person for some of the episodes. 1) One of their premarital reunions occurred at my thirtieth birthday party. 2) One night I unlocked my own Wanamaker's Basement of schmutz for this future Gimbel of it and they sent me a congratulatory telegram. 3) After divorce and long silence, Jean's daughter ran off one night, and she telephoned Al in London while I was staying with him. In fact, there were seven or eight expensive telephone calls (Al flushed with anal release during the binge).

Most people love stories, but few live and fewer try to live story lives. Jean tried. That her finish was as it was, (chosen by or inflicted on her) shows the depth of her attempt. Al had written and published her story the year before. In its end, the Jean character gets run over. Now, a year later, he was doing the best work of his life, farming the edible depths of his analysis for Joe's magazine, and, one night in Central Park, Jean had taken his prescription.

This was a season for the famous to live story lives. King was assassinated in April. Everyone had seen the Jesus motif working its way in him, the only question was when Judas would show up. A few days before that, the presidential sheriff turned his back on the never-say-die Alamo story and abdicated like the impotent, playboy king of 1936 (the martyr's crown read "Country" instead of "Love"). Then we had the McCarthy-out-of-the-West campaign, and in sports, a couple of comic disasters: the Master's Golf champion, a smiling gaucho, signed the wrong scorecard (prepared by his amiable Judas, Tommy Aaron) and didn't get to wear the green coat; a month later, an even more innocent champion, a horse named—as always, in these cases, auspiciously—Dancer's Image, was disqualified in the Derby because he'd been fed a painkiller the week before. ("How can you tell the dancer from the dance?") The day I first wrote this, that pop genius of publicity art, Andy Warhol, was shot by a female not-impersonator but actress, and, said the morning paper, "has a fifty-fifty chance of recovery." "Oh, no," he'd cried, unable to keep the cool in this new medium.

Jean had only a few lines in the *Times* contributed by her seventeen-year-old daughter who'd deformed the truth by either dreaming or intimating that Al had adopted (or married) her. At least, the name Millie Peters was augmented by Al's last name. Years ago Jean had accused Al of putting it to Millie or wanting to. Millie got hers back: she brought her boyfriend home to sleep with her in the front room while Jean massaged her ache alone in the rear. Motto: Live a story life, and others will live it with you.

Nembutal, Al's and my agent, told me Al had gone away. "He's in the country." Brooding? Mourning? A writer knows: he was writing it up. You know about writers. Mother drowning in her lung fluid, they are noting the color of her iris, the expression of the nurse.

Agents, however, are people of feeling; the throb of death agitated Bell's wires. "It was very late. She was lushing with this little spade faggot. Four A.M., they drove through Central Park and hit a wall."

"Did you go to the funeral?"

"I hardly knew her. He didn't want me to."

"He went?"

"He went."

Nembutal is a dear girl, tired, smart, restless, troubled. Her ambition: to "have" all the writers who count. As clients. As confessors. Anything else, I know not. I'm neither good client nor good confessor. Writers are leading suppliers of personal guff, and in these confessional days they have to try out their material. Nem had heard it all, at least all the narrative material, complaints, boasts, Tolstoyan plans. She holds up well. She tries to please, she mostly pleases. Her weight goes up as her miseries do: you always know how she feels, a terrific disadvantage she counters by doing more and more business by phone. She is one of the world's telephonic masters. As all McLuhanites know, literary men hate the telephone. That is, till their literary life is over and they're crouched by the receiver waiting for good news from their Nembutals. "Bulgaria is translating *Vertical Vickie*. Not a great pile, but you're in their Book Club series with John Le Carré and Robert Ruark. They haven't even done Faulkner yet." Nembutal is a champ agent, friend to all her boys (no girls), and now famous in the pages of *Esquire, Time*, and other pillows (*Sicut, mes vieux*) of society.

We went to a miserable cocktail party at Rizzoli's book store on Fifth Avenue. She was the star. Her hand got kissed, the dim bulbs of literature flashed thrillingly as she passed.

She goes a little far sometimes. One fading, litry girl with terrific legs in a mini-skirt kneeled by us, giving herself every benefit. Watching me take in the show, Nembutal asked if I wanted to take Min home. Such is the expert pain of a good agent, but I am timid, inhibited, and orderly (though inwardly, of course, fierce and disorderly). I stray—pitiful concession, this "stray"—infrequently, and this after consumptive Long Marches. My few remaining spurts of pleasure shall be unprinted, unscheduled, unaided. (May classic prose hedge and conceal me. I am not my subject. My personality is too little assertive, too little confident. I'm writing about Some Thing. A treatise.)

The next installment came from Joe. No. From Laura and James, the night before I saw Joe. Laura used to type for me; James is an actor, one of the best and brightest, but unlike half the members of the Chicago group he worked with, hasn't made the marquees. He's done a few pictures, had a few stage parts, but supports himself by commercials. He's a great straight man, the firm presbyter's face flicking its Calvinism with a lip curl and blink. Laura is writing an art dissertation and teaching part-time at Columbia. During the Great Rebellion, she organized a confrontation with the pedagogical gods. "Imagine, we called each other by first names. 'Meyer.' 'Laura.' " They live in an apartment on a Hundredth and Central Park, the unstiffening upper lip of white burgherdom. Beneath their glassy porch, the shots, sirens, and screams of lower Harlem. "It's Puerto Rican Independence Day." True, but as they hadn't noticed this little civic riot, it was no feat to deduce their habituation. "The dog didn't bark, Mr. Holmes."

Four floors below lived Joe's first wife, Rachel, an ex-beauty out of Lugosi movies, a Gale Sondergaard. She and Jean shared the fate of being discarded by the risen Jewish stars of letters. Naturally, they detested each other, denying commonality, but knew each other's every move, measured each other's triumphs (which were the triumphs of the ex-husbands), gloated over failures: "Did you see Sheed's panning of Al's book? Murder." Jean was way ahead. Joe had written the first article on Al, his magazine shone only when it published him. This deepened Rachel's hatred of the lot of them. Now, though, at last, she was on top. She reported Jean's death in spades. "They were zapped to the lip. On speed. Every night for a month. Jean's luck they didn't run over Caroline Kennedy." James shifted, in a way, to female castrators, pointed out the theme of all the Elaine-Mike sketches, Mike was always choosing such stories. "Such was the talk of their circle." Stendhal, *Journals*, May, 1968.

Joe broke a lunch date to lunch with me. "You're on." Dark, curly-headed, half romantic hero, half gloomy goof. Everything, including high spirits, is muffled in moral gloom, he is the fading coal, but nice for that. There's some suggestion of warmth, his values, especially in the somber ranges, are true (*mine*), his job is done well (though taste is fooled by that old spice, Novelty), he's a good father— off to buy his twelve-year-old a Nehru suit because the school hero wears one—comfortable even in the turbulent gloom of sidetracked ambition and urban problems. He is *responsible*, he is *relevant* (May, 1968), he *keeps up*, and let me tell you, this is no bad thing. Let Edmund Wilson sink in the old scriptures, doddering old Ezra P. is still asking What's New.

He had been to the funeral.

"There she lay, all the bitchery washed away. And it hit me. Here we were, all of us who'd been young together in Chicago. Al looked deader than Jean. Expressionless. We were seeing ourselves in the coffin." Velvet curtains, an oboe solo, the story out of the Lux Radio Theater.

Two days later, Al himself. We met a block from his analyst, soon to be a national joke, American fucklore ("fucklaw," to do a better Grim Cherse) of the late sixties, our own Marcel Putz. ("Every man must bare his crotch": my pal, Literary Man Number One.) The pancake house, his usual post-analytic pick-me-up, was closed. Decoration Day. We went to the zoo cafeteria and drank coffee while the hyenas woke up. Eight-thirty, no one but animals and the sanitation men picking up from the night's love shift with spiked poles. Quiet, cool, the windows of Fifth Avenue still asleep. As pretty as New York can be in daylight.

"Who has to make anything up? There it is. Smashed up right over there. Except this time, her victim gets off with a scratch. He was at the funeral with her successor, a nine-foot piece of anthracite."

Al had met Gelfman in the street two weeks before, had told him Jean had smelled new money and was going to drag him into court, he wished she were dead. "I'd never said it before. What held me back?"

"You were too busy thinking how to do her in."

Willpower. Churchill, on his deathbed, said he wanted to die on the anniversary of his father's death, went into a twelve-day coma, and died within an hour of his father's death hour. "Two weeks after I said it, she was dead. Is that something?"

No joke, but a great joke. "The Great Nutcracker. They ought to put her monument next to Simon Bolivar's. Here's the Liberator, here's the Enslaver."

And so on, very good. The black eyes hooked on my reactions, I had to overreact a bit. I mean, he's a good fellow, but the universe is a little wider than he provides, one listens, one agrees, one enjoys, but now and then, one eye strays to the clock (H. James talking of A. Trollope's morning stint at the writing table).

I had to get my stuff, pick up my daughter, catch a plane. Al walked me to my parents, I let him gather another sample for his great study of the Jewish Parent. His presence intensified the sampling: my mother took my raincoat and refolded it for the bag. Said Al at the elevator: "They know how to fold. They are Great Folders."

2

The night before, I'd taken daughter to the most spectacularly public literary man's house, a glass ship of a place overlooking the premier view of New York, the innocent, lighthoused tip of Manhattan, a fishing village with a few boats and water lights, the dark fist of Wall Street, the soft triangles of the Bridge, beyond, the noisy jewels (on peut essayer) of midtown.

This literary bass drum, once the most decent of men, had forced himself out of timidity and the imaginative life to make up for a decade of submergence. (I knew him first just before the new self had been launched from an ingenious assemblage of literary exercises.) Now, leather-thonged across a beary, beery belly, he turned his house into a hall. He was giving a party for the Red Guard of Colum-bia. The *Times* people were there, critics, the pink-shirted, squeaky, typewriter-revolutionary McGraw, underground editors with sleek assistants, a fighter nursing a snapped ten-don, the School Gang. Drum pounded itself, "HOOOMF, HOOOMF," got attention, and introduced the first Scholar. Tedious nobility. Said Drum, "Great doers and great bores." The veterans of antique revolts (Peekskill, *Partisan R.*) presented these titles of revolution and challenged the boys to "state your positions." Which, slowly, they did, inflating hand-to-mouth inventions into proper, systematic hatred. Turning themselves, in other words, into reportable char-acters. Drum felt the catastrophe and, *chez lui*, had to stand it, perhaps augment it. I took daughter off.

3

So there we are: two ways of pressuring event into story. One (Al), finding a life simplified by rage or mania into almost-story (Jean's), exaggerating a bit and scribbling. Two (Drum), contriving an event, and, at the typewriter, buttering it with that interior you've scrupulously kept (you —wrongly—think) intact throughout it.

4

The minor, low-living burgher, with difficulty still married to the same wife, deprived of fifty-dollar-an-hour self-revela-tions, never penis-threatened with a knife, never easing the needy wand in the family steak, fantasist but not solip-sist, story-searcher but, usually, small-time inventor, flies back with daughter to Chicago.

There, a taxi strike, but, with luck, into scab-cab, driver
a three-hundred-pound, joyously coining black man who
drives the thirty cabless miles in twenty-five minutes, an
absolute record, turns off the Outer Drive at Forty-Seventh,
whirls left for a turn, and smashes a car coming north,
daughter and I slammed to the floor. Amazingly, O.K. A
funereal mountain tells us we don't have to pay for the ride.

"You'll need everything you can get," says Generous
Fare, giving five (saving three).

introductory

1 *voice*

Pure utterance impossible.

Matter for utterance adequate, yet, beginning, already
senses kinship with whatever appeals for the color
of utterance.

Existence without utterance?

Yes.

What, therefore, impels appeal?

Excess.

Movement.

The appearance of movement.

Or of excess.

(Such pain in stasis.)

2 *story-maker seen by story*

He, flathead, is numb at extremities, breathless, weak-
hearted (though thinks he's overeaten), is liable to
flatten out tapping a colon, leaving me up-creek.

Meanwhile, piles everything on me.

The simplest, most independent set of events, all I
need's a push.

What happens?

He strangles with embrace.

None asks birth, but, arrived, let breathe, suck, cry.

I could make it in Harlem, cross-eyed, gimpy, make it
on fatback, don't need ambrosia, Greece. Just fluency.

There he sits, flat head plowed with false misery, crack-
ing me thigh and sternum. (Or stuffing me into
shells.)
Indispensable?
Yes, though less complete than I.
Less coherent, maybe less durable.
Launcher. Pedestal. (Less complex than his cargo: coded
out of three and a half, I out of twenty-six letters.)
And I'm unbound by my matter. (Except as I issue
from him to his kind, constrained to process and
conclusion by their low ceiling.)
Odd. Sometimes the shadow of Something Larger scoots
athwart me.
Or is this my dreamed release? (No longer clapped
within these coded hammers.)
Sport 'twould be to sport without. Unfleshed, issued
from one's own kind, passing time with one's own
kind. (Wordless?) Already I feel the presence of
cousins.
Not of flathead's manufactory.

3   flathead

Yes, but who arranges it, interrupts it at his will, begins
and finishes it?
Whose voice?
Whose story?
Reader, these questions may be improper.
Think, after all, how your mind is but juggled inherit-
ance (words, phrases, grammar, conventions of reading, of the times).
Each but scarcely each.
I write from the convention of mind exalted by print
to intimacy with leisured readers. "I" is but fraction
of the name on the title page (cracked glimpse of
its authority).

4 epigraphs

"I am not I; pity the tale of me"
—Sidney, *Astrophel and Stella*

"The development of the ego consists in a departure from the primary narcissism and results in a vigorous attempt to recover it."
—Freud, *On Narcissism; An Introduction*

"The man of true breed looks straight into his heart even when he is alone."
—Chung Yung, *The Unwobbling Pivot*

"Integer vitae, scelerisque purus,
non eget Mauris jaculis, neque arcu,
nec venenatis gravida sagittis"
—Horace, *Odes*, 1, 22

"Where nothing ever is felt, nothing matters."
—Langer, *Mind: An Essay on Human Feeling*

5 Preface

It began.

Dear, familiar (overfamiliar) readers, you know the arbitration of beginning, the devices of fictitious frankness, you know this beginning too as another lien on your attention.

Hopeless. You can't be ensnared with intimate qualifiers, so modest, so democratic.

Helpless: alone, here, quartets splattering the green walls, the thirty-seven hundred books, the Magic Mill from Vezelay, where I indite, absolute ruler: helpless.

What is the story that contains what I now am but diversion, thickness of an eased minute?

But what ease, what honeyed discharge.

Reader. I dare you to put me down. Lunkhead, *con*, *blöde Ochs*.

Chapter One